WE LIVE
NEXT
DOOR

BOOKS BY LAURA WOLFE

Her Best Friend's Lie

She Lies Alone

Two Widows

Laura Wolfe

WE LIVE NEXT DOOR

bookouture

Published by Bookouture in 2021

An imprint of Storyfire Ltd.
Carmelite House
50 Victoria Embankment
London EC4Y 0DZ

www.bookouture.com

Paperback ISBN: 978-1-80314-006-3
eBook ISBN: 978-1-80314-005-6

For Lisa, my most treasured cousin and friend

ONE

The best time to walk down my street was at night. A stroll in the dark was peaceful and anonymous; it didn't hold any expectations. Cars rarely passed, and neighbors didn't linger in their yards, looking for small talk. After a day of catering to the demands of a three-year-old, I embraced the feeling of being invisible for a while, of clearing my head. Now a spring wind brushed against my cheeks as Roo tugged me along by his leash. I glanced back at our front door, wondering if I'd ever adjust to the daily suburban grind. These few minutes to roam the streets felt vital to my survival.

Fresh air filled my lungs, causing the tension in my shoulders to blow away with the breeze, swirl over the rooftops, and fade into the night. I stepped beyond the faint splash of light cast from our front porch and onto the shadowy sidewalk, where the distant windows of neighboring houses glowed warm and yellow. My dog pulled with determination, straining all fifty pounds of himself against my grip to reach a patch of shrubs near the driveway next door. I gave up and followed him, holding another gulp of May air in my mouth, thankful the bitter sting of another Michigan winter had vanished.

It was just after 9 p.m. Mom had surprised me a couple of

hours earlier by stopping by with a casserole—any excuse to see her only granddaughter. I pictured her humming a lullaby, keeping watch over Isabelle as she slept. I envisioned Mark at his business dinner, trying to land another client over dessert and coffee. But mostly, I focused on the sturdy feel of the cement beneath the rubber soles of my sneakers and the breath expanding and releasing from my lungs. This nightly walk with my dog had become a meditation.

Roo sniffed the shrubs and lifted his leg. A picture window glowed beyond the darkened lawn of our next-door neighbor's house, a basketball game flashing across the flat-screen TV. A tuft of Mr. Delaney's fluffy white hair peeked above the edge of a leather chair. His wife had passed away a few years back, and I imagined he was lonely.

I'd grown up here, in the Detroit suburb of Glenn Hills, and in the same brick colonial where Mark and I and Isabelle now lived in the Ridgeview Pines subdivision, where oak trees reached their knotty branches over the sidewalk, roots burrowing deep beneath the well-kept lawns. These streets were as familiar as the veins on the back of my hand. As someone who'd always considered herself an urbanite and a risk-taker, the last place I thought I'd end up was back in my childhood home on Mapleview Lane.

Sometimes it was strange to walk past the bus stop where my teenage self had languished every morning for years while dreaming about escaping to someplace more exciting. It felt awkward watching my daughter digging in the sand at the same playground where I'd met up with my band of outcast high schoolers every Saturday night to sneak alcohol and cigarettes. A few times, I'd hidden behind the cement tunnel and made out with Dean Michaels, his breath laced with cheap beer, his grubby, greedy fingertips burrowing beneath the thick band of my bra as our friends sat on swings, talking and laughing in the distance.

But a lifetime had passed since I'd kissed Dean Michaels, who now lived in Tucson with his wife and four kids. A little more than two years ago, Mom announced she was selling the family home to move to a low-maintenance condo on the other side of town; she had a deal for us. The decision had seemed obvious—the positives of leaving our overpriced loft in Detroit and returning to Glenn Hills for a fresh start far outweighing the burden of a few uncomfortable memories. Despite my reservations, the place had welcomed me back with open arms.

Roo's nails clicked against the cement as we continued toward the beige Tudor house two doors down, where a miserable woman named Barbara Draper lived with her adult son, Phil. Rumor had it that Phil moved back in with his mom after fighting a losing battle with his addiction to painkillers. Barbara had resided at the address for as long as I could remember, and in my mind's eye, she'd always been the same age: old. Stories about her had put the fear of God in me when I was younger, although I'd never experienced any altercations with her myself. I kept my distance from her now, too, especially after last year when rumors circulated that she had poisoned the Morenos' dog. There'd never been any concrete evidence.

I usually kept my eyes down and scurried past Barbara's shadowy residence as quickly as possible, keeping Roo close to my ankles. I didn't want her to accuse me of some imagined transgression, like stepping on her grass or failing to clean up Roo's droppings. But tonight, my chin jerked up as I stood in front of Barbara's house, noticing my friend Bree's Mercedes in the driveway. I inched closer to the vehicle and checked out the license plate. The characters SOLD4U came into focus, confirming the car was definitely hers. Bree was a realtor and occasionally worked in this neighborhood.

Roo wagged his tail and yipped as a cat darted out of a clump of bushes and scurried across the road. My eyes followed the cat's path toward the ranch-style house across the way that Bree had recently sold to an investor. The scent of freshly cut grass swirled around me, and I was happy the new owner was giving the rundown property some much-needed TLC.

I tugged Roo along, widening my step to avoid a crack in the sidewalk. This street held a different aura under the light of the moon. In the glare of the afternoon sun, Mapleview Lane bustled with activity. Kids traveled in packs on their bikes, neighbors yelled from their front porches and commented on the weather, drivers waved as they passed or stopped their cars to chat. But now, as Roo pulled me through the shadows, only thick silence surrounded me. Quiet scenes flashed behind lit windows, offering a momentary escape, like I'd peered into a snow globe or stumbled across a Norman Rockwell painting. Nothing too exciting happened here.

A car rolled past, with headlights on. Shadows shifted up ahead, and a lanky man in a baseball cap materialized, wandering past the corner with his shoulders hunched and hands shoved in his pockets. It was my neighbor, Sean Peale. He and his wife, Stephanie, lived with their twin boys in the house behind us. Sean was friendly enough, but his curved lips and dodgy eyes always made him seem like he was silently laughing at an inside joke. I shortened Roo's leash, pausing to avoid another uncomfortable run-in with my backyard neighbor.

I faced the rare glare of the Drapers' front porch light. Barbara's residence usually nestled in the shadows, but tonight lights glowed from within the house. The downstairs curtains were drawn, and I couldn't spot anyone inside. I knew Barbara requested a price analysis of her property a couple of times a year —a free service Bree provided to potential clients. After four years of visits, the woman hadn't listed her house, and Bree doubted Barbara would ever pull the trigger. I hadn't been aware of tonight's meeting though, which seemed to be running especially late. I gave my friend credit for humoring the difficult woman. Maybe the recent sale across the street had urged another pricing re-evaluation.

The jangle of metal drew my attention away from the Tudor house. A dark-haired woman walking a golden retriever approached from the opposite direction, shining a flashlight ahead of her. She angled her beam down, and I could see it was Avery Moreno with their new dog. Her teenage boys were much older than Isabelle, and I didn't know her well, but we occasionally passed each other on our nighttime walks.

"Evening," Avery said, tipping her head with a smile. "Enjoy the warm weather."

"You too." I pushed Roo to the side to give them room. The woman's eyes flickered toward Barbara's house, and her lips flattened. I wondered if she suspected Barbara of murdering her last dog, like the rumors had suggested. I continued walking in the opposite direction as Roo sniffed the air behind him.

I trekked along my usual loop, passing the gated neighborhood playground where a couple of shadowy figures huddled on a bench, lowering their voices as I passed. *Teenagers probably*. Their muffled laughter reached my ears as I blinked back ghosts from my past and continued past the attractive variety of 1960s and 1970s houses sitting on manicured half-acre lots. Some of the homes had been torn down and rebuilt in recent years. Many had changed owners, following a neighborhood's typical life cycle, with young families replacing the octogenarians.

Several minutes later, I completed the loop, heading back down Mapleview Lane toward home and finding the fresh air and quiet had worked its magic. The day's stress had left my body. My jaw loosened as I neared the Drapers' house again from the opposite direction. Bree's car was no longer in the driveway, and someone had turned off the light over the front door. I smiled, wondering what stories Bree would tell me about her meeting with the surly widow.

Roo halted suddenly, and I nearly toppled over him. He perked his ears toward Barbara's blackened yard. Then I heard it too—a rustling behind the bushes lining Barbara's front fence, followed by soft footsteps. I wasn't sure whether the crunching of hurried steps was from a human or animal. Only faint shadows wavered before me. Roo growled toward the noise. Then, his deep, throaty bark tore through the quiet. I waited and listened, wondering if the cat had returned and hoping a skunk or raccoon wouldn't leap out from the shrubbery and attack. I half expected Barbara herself to spring forth and yell at Roo to shut up.

Roo fought against me as I pulled on the leash. My fingers dug into my pocket for the flashlight on my phone. I aimed the beam toward the bushes, but the shrubs sat silent and motionless. I exhaled when Barbara didn't emerge. Nothing was visible through the thick tangle of branches. Whatever movement I'd heard had stopped. Roo sniffed the air, but his muscles were rigid and his hackles up. I moved the beam across the fence line and into the backyard, finding nothing but the solid trunk of a maple tree reflected in the light.

"C'mon, boy." I jerked the leash, and Roo snapped out of his trance. I relaxed my fingers and continued along the sidewalk, allowing myself to breathe again. Beyond Mr. Delaney's house, our front porch light gleamed like a candle.

Just as I put my head down to hurry home, a blip of movement in my peripheral vision caused me to turn toward the Drapers' upstairs window. I flinched, finding a pale, disapproving face staring down from a gap in the curtains. It was Barbara Draper, her gray hair cut severely close to her scalp and her black eyes pressing into me. I had the strange feeling I'd glimpsed something dangerous, that I'd stumbled into a trap. Still, I couldn't pull my eyes away. She must have heard Roo barking. My instinct was to run, but it felt as if the sidewalk had hardened around my feet. Her steely stare held me in place, making me feel as if she'd caught me cheating or breaking the law, even though I hadn't done anything wrong.

Barbara leaned toward the glass, her hands jiggling with the window frame as if she was clearing a path to scream at me. I'd never been a direct target of Barbara's wrath, but there was a first time for everything. As she rattled the pane of glass, I snapped my eyes toward my dog, my heart thumping. I had a choice: fight or flight, and I was definitely going to flee. Maybe my panicked reaction was silly, but something about Barbara's hardened glare felt off. Dangerous, even. Hands shaking, I yanked Roo's leash, jerking myself out of my frozen state. I turned away, feeling the weight of her watching eyes on my back. My feet picked up speed, tumbling over each other as the muffled sound of a woman's scream chased me all the way home.

THE NEIGHBOR LIST

POSTED MAY 6

Username: BDraper

Subject: CONTROL YOUR CATS!

Yesterday I witnessed a cat prowling through my yard trying to kill songbirds and digging in my flower beds. YOUR poor decision to own a cat should not be a burden on ME!!! Please have some respect for your neighbors and keep your cats INSIDE!

LMcMahon: Is this a joke? Why not get upset about something worthwhile like starving kids or climate change?

SurfsUp77: I thought BDraper was banned from this app.

Daisy00: Can U post a pic of the cat? Mine has been missing since last week.

Click to view ninety-seven more comments

TWO

The doorbell chimed. I walked away from the living room, where cartoons buzzed on the TV and Isabelle sat on her blanket, enthralled.

"I got it." Morning light poured through the front door into our foyer. Bree stood in the doorway. I opened the door wider. "Good morning."

Mark popped his head out of the kitchen and stepped closer. "Hi, Bree."

"Jessica! Mark! Oh my God. Did you hear?" Bree stood up, her sea-blue eyes moving from side to side as she entered our house, her purse pinned under her arm. She looked too formal for a Saturday morning, dressed in slim black pants, heels, and a patterned silk blouse. But I supposed Saturday was a workday for realtors.

Mark lowered the dish towel in his hand.

I ushered Bree inside, where our house smelled of pancakes and maple syrup. "No. What's going on?"

"Barbara Draper is dead." Beads of perspiration glistened through the powder on Bree's forehead.

I shook my head. "What? That's impossible. I saw her in the window last night when I was out walking Roo."

"I was inside her house earlier yesterday too! She wanted *another* price analysis." Bree made a pained face. "But didn't you hear the ambulance and police go by?"

Wrinkles creased across Mark's forehead. "I did hear some sirens, but I didn't give it much thought."

"I must have slept through it," I said, not remembering hearing anything. Sleeping late on Saturday mornings was my luxury. Mark got the same deal on Sundays as we took turns getting up with Isabelle.

Roo danced around our visitor, wagging his tail. Bree bent down to hug him, the same over-the-top greeting she always gave our dog. I slipped past her in my socked feet and sweatpants and leaned out the door toward the Drapers' house. Sure enough, two police cars sat in front. If there had been an ambulance at the scene, it had already left.

I returned to the foyer and stared at my friend. "Do you know what happened?"

"Yeah. The police called me about an hour ago and asked me to meet at the house and answer a few questions. Phil told them I'd been there last night. I guess he'd been under the influence and couldn't remember much. I said I'd be happy to help." Bree pursed her lips. "It turns out that Barbara drowned in her bathtub sometime after I left. She was still wearing her bathrobe."

"The bathtub?"

Bree nodded. "It's so crazy. They said it looked like a tragic accident, but they wanted to cover their bases."

"How do you drown in a bathtub?" Mark looked toward the ceiling. "Couldn't she just stand up?"

I giggled at the absurdity of it, although a sour swirl of nausea rose in my stomach. I craned my head toward Isabelle, who remained glued to the TV. Visions of Barbara's disapproving stare floated through my mind. I waved everyone forward. "Let's sit down in the kitchen." As we gathered around the circular table in our outdated kitchen, Barbara's muffled scream echoed in my ears.

I thought she'd yelled something along the lines of, "Go away!" but maybe I'd gotten it wrong.

Bree scraped her chair forward, gazing at the floral wallpaper. Since moving into our house two years earlier, Mark and I had modernized much of the house with fresh paint, new windows, and flooring. But the kitchen was one of the rooms we hadn't tackled with updates yet. The mustard-yellow wallpaper and worn Formica countertops were remnants of my childhood, a "Marilyn Tyler special," as I often referred to Mom's decorating choices. The kitchen still felt like it belonged to her. I poured a fresh mug of coffee and set it in front of Bree. Mark offered her pancakes, and she declined.

Bree leaned in and lowered her voice. "Well, I'm probably not supposed to tell anybody this, but I overheard the medical examiner talking to the lead detective in the next room. She said Barbara's injuries were consistent with an accident. She said there was a puddle of water on the tile floor and that Barbara most likely slipped and hit her head on the marble shelf above the tub, knocking herself unconscious before falling into the water and drowning. I guess they found some blood or hair or something on the edge of the shelf too."

"What are the odds?" I laced my fingers together, wondering if Roo's barking had gotten her so worked up she'd slipped and fallen to a watery death.

"Who knows?"

I leaned back in my chair and studied Bree's berry-stained lips and sparkly necklace, wondering how she could look so put-together so early on a Saturday morning, especially after she'd just discovered her potential client was dead. I didn't think I'd ever seen Bree come undone, not even on the spring day last year when she revealed to me her husband had moved out and they were getting divorced. She'd been fully made-up with a sleek braid in her blonde hair that day too. I supposed she was used to keeping up her image.

Bree and I ran in different crowds back in high school, and

while we'd been friendly toward each other, we hadn't been close. Bree had been a cheerleader, a confident trendsetter, and a fixture on the homecoming court. Meanwhile, I preferred to focus on what felt like more alternative hobbies like designing tattoos, volunteering at the humane society, and smoking weed. I'd left Glenn Hills for college on the east coast, eventually giving up the weed and returning for a marketing job in Detroit. Mark worked in the same downtown building. That's how we'd met.

I'd only connected with Bree since moving back to Glenn Hills two years ago. Mom had hired Bree from a real estate flier a week before realizing Mark and I were the perfect buyers for her house. Bree still helped coordinate the deed transfer though, and only accepted a fraction of the commission for her work. Since then, my old acquaintance from high school had surprised me with her easy-going nature and sharp sense of humor. The two of us hit it off instantly and had gotten together almost weekly ever since.

Bree cradled the warm mug in her manicured fingers. "The policeman was asking me if Barbara had been drinking or taking any pills. She could have passed out before she fell in the tub, I guess."

"Was she? Drinking or popping pills?" I asked.

"No. Not that I saw anyway. But I was only there for an hour. Phil was definitely out of it by then. His eyes were glazed and he kept twitching before he disappeared up to his bedroom."

"Oh my God. What if it was suicide? Did she seem upset?" I ground my molars together, hoping her sighting of Roo and me tramping near her perfect lawn hadn't pushed my neighbor over the edge.

"She just seemed a bit annoyed that her house hadn't gone up in value since the last time I met with her. She blamed it on the surrounding neighbors for not keeping up their homes." Bree fluttered her long eyelashes.

"Sounds like Barbara."

"I bet Phil did it." Mark's mouth stretched back in distaste.

"Any guy pushing forty who lives with his mother has to be a little off."

"Mark!" I batted his arm. "That's horrible. We shouldn't accuse the poor guy. He's probably devastated."

"Can you imagine what it must have been like growing up with Barbara Draper as your mother?" Bree asked. "Mark might be on to something. Maybe Phil slipped a few painkillers into his mother's nightly Scotch and waited for her to topple over."

Mark's lips twisted to the side. "Or maybe he pushed her."

I knew almost nothing about Phil, despite having lived two doors down from him for years. When we were growing up, we had barely acknowledged each other's existence. He was five years older than me, and as school-aged children, this meant we might as well have been twenty years apart. My memory of him was one of a loner who occasionally materialized from the shadows to skateboard around the neighborhood, then vanished just as quickly. I remembered running into him one summer night when I met up with some friends at the playground. I was probably fifteen and he must have been home from college. The boys in my group referred to Phil as the "son of the bitch," and "Draper the Raper," saying the words just loud enough so Phil could hear them. It shamed me now to think that I'd stood by silently as the young man rose from the bench and left the park with his head down, never defending himself. Through Bree, I'd heard about Phil's battle with addiction in more recent years. Presumably, he couldn't hold a job and had no friends, explaining why he lived with his mother.

I leaned forward on my elbows, remembering Barbara's muffled scream but feeling a sudden need to defend Phil. "Maybe someone else pushed her."

Mark shook his head. "There was only one other person in the house with her."

Bree crossed her arms, clutching her elbows in opposite hands. "But Jessica is right. Barbara had plenty of enemies."

"There's probably fifty suspects from The Neighbor List, alone," Mark said.

We sat in silence, no one disagreeing. Barbara had complained about everything and everyone, often airing her issues publicly on The Neighbor List, an app used by people in the area to connect with neighbors on a variety of topics. While most people used the platform to post about lost pets, job openings, or restaurant recommendations, Barbara only moaned about property taxes, barking dogs, loud children, road construction, poor service she'd received at various neighborhood businesses, and the incompetence of local politicians. She'd been banned twice for abusive comments but had somehow kept making her way back into the forum.

I cleared my throat. "I saw something weird last night. After Bree left."

Mark tilted his head.

"Roo barked at a noise in the Drapers' yard. Barbara was looking at me through the upstairs window. She had the strangest look on her face. Like she was angry or upset, but there was something even more sinister in her eyes. It was creepy. Then she started rattling the window like she was trying to open it. I thought I heard her scream at me as I ran away."

"She was probably yelling at you to keep off the grass. I'm glad you saw her, though." Bree tapped the table with her fingertip. "That's proof she was still alive when I left."

"Hi, Bwee."

I turned to see Isabelle's pudgy cheeks in the doorway.

Bree's eyes lit up. "Hi, angel. It's so wonderful to see you."

"Want to play hide and seek?"

"Oh, I wish I could." Bree glanced at her watch. "I've got to go to work. A nice lady is looking for a new house today, and I'm going to show her some places. And then I'm visiting your new neighbor across the street to see what renovations he has planned for the house I just sold him."

Isabelle tugged at her choppy hair. "Okay."

"I promise I will next time. Okay?" Bree said as she stood.

I grinned at Bree. "The new neighbor wants your advice?"

Bree's eyes sparkled in the morning light. "Yeah. His name is

Rick. He's handsome. And single. And so what? It's a professional courtesy."

"Uh-huh."

Mark and I chuckled.

"Go get him, tiger," I said.

Isabelle stepped next to Bree and did a little hop. She looked so small and huggable in her pink, footed pajamas. "I'm going to the zoo today."

"The zoo? I love the zoo. Will you say hi to the penguins for me?" Bree chatted with Isabelle in an animated voice as we made our way to the front door. I got the feeling Isabelle was the perfect dose of a child for Bree, just a teaspoon here and there. She could bask in Isabelle's admiration and then leave as soon as the responsibility became an inconvenience. Bree looked over her shoulder at me as she opened the door to let herself out. "Let me know if you notice any more developments at Barbara's house."

"Yeah. Keep us posted from your end too."

"Bye, Bwee!"

Bree blew a kiss toward Isabelle then closed the door, leaving a swirl of vanilla-citrus perfume in the air.

Mark puffed out a breath. "Wow."

"It's unbelievable. Isn't it?" I crossed my arms and leaned against the wall. "Barbara was just there, and now she's not. Do you think it was an accident?"

"I have no idea."

I looked toward the window. "It's just—"

"What?"

"The look in Barbara's eyes last night, when she was peering out the window at me. And the way she yelled. Something wasn't right." I swallowed, finding my mouth had gone dry.

"Was anything ever right with Barbara Draper?"

"I guess not." I shifted my weight to the other foot as another distant memory forced its way to the surface. "But she was nice to me once, when I was a kid."

Mark threw me a questioning glance. "Really?"

"I was only about seven years old and I fell off my bike in front of her house. I skinned my knee pretty badly. I'm not sure where Mom was, but no one was around to help me. Barbara ran out from her house with a warm washcloth and some Band-Aids. She fixed me up and told me I'd be fine. She even gave me an orange popsicle and walked me home. All the other kids in the neighborhood were always scared of Mrs. Draper." I paused, biting my lip as I remembered the time Barbara screamed at a little girl for letting her dog pee on the grass near the Drapers' driveway, and recalled Barbara's yearly ritual of scolding kids who dared to approach her darkened door for candy on Halloween. "Barbara yelled at them for all kinds of things, but was never mean to me. Not once. It's weird."

Mark rubbed his forehead as Isabelle and Roo wove in between our legs. "Well, her singular act of kindness happened almost twenty-five years ago. I think it was a fluke."

I began to step away, but Mark wrapped his arm around my waist. "Hey. After our big day at the zoo, how about dinner at Frederick's tonight?" He waved his arm toward the door. "Get our minds off all this."

"Ooh. Frederick's." I imagined the aroma of the crusty rolls and the firecracker shrimp appetizer we always ordered at our favorite local restaurant. "That sounds wonderful. I'll call Sophie and see if she's available."

Sophie was the babysitter we'd hired to take care of Isabelle every Thursday morning and occasional weekend nights. I'd found her a few months earlier via The Neighbor List. The baby-faced nanny had left her clerical position at the hospital and was saving money to finish her classes at community college. She wanted to become a kindergarten teacher and had glowing recommendations from previous families whose kids she'd watched. Sophie was a lifesaver. More importantly, Isabelle loved her.

Mark clapped his hands. "C'mon, Isabelle. Let's get you dressed. We're going to the zoo."

Isabelle hopped after him toward the stairs. I turned, hugging my arms in front of me. I inched forward and gripped the front door's metal handle. Still wearing my lounging clothes and without the benefit of make-up or combed hair, I stepped outside into the brisk morning air and squinted into the sunlight. It would be a perfect day for the zoo. My gaze traveled past Mr. Delaney's house toward the Tudor two doors down. I half expected to see a crowd of people gathered around the Drapers' house, whispering theories to each other, but Mapleview Lane stretched long and empty. Only a lone jogger rounded the corner at the other end of the block.

Without any flashing lights or fanfare, a police cruiser slowly backed out of the nearby driveway and approached our house. Maybe Barbara's death had been nothing more than a tragic accident after all. I froze on the cement step as the car rolled past. The outline of a head materialized in the back window as someone turned to face me through the glass, his features slowly coming into focus—deadened eyes, thin lips, ruffled hair, and pasty skin. My breath hitched in my throat. I hadn't seen the secretive man in a few months, but I recognized him immediately. It was Phil Draper.

Was Phil going to the station voluntarily? Or had they arrested him?

Son of the bitch. Draper the raper. I couldn't stop the boys' cruel taunts from escaping the past and entering my thoughts. As soon as I blinked, the car was gone. I stumbled inside, thrown off-kilter by the unexpected sighting. More questions swarmed my mind. I'd only glimpsed Phil for a moment, but there was something familiar —and troubling—about his worn demeanor. It could have been the drugs, I supposed. Still, his dazed stare and blank face didn't quite match that of a man devastated by the loss of his mother. Bree mentioned that Phil discovered Barbara's body this morning, but the man in the back seat of the police car had the same disoriented expression I'd seen on myself so many times since Isabelle was born. It struck me as the spaced-out, shell-shocked appearance of someone who'd been awake all night.

THREE

I smoothed down the front of my little black dress with my palms. "Isabelle had her bath already. She can have a fruit cup before bed."

Sophie sat cross-legged on the carpet next to Isabelle, nodding along to my instructions.

"We went to the zoo!"

The babysitter's blonde ponytail bobbed up and down. "I know. That sounds so fun. Maybe we can draw all the animals you saw today after your parents leave."

"Yeah!"

Sophie flashed a smile in my direction, revealing an endearing gap between her two front teeth. She wore the imperfection well.

Her eyes paused on me. "That dress looks stunning on you. Where are you going?"

"Oh, thanks." I looked down, blushing involuntarily. I was only thirty-three, but I'd lost my edge. I'd been feeling old and frumpy lately. In my teens and twenties, I'd been so much cooler. I used to flash my anti-establishment appearance like a switchblade, taking pleasure in my ability to make the mindless masses stare. I'd had pink tips in my hair, a silver stud in my nose, black lipstick, a glimpse of the dying rose tattoo visible on my hip—the one Mom didn't find out about until a year after I'd gotten it, and then she'd absolutely lost her shit. She'd told me over and over that, someday, I'd regret the permanent mark on my body. So far, I still cherished my tattoo, hidden under my waistband like a little secret. But my style had definitely dulled since my marketing job in the corporate world, followed by marriage and a baby. Sophie was only about five years younger than me, but our age gap felt more dramatic. Her face held the soft curves, smooth skin, and the trendy make-up of a hip twenty-something. A compliment from her didn't go unappreciated.

I smoothed back my hair, which was now colored a basic brown with a few subtle highlights. "We're going to Frederick's again. We'll be back in about two hours, but text if there are any issues."

"Of course."

Sophie straightened her shoulders. "Oh, before I forget, I noticed Isabelle's booster seat in the kitchen is the Tadpole model by Toodaloo."

"Yeah. My mom gave her that one."

"Oh okay. Well, I'm not sure if you heard, but the manufacturer recalled that model. It's been in the news the last few days because it slips off the chair too easily, and kids are getting injured."

"Oh, no. I didn't even hear about that." I studied Sophie's solemn eyes. She frequently offered helpful information related to Isabelle, making me feel slightly unqualified to be a mother. Then again, Sophie was wise beyond her years. "Thanks for letting me know. I'll buy a replacement."

"Sure thing."

Four knocks cracked at our front door. I walked toward it and peered through the peephole, finding my mom hovering on the front step. Annoyance needled through me at another one of her unannounced visits, but I took a breath and pulled open the door.

"Hi, Mom."

"Hi, Jessica." She widened her eyes at my dress as she stepped

WE LIVE NEXT DOOR

inside. "Oh. You're all dressed up. I hope I'm not catching you at a bad time."

"Actually, Mark and I are heading out for dinner in a minute. Did you need something?"

"I forgot to get my casserole dish back from you. I wanted to make another recipe tonight so that I can deliver it to my neighbor in the morning."

"Okay. I'll get it."

Mom stretched her neck toward the living room, eyes searching. "And where's my sweet girl?"

"Gwamma!" Isabelle squealed.

Mom skittered forward, finding Isabelle and Sophie crouched over a game on the living room floor, and I suspected Isabelle was the real reason she stopped by.

"Mom, you remember Sophie?"

"Yes, of course. Hello."

Sophie stood up. "Hi, Mrs.—"

"It's Tyler. But call me Marilyn, please."

The babysitter grinned. "Hi, Marilyn. Isabelle was just telling me all about her trip to the zoo."

Mom clasped her hands together. "How wonderful!"

I left them talking and retrieved the dish, running into Mark coming in from the garage. Mom's laughter bellowed from the next room.

He stopped mid-stride and raised an eyebrow. "Is your mom here again?"

Mom's failure to shift her mindset about who owned this house had been Mark's biggest concern about buying it from her. He worried she would continue to think of it as her own, and it turned out his concerns were valid.

"She just showed up." I held up the dish. "But she's leaving. Now."

Mark dropped his head but followed me into the living room. "Hi, Marilyn."

"Hi. Thanks for this." She took the dish from me and kissed Isabelle on the head.

I walked her to the door, realizing that she probably hadn't heard the news about the untimely death of her longtime neighbor.

"Mom, I almost forgot to tell you. Barbara Draper died last night."

Mom's mouth fell open, her eyes blinking. She touched her head and steadied herself against the couch as if she might faint. "What? How?"

"According to Bree, Barbara slipped, hit her head, and drowned in the bathtub. They found her body this morning."

"Oh, my. The bathtub." Mom made a face like she'd eaten a sour grape. She placed a hand on her hip and fixed her gaze toward the wall. Her mouth opened slightly as her thoughts seemed to drift somewhere far away. "Well, I can't say she was a close friend, but that's too bad. She was a fixture in this neighborhood. I think she meant well, in her own way."

"Bree said the medical examiner ruled her death an accident at the scene. But it's a suspicious way to die, don't you think?"

"Plenty of people on this street disliked Barbara—myself included—but I can't imagine someone would kill her." Mom stepped to the side and lowered the dish. "I had an acquaintance years ago—Jane something or another—who fell in the shower and died on the spot. Accidents happen sometimes. Although, now that I think about it, there were lots of whispers about Jane's husband afterward."

A breath released from behind me, and I turned to see Sophie staring at me. A nervous twitch on her lips conflicted with her usually calm demeanor. I hadn't meant for her to overhear us.

"Sorry, Sophie. There's no need to worry. Our neighbor's death was a freak occurrence. This is a very safe neighborhood." As I said the words, memories from last night and this morning swarmed my mind—the rustling in the bushes, the indiscernible footsteps, Phil's face in the back seat of the police car. *Had Phil been the one I'd heard outside?*

A smile forced its way onto Sophie's face as she leaned down to pet Roo. "I'm not worried. I always keep the doors locked at night. And I know how to swim."

The rest of us laughed at Sophie's remark. Mom said her good-byes and returned to her car. Mark and I said goodnight to Isabelle and left through the garage.

Thirty minutes later, Mark and I sat across from each other at a secluded table in the corner of Frederick's. The waiter set our drinks and a basket of steaming bread in front of us.

Mark leaned back and shook his head. "Man, what a day. A dinner out is just what I needed."

"Yeah. Bree isn't the only one with an exciting dating life." I winked at him, admiring the crinkles around my husband's eyes and the dimple that had formed in his cheek. My feet ached from the miles we walked at the zoo, and I rotated my ankles under the table. "By the way, Bree texted me earlier. I guess Rick asked her out on a date. A real one."

Mark took a sip of his drink. "Bree likes to play the field, that's for sure."

"I hope she finds someone good for her. Alex was such a jerk."

"How does she pay for that car?"

"No idea. She leases it, I think. She's always complaining about business being slow. It must be so stressful not to know where your next mortgage payment is going to come from."

Creases formed on Mark's brow as he shook his head. "There's something to be said for the nine-to-five grind." He reached for a piece of bread. "Speaking of business, how's your job search?"

I swallowed two large gulps of my wine and stared at my silver-ware. I'd hoped to avoid discussing my job search for at least a couple of more weeks. The prospects weren't great. Even the jobs that matched my marketing background sounded so mind-numb-ing. Before Isabelle had arrived, I'd never had a problem grinding through hours of tedious tasks and submitting to the demands of self-important bosses. But now, Mark made enough money to allow us to live comfortably enough. The freedom was contagious. Any job that took me away from my daughter had to be worth it.

"The job search is okay."

Mark set down the piece of bread in his hand, waiting for more information.

I cleared my throat. "I mean, I haven't really found anything worthwhile." I needed to tread carefully. Staying home with Isabelle full-time was a temporary arrangement as far as Mark was concerned. Thursday mornings, when Sophie watched Isabelle, were supposed to give me time to locate and apply for a new position. But I'd been using the time for other things.

"Maybe I can help with your search. I know of some other sites than the one you're using."

"Thanks." I forced a smile into the corners of my lips. "It's just that I'm not sure anymore. About marketing, I mean."

Mark stared at me for a second and then cocked his head. "But that's your background. What else would you do?"

I took a long swig of my wine, gathering my courage. Another idea had been taking form in my mind for months. "This might sound crazy, but remember when I used to dream about opening a neighborhood bakery?"

Mark straightened his shoulders and coughed. I hoped a piece of bread hadn't lodged itself in his throat.

"A bakery?"

"Yeah. More of a cake shop, really. You know, those cakes with the tattoo designs I've been making? They're a big hit with everyone. No one's ever seen cakes like mine before." I stopped talking long enough to measure the shock level on Mark's face, which was approximately a nine out of ten. "It would be a risk, I know. But I've been doing a lot of research on everything that goes into starting this kind of business and creating a few new designs. I've gotten so much praise for the cake I made for Bree's birthday party." I paused, remembering the design adorning Bree's white chocolate cake: a red rose with overlapping petals swaddled by an

S-shaped ribbon with the words *Happy Birthday!* printed in gothic blackletter font. "And the cake I made for my cousin's wedding." I'd gone old school with that one, painting the newlyweds' initials in a simple style—*JW + LP*—inside the crude outline of a red heart to replicate the artwork of young lovers sometimes graffitied in alleys or carved into trees. The guests had gone nuts over it. I looked at Mark, trying to explain, "People get to experience the thrill of a tattoo without the commitment. There's a little rebellion hiding inside everyone."

Mark stared at his drink.

"And I've come up with even more recipes and designs since then, including a whole vegan line. You know I'm passionate about baking, but this allows me to use my art degree. Plus, I could make my own hours, more or less."

Mark rubbed his temple and exhaled. He reached his hand across the table to touch mine. "Jess, I agree that you're a fantastic baker and a skilled artist, but you're getting a little ahead of yourself. Baking is more of a hobby than a career, don't you think?"

"Not necessarily."

His eyes darted toward the people at a nearby table and then back to me. "And how many people really want tattoo designs on their cakes?"

"A lot of people would. It's something new. Edgy."

A look of pity washed over my husband's face, like a parent about to tell his eight-year-old she would not be getting that pony for Christmas. "Look, Jess, I'm not trying to kill your dream. You're free to bake cakes anytime you like—from our kitchen at home. But opening a store is a huge risk. Something like that could ruin us financially, especially if it doesn't go the way you've envisioned. I read that something like half of all small businesses fail in the first year."

My insides coiled, my hands clenching under the table. Why couldn't Mark at least play along and entertain the possibility before smashing my dream to bits? "I can't sell the cakes I make at home. I have to be licensed by the state. I need a commercial kitchen to do that."

"You mean people don't want Roo's fur stuck in their frosting?" Mark smiled. He was trying to make a joke so we could relax and move on, but his words felt like cold water spewing from a hose, dousing my flame of hope. I jutted my chin forward, not responding.

Mark shifted in his chair and tried again. "Have you thought about supply and demand? Aren't there already a few bakeries in Glenn Hills?"

"Yes." I looked away, annoyed that he was only viewing this from a business standpoint. Our suburb was already home to four independently owned bakeries, to be exact, but I wasn't going to share that information now. I held my breath and found Mark's eyes again. "There is only one high-end bakery in Glenn Hills, and it has horrible reviews online. Apparently, customer service isn't their strong point." My memory tumbled back over one particularly colorful and damning one-star review left by none other than Barbara Draper, complaining that her cake tasted like cardboard and sawdust. "Anyway, mine would be different—a novelty. No one makes cakes like mine. They're like edible art. Did you know people will pay thousands of dollars for a wedding cake?"

Mark sighed and adjusted the napkin on his lap. "I don't doubt it. But this is the first I've heard about this dream of yours. It's a lot. Maybe we can put the idea on hold for a while? See if you still feel the same a year or two from now. I know the job search has been stressing you out. Why don't you take a break from that for a while and enjoy being with Isabelle? I'm sure you'll know the perfect job when you see it, even it's six or eight months from now."

"But why can't we—"

Mark raised his fingers in the air, signaling for me to stop. "Jessica. It's not happening. I'm sorry. We just took on a new mortgage payment. We haven't remodeled the kitchen yet, and there's barely any money in our daughter's college fund. I'm not going to risk Isabelle's future. Or ours."

I felt my cheeks reddening and tears swelling behind my eyes, but I swallowed back the emotion. Mark had always been the voice of reason in our relationship, which was probably why I'd held off mentioning my idea to him for so long. I was the spontaneous one, the dreamer who sometimes acted on my emotions without thinking things through. Maybe he was right that my pipe dream wasn't worth the financial risk to our family, especially after we'd just gotten a fresh start.

Mark crossed his arms in front of his chest. Whether he realized it or not, he'd switched into combat mode. I didn't want to ruin our dinner out. We only got the chance to eat out on our own once a week, at best.

"Okay. I'll put the cake shop idea on hold for now. It's just something I've been thinking about." I pinched the stem of my wineglass, noticing the tremor in my fingers.

He uncrossed his arms. "I love you, Jess. And I support you. But some things are better left as hobbies."

I nodded.

A waitress in black pants and a pressed shirt swooped beside our table, all sparkles and smiles. "Hi, folks. Do you have any questions about the menu?"

"No," we both said at the same time.

FOUR

An hour later, I leaned against the passenger seat as Mark drove us home. The rest of our date at Frederick's had been quiet and uneventful. I continued answering questions and forcing smiles as if losing my dream of opening a cake shop hadn't been a big deal, but my insides felt deflated, and my appetite had all but vanished. While Mark had nursed his single vodka and tonic over appetizers, dinner, and dessert, I'd ordered two more glasses of wine—at least one more than I should have consumed. Mark had turned our conversation toward Isabelle's newest funny phrases and his latest drama with his boss, George, at the financial planning company where he worked. George was becoming more demanding of Mark's time, which I'd already known because of my husband's late arrivals home in recent days.

Now the car rattled along the road, making my overly full stomach even more queasy. Lights flitted by as we turned into our neighborhood entrance and toward home. Instead of taking a right into our driveway, as I was expecting, Mark continued straight.

I turned a questioning glance toward him.

"I thought we'd drive past Barbara's house. See if anything's going on," he said with a shrug.

A thread of curiosity pulled through me, replacing the sinking feeling that had been nagging me all night. I wondered if I was as bad as the people who gawked at car crashes and train wrecks. Maybe my need to witness another's tragedy was human nature. But Barbara's demise was more than that. It was a mystery too. A strange death had occurred too close to home. *Had it been an accident? Or Suicide? Or something even more sinister?* We rolled past the lit windows of the nearby houses.

Our backyard neighbor, Sean Peale, strolled along the sidewalk but disappeared into the shadows once we'd passed him. I'd seen him last night, too, and I hoped his after-dark walks weren't becoming routine. Making conversation with the man could be painful, his sideways grins always making me feel as if I had a rogue chunk of spinach stuck between my two front teeth. Mark slowed in front of the Draper house. A lamp illuminated a downstairs window, but the shades were partially drawn.

"Looks like someone might be there."

"Do you think it's Phil?"

"Probably. Unless he's in jail."

I couldn't stop myself from giggling, aware my reaction was wholly inappropriate.

We stared at the silent house for a moment, finding nothing of interest—no clues or suspects or information to shed light on our neighbor's strange death.

"Well, that was exciting."

"Yeah. We really cracked the case."

Mark accelerated up the street and circled the block. As we headed back toward our house, something jutted out in front of our car, our headlights illuminating a boy on a bike. Mark slammed on the brakes to avoid colliding with him.

"Watch it!" Mark huffed as the teenager turned to glare at us, then crossed the street and pedaled away. "He's wearing all black. Doesn't he know we can't see him?"

"That's Avery Moreno's son, I think. The older one. Thank God you didn't hit him."

"He was in a hurry."

"Probably heading to the park to meet his friends."

Mark threw up his chin. "Ha! Does that remind you of your high school days?"

"Kind of. I preferred walking, though." I looked away, banishing the vision of me and Dean Michaels behind the cement tunnel.

Mark drove toward our house, this time at a much slower pace. "I hope Isabelle didn't give Sophie any—"

"Wait. Stop the car! What's that?" A wavering outline moved somewhere outside my window.

Mark hit the brakes, and I lurched forward against the seat belt. A tall, shadowy figure stumbled out from behind the same hedges where I'd heard the rustling noises the night before. A man ambled across Barbara Draper's front lawn. Then he collapsed, laying murky and motionless.

I grabbed Mark's arm. "I think that's Phil."

"Oh, shit. You're right." He blinked out the window before turning toward me. "What should we do?"

"We should probably help him." My fingers went cold as I said the words. I remembered the wild hair and empty eyes I'd spied through the window of the police car this morning.

Mark closed his eyes and tipped his head back. "Okay. Yeah. We should." He edged the car closer to the curb and turned off the ignition. I opened my door at the same time he opened his.

Mark held his hand up. "Wait here."

"What? No. I'm coming with you."

"Jess!" Mark spoke in a loud whisper. "Who knows what this guy is capable of?"

"Look at him. He can barely stand up. You might need me."

My husband lowered his head and sighed. "Fine." He waved me forward. We closed the car doors. The heels of my shoes sunk into the grass as we inched toward the body splayed on the lawn. The motionless figure resembled a decaying log, but I feared Phil had a hidden violent streak. What if he was more like an alligator lying in wait? The car headlights clicked off. Now we could barely see anything.

I crouched near the toppled body, remembering how I'd stayed silent that night at the park as the boys taunted him, how Phil's mom had gently washed my bloody knee as I lay crying on the sidewalk. Helping him now was the least I could do. "Phil. It's your neighbor, Jessica Millstone. I'm Marilyn Tyler's daughter." I paused, waiting for a response, but there was none. "And my husband, Mark, is here too. We live two doors down."

"Huh." The man's eyes were closed. He rested his head on his arm, his chest rising and falling.

"He's passed out," Mark whispered.

"Should we call an ambulance?"

"What? No. It looks like he had a little too much to drink." Mark paced to the side and back again.

I stood up, remembering the rumors of painkiller addiction. "What if it's more than that?"

"I know what it looks like to be drunk. You were one glass of wine away from being in the same state." Mark nudged me with his elbow to let me know he was kidding.

I lifted my chin, slightly offended. My alcohol-induced haze had all but evaporated as I wavered in the chilly night air. "What do we do?"

"Let's help him into the house and get him some water." Mark crouched down. "Hey, buddy. Let's get you back inside so you can sleep this off."

"Okay." The mangled word managed its way from Phil's mouth. With a ridiculous amount of effort, Phil propped himself on one elbow. Mark grabbed the other elbow and pulled the man to his feet, supporting his weight. I followed a step behind, ready to break the fall of anyone who stumbled or needed help. They lumbered toward the front door, one awkward step at a time.

I wondered if Phil had tried to drink away the pain of his mom's death. Or was he attempting to drown his guilt?

"Great job. Almost there." Mark matched the man's slow pace.

Just as they approached the front step, Phil lurched away and bent over the bushes. He steadied himself against the wall as he vomited. His breathing was heavier now. He threw up again. Mark and I scooted away from him. I closed my eyes.

"Sorry. Sorry." Phil straightened and took a giant step toward the front steps.

"That's okay. It's probably good to get that out of your system." Mark looked over his shoulder and made a face at me. He grabbed Phil's arm and helped him up the steps while trying to leave space between them. Phil had left the front door unlocked, and I followed them inside. A small, dark foyer led to a more open living room, where wooden beams ran across a much higher ceiling. The kitchen doorway sat beyond the main living space, and stairs to the second floor rose from the room's far corner. Phil made a beeline for the couch and fell into it.

"I'll get some water." I hurried past them toward the kitchen. A collage of family photos hung from the living room's back wall. In the center photo, a curvy woman wearing a beaded ivory wedding dress tossed her head back in laughter. Her much taller groom gazed at her with a look of adoration. It took me a second to realize the woman in the photo was a young Barbara Draper. Somebody had captured the image decades earlier. I gasped. Other than the shape of her forehead and the slope of her nose, the woman in this picture looked nothing like the Barbara Draper I'd known. I wondered what had happened to Barbara in the intervening years. How had she gone from the happy woman on her wedding day to the miserable old hag who saw the worst in everyone and complained about everything? According to Mom, Barbara's husband, Ed Draper, had died about thirty years ago—when I was still little—but I didn't remember him at all.

I leaned forward to study the groom's face, but the only famil-iarity came from Phil's features. Phil shared his dad's narrow nose, lazy eyelids, and mud-brown eyes. The surrounding photos were of Phil as a baby and a toddler. A couple of images pictured family vacations with palm trees in the background. Then there was Phil at his high school graduation, forcing a stiff smile from under his purple and gold cap and gown. He'd graduated five years before me from Glenn Hills High School.

Phil groaned from the couch, and I yanked my gaze from the frame, remembering what I was doing. I hurried into the kitchen for the water. The decor was outdated by at least twenty-five years, just like our kitchen. However, the room was immaculate. The air smelled faintly of eggs and onions, but no dishes sat out anywhere. I opened a couple of cupboards before finding one that housed the glasses. I filled the glass with water from the kitchen faucet and carried it into the living room, where Mark pulled the shoes off Phil's feet.

"Here you go. Can you drink this?" I asked, holding the glass to his mouth.

Phil's eyes popped open as if seeing me for the first time. He struggled to raise his neck from his prone position and sipped from the glass. Then he flopped his head back onto the cushion and closed his eyes.

I set the glass on the end table next to him.

Mark tipped his head toward the door. "He'll be fine. We should go."

"Yeah." The air felt thick. The place gave me the creeps, especially knowing what had recently transpired in the bathroom upstairs. We'd done our good deed for the day by helping Phil. We had no proof that he had anything to do with his mother's death. The medical examiner had already reached a different, albeit somewhat rushed, conclusion.

I took one last look around the inside of the house. I must have walked past thousands of times over the years but I had never seen inside its walls. It bore the stamp of Barbara Draper everywhere—from the evenly spaced pictures on the walls to the vacuum lines on the carpeting to the outdated, dust-free furniture. A monument to order and cleanliness. Mark strode toward the foyer, on a mission to leave before anything else happened. But just as we reached the front door, I heard mumbling from the living room. It was Phil, speaking in tangled half-sentences, attempting to convey a message through his stupor.

Mark narrowed his eyes. "He's talking gibberish. Let's go."

I held up my finger as curiosity got the better of me. Phil had been through so much. He must have known more about what had happened to his mother than anyone. I turned on my heel and returned to the couch, where Phil lay silent. "What did you say?"

There was no response.

"Jessica. Let's get out of here." Mark's feet stomped from the foyer.

I ignored him. "Phil, what did you say a second ago?"

The man's eyes were closed. He breathed heavily and slowly, like someone asleep. I realized I'd lost my opportunity to glimpse through the murky window of Phil's tortured soul. I turned and took two steps away from him, heading back toward Mark.

All at once, Phil's scratchy voice cut through the air again, his chilling words causing my spine to straighten and my toe to catch on the floor. I steadied myself against the wall, swallowing against my dry throat as my mind registered his statement.

"It wasn't an accident."

FIVE

"He said, 'It wasn't an accident.'"

"Really?" Bree's black mascara weighed down her eyelashes. "Wow. That's creepy."

A toddler squealed from across the park. My gaze landed on Isabelle, who sat in a communal sandbox a few feet away from the bench where I perched next to Bree. My daughter was easy to spot in her blue-and-pink striped sweatshirt. She shoved a flimsy shovel into the sand and poured its contents into a plastic bucket. I admired the sheer determination on her face.

Bree dropped her phone into her purse. "What did you do then?"

"I shook Phil's shoulders but couldn't get him to talk anymore. He'd completely passed out. Mark wanted to get out of there as quickly as possible, so we left." I pressed my back against the wooden bench.

"What do you think he meant by 'It wasn't an accident'?"

"Well, probably that his mom's death wasn't an accident." Bree raised a plucked eyebrow at me and grinned.

"Come on! What do you think he really meant?"

"I don't know. Maybe Barbara died by suicide, like you said yesterday. It couldn't have been easy to lose her husband at such a young age, to be hated by literally everyone, and to have her only child end up as a drug addict. She could have gulped down a bunch of pills and climbed into the tub. Being under the influence, she probably lost her footing on the wet floor and hit her head on the way in. She seemed especially grumpy when I saw her that night. I've never seen anyone take flattened property values so personally."

"Did she seem depressed?"

"Not particularly. Then again, I've heard that depression can reveal itself in different ways, including anger."

"Huh." A cloud blocked the sun, and I propped my sunglasses on top of my head. "I got the feeling Phil was talking about himself."

Bree tipped her head back. "Why? I mean the guy is a creeper, don't get me wrong, but his mom was pretty much all he had. She stood by him when no one else would. Plus, it felt like he was on another planet when I was there. You should have seen the glazed look in his eyes. I wasn't sure if it was the drugs or if my presentation was boring him to death."

"What do you mean by a creeper?" I pressed my palms into the bench and watched Isabelle carry an empty bucket to the other side of the sandbox. Other than that night in the very park where we now sat, my knowledge of Phil was limited to vague childhood memories of a secretive older boy who lived two doors down and mostly kept to himself. Over the last two years, I'd only spotted him a handful of times getting the mail or mowing the lawn. He'd always averted his eyes and bolted at my approach.

Bree fiddled with her bracelet. "Phil stares at me a lot, for one thing. But only when he thinks I'm not looking. It can be uncomfortable. I've been over to their house a few times now. He's usually lurking somewhere in the shadows, pretending to be interested in the price analysis, but really he's just... watching. Watching *me*, specifically. When I acknowledge him by saying hi or whatever, he pretends like he was looking out the window or doing something else."

"Sounds like he's unnerved by your beauty. He probably has the hots for you."

"Ha." Bree waved me off. "Phil has the maturity of a twelve-year-old boy, but I've always thought of him as harmless, at least to everyone except himself. He's like a mouse that's scared of the daylight."

"Do you think he inherited the house?"

"Probably. I'm not aware of any other immediate family."

"Maybe money was his real motive." I flashed a sly look toward my friend. "Maybe he'll be more motivated to sell than his mom."

Bree shook her head. "That's horrible, Jess."

"Sorry."

Bree lifted her chin. "To be honest, the thought did cross my mind. It's way too soon to broach that subject, though."

I ran my fingertips over a metal bolt in the park bench. "I just can't stop thinking about Phil muttering that it wasn't an accident. How would he know that unless he was involved?"

"Why would he incriminate himself?" Bree asked, pinching her lips together.

"Guilt? He was totally out of it. He probably didn't even realize he was talking out loud."

"Still. It's most likely Barbara's death was an accident. Or, at worst, suicide. I told you what the medical examiner said."

"What about murder? By someone other than Phil."

Bree fluttered her thick eyelashes. "Barbara had plenty of enemies, but I don't see it. No one would kill a sixty-five-year-old widow over being yelled at to keep off her grass or because of a bad review she left on The Neighbor List."

"People have done crazier things. Haven't they? Maybe Phil saw or heard something the other night. Something that didn't seem important until later." I thought back to the people I'd seen near Barbara's house that night: Sean Peale and Avery Moreno. But Bree and I had been nearby too.

Bree faced me, frowning. "Listen, you had a weird experience, and I'm sorry for that. But I think you've been watching too many real-life crime documentaries. My advice is to mind your own business and let the police handle it. You said yourself that you saw Phil in the back of the police car. I'm sure he already told the detectives everything he knows. Focus on your daughter and your perfect life."

"Huh." I crossed my arms. I wanted to tell Bree how unperfect my life was, but she was going through a rough time, and I didn't want to be insensitive. I angled myself away from her, setting my jaw. As much as I tried to shutter away the past and block out my unsettling memories, they whirled through me. It had been nearly four years since I'd been mugged in the underground parking garage beneath our trendy Corktown loft building in Detroit. The event caused something inside me to shift, shattering my confidence; it was the moment I'd realized I wasn't as tough as I thought I was.

I'd been weighed down with a layer of pregnancy weight and sweating in the summer humidity as I heaved two bags of groceries from the back of my SUV, keys clutched in my fingers and envisioning the Asian-inspired stir-fry I was going to make as a surprise for Mark. He'd been working such long hours, too tired to do much other than watch TV when he got home. In the preceding weeks, Mark had seemed more interested in helping Sharon, our new neighbor across the hall, with her household repairs than with taking care of our own condo or in daydreaming with me about my decorating ideas for our baby's nursery. Mark's sudden friendship with our attractive neighbor had been on my mind as I turned to carry the groceries through the shadowy rows of cars. The elevator sat on the far wall and I'd been so focused on getting there that I hadn't noticed the silent figure lurking behind a nearby pickup truck. He stood and strode toward me with purpose, the man's sheer size causing terror to ripple through me. That was before I even spotted the focused gleam in his small eyes and the gun in his hand.

"Don't scream." He'd spoken calmly as he lifted the weapon, eyes darting from me to the garage door.

A bottle of pepper spray sat buried somewhere in the bottom of my purse. I often held the spray close at night but hadn't thought to have it handy at 4:30 in the afternoon in my building's supposedly secure garage. The tiny baby growing inside me had been the only thing I could think about as I stared at the gun, stunned into silence. The man was several inches taller than me with broad shoulders. Even if the gun wasn't loaded, I'd surely lose this battle. Still, I had to protect the baby. Ignoring the man's orders, I attempted to scream, hoping someone else in the garage would hear me and call 911. But when I opened my mouth, my cry for help emerged more like a croak, my voice lodged in my throat as only tears flowed from my eyes instead.

The man lunged toward me with a grunt, ripping the purse from my body so hard that the straps broke. The grocery bags fell from my hands, a can of coconut milk, bok choy, onions, and limes spilling out onto the concrete floor. I cowered, bracing myself for a gunshot, but footsteps sounded instead. The man sprinted away with my bag, fleeing between the parked cars and through the emergency exit, leaving me slumped on the ground, crying.

A young couple pulled into the garage a minute or two later and rushed to help me. The mugger had only stolen my purse, I explained as I stood and brushed myself off, my key ring still intertwined in my fingers. But now I knew, in fact, he'd taken much, much more. My sense of security had been destroyed. Between the mugging and the lingering presence of our younger, skinnier, more effervescent neighbor across the hall, I realized I didn't want to stay in our city loft any longer. Several months later, Mom told us her house was for sale. I'd thought moving back to my safe suburb and into my childhood home was the clear answer. But now here I was living two doors down from a woman who'd possibly been murdered. Maybe my plan hadn't been a good one at all.

Bree's bracelets clinked against each other, pulling me out of my sinking thoughts. As she crossed her arms and watched Isabelle, I could see she wasn't in the mood to listen to my wild theories. It was the same response I'd gotten from Mark after the incident last night when I'd suggested we report Phil's statement to the police.

"What's Mark doing today?" Bree asked in an obvious attempt to change the subject.

"He went for a jog. Now he's out running some errands." I picked my fingernail, remembering that I hadn't asked Bree about her rendezvous with our new neighbor. Last night's events with Phil had consumed my thoughts. "Hey, tell me about Rick. What's he like? When are you going out?"

Bree's jeweled eyes came alive. "I think this one's a catch. He's got this southern accent that's so charming. There aren't any issues in the looks department." Bree winked. "And his business seems like a success."

"A house-flipping business?"

"Yeah. Rick works for himself. He does some smaller remodeling projects too. His company is called Kensington Renovations."

"Wow. It sounds like this guy checks all the boxes." I gazed across the park. "Bree Kensington. That has a nice ring to it."

Bree swatted my arm. "Oh, shut up. We haven't even gone out on a date yet. Anyway, his last name is Smith, not Kensington. And I'm never going to change my name, even on the slim chance that I remarry."

I laughed. "Smith doesn't sound as fancy."

"It's not that. In real estate, your name is your brand."

"No kidding, Bree Bradley, *I Sell Glenn Hills*," I said, repeating her well-worn tagline. "Everyone has heard your name around here. By the way, I just saw your shiny full-page ad in *The Scene*. How much did that set you back?" *The Scene* was a local magazine highlighting social events for the area's most prominent socialites and business people.

"More than I care to share, but that's why I have credit cards. Right?"

I bit my lip, hearing the crack in her voice.

"I'm joking," she said. "The payment was nothing an extra commission can't cover."

"The ad looked great. I hope you get some new business from it."

"Yeah. Me, too. Anyway, I'm meeting Rick at that French Bistro on Main Street on Wednesday."

"Ooh! Sounds romantic. I can't wait to hear all about it."

"Thanks." Bree pulled her phone out of her purse, read a text, and put it away, a routine she'd performed every three minutes since I'd reconnected with her two years ago. "You know, Rick mentioned that he hadn't met any of the neighbors yet."

"Yeah, I tried to catch him outside the day he was moving in, but I missed him."

"No big deal. It's just that he was unsure about writing a contract on the house initially, so I gave him the hard sell on the neighborhood. I don't want my client to think I lied and that his neighbors are unwelcoming. And now, with everything that's happened with Barbara Draper. I'd hate for him to have buyer's remorse."

I sat up straighter. "Rick probably won't be living there too long if he's planning to flip. But you're right. We should have been more welcoming. I'm going to make a cake for him. I'll take it over in a day or two."

"Oh, you don't have to go to that much trouble."

"No. I want to. Baking is fun for me." Mark's words from the night before echoed through me: *"Baking is more of a hobby."* Maybe he was right.

"Okay. I'm sure Rick would appreciate that. And so would I." Bree elbowed me. "And maybe put in a good word for me as long as you're there."

I gave Bree a mock salute. "Will do."

Isabelle staggered toward us, carrying a bucket full of sand. "Mommy! Bwee! Your cake is ready!"

Bree clapped her hands. "Oh! Looks delicious."

Isabelle grinned and jumped up and down as Bree and I pretended to devour her sand creation.

A high-pitched voice chirped behind us, and I turned to see

Stephanie Peale and her head of auburn curls heading toward the park. She lugged an oversized tote bag on her shoulder as her two-and-a-half-year-old twin boys hopped alongside her.

Bree followed my gaze. "Well, that's my cue to leave."

Bree didn't like Stephanie, and I suspected the reverse was also true. Unlike her recalcitrant husband, Sean, Stephanie possessed the gift of gab. She was one of those women who'd seemingly prepared her entire life for motherhood, wholly absorbed in her boys' every activity and possessing more knowledge on every stage of childhood development than any regular person should know. She ran a natural motherhood blog where she posted daily tips, recipes, and anecdotes to help struggling parents. Oddly, reading her blog only made me feel worse about my parenting skills, as if I was always falling seventeen steps short. The mommy blogger wasn't someone I'd typically be close friends with, but the proximity of our houses and having kids roughly the same age had forced a bond.

When we'd first moved in, Mark and I had made an initial attempt to befriend the couple bordering our backyard fence before realizing we weren't a great match with the Peales. We'd had them over for dinner, which had turned into an awkward two-hour affair. That night, we'd learned that Sean was a podiatrist who owned a small practice in town. We'd also discovered his talent for making whoever he was talking to feel incredibly uncomfortable. Mark had stretched his face toward me several times throughout the night as if to say, "help!" The four of us had never made plans again, although I ran into Stephanie at the park several times a week.

Bree dabbed her lips with an invisible napkin and winked at Isabelle. "Mmm. Sorry to eat and run, but I have to get ready for my open house on the other side of town. The place has been sitting on the market for over four months."

I brushed some sand from my lap. "I hope it goes well. Thanks for meeting us."

"Any time." Bree dug through her purse and sighed. "Ugh. I forgot my cardholder."

"A realtor with no cards. Sounds like the kiss of death."

"Boys! Stay together!" Stephanie called in the distance. "Hi, Jessica." Stephanie waved at me and dipped her head toward Bree as she neared, offering the kind of forced smile that isn't a smile at all, sugary sweet and laced with arsenic. Stephanie's shadow blocked the sunlight as she thrust two pieces of paper at us. "I'm sure you already heard, but Sean is running for the open seat on City Council. There's a special election in five months."

I stared at the flier in my hand.

Dr. Sean Peale for Glenn Hills City Council. Vote for Family Values First.

Bree grimaced and looped a finger through her key ring.

"Wow," I said. "No. I hadn't heard." I looked down to hide my shock, wondering if Sean's "Family Values First" tagline was some sort of far-right dog whistle to homophobic voters. A hundred smart remarks flew through my head, but my mouth had gone dry and I couldn't speak. I was astounded that someone as socially inept as Sean Peale would throw himself into the political arena, even one as limited as the Glenn Hills City Council.

"Hope it works out," Bree said, her flat tone conveying she couldn't give a crap. She stood and crossed in front of me, offering a curt nod to Stephanie as she passed.

I wished Bree wasn't abandoning me as I braced myself for conversations about Sean's venture into local politics, followed by lectures on sugar-free applesauce and toddler sleep patterns.

As Stephanie began talking, Bree slipped through the gate and fled toward her car, dressed in her fitted pencil skirt and silk blouse. Her bright lipstick and smoky eyeshadow popped beneath her sleek low ponytail. But her attractive exterior failed to hide the fault lines in her voice when she said, "The place has been sitting on the market for four months," or "That's why I have credit cards." I pictured Bree's leased Mercedes, the mortgage payment on the condo she used to share with her ex-husband but now covered herself, and the array of designer clothes and purses she collected to keep up her image. I wondered how desperate my friend's financial situation really was.

SIX

I loaded the groceries in the back of my SUV. Unlike Bree's gleaming Mercedes, my vehicle was bruised, battered, and paid in full. This morning, Mom had made another one of her unannounced visits, insisting that I get out of the house and *do* something while she played with Isabelle. I promised Mark I'd talk to her about the increasing frequency of her pop-in visits, but Mom's eyes had shone when she spotted her granddaughter. We'd been low on food, and I'd already been planning on heading to the grocery store, so I avoided the subject, thankful for a shopping trip that didn't involve Isabelle whining for every box of donuts and carton of ice cream we passed.

Now I sat in the Kroger parking lot, stifling a yawn. I turned over a "Sean Peale for City Council" flier someone had wedged beneath my windshield wiper and sighed, wondering about the cost of the Peales' relentless marketing, and remembering my encounter with Stephanie at the park yesterday. I'd mentioned to her that I'd seen Sean walking outside the night Barbara died, and she confirmed that her husband often strolled at night to get some air and gather his thoughts. I hadn't meant to insinuate anything, but Stephanie immediately suggested that Barbara's son was likely responsible if any foul play had been involved and that she and Sean were fast asleep by 10 p.m. Then she steered the conversation toward her newest blog post on the best organic cotton pajamas for kids. I'd nodded along but couldn't ignore the fact that Stephanie had defended her husband against an accusation that had never been made.

I crumpled the flier, realizing I was probably reading into clues that weren't really there. A check of my phone revealed my shopping errand had only taken thirty minutes. Mom would probably be disappointed if I returned so soon, so I debated hitting a nearby coffee shop or maybe even a bookstore. Just the thought of sipping a latte while browsing for a page-turner felt like a luxury, but I quickly discounted the idea. My fingers scrolled past The Neighbor List icon on my screen, then back again. A post I'd seen on the app a couple of days earlier called to me, and I couldn't resist indulging my daydream for a few minutes. I scrolled down to the listing I'd bookmarked:

> Retail Space Available in Oak View strip mall. 300 sq ft. Easy parking. Formerly Baked bread shop.

I knew the location of the Oak View strip mall, only a couple of miles away. My insides hummed with anticipation as I entered the address in my GPS. But just before I backed out of my parking space, a notification popped on my screen, indicating a private message from someone on The Neighbor List. I clicked the message box, finding a message waiting from a user called Admin1. Was that the administrator? My eyes scanned the words:

> Enjoy your perfect family.

I blinked, my breath suddenly shallow. Was it a compliment or a threat? I swung my head over my shoulder, searching the surroundings for anyone suspicious or familiar. I couldn't imagine why someone claiming to be an administrator of the app would send this message to me. I reread it, looking for any clues I may have missed the first time. There was no real name linked to the account, just Admin1. The sentence sounded like something Bree often said to me as she operated under the illusion that my life was some kind of fairy tale. But I couldn't imagine my friend doing something like this, even as a joke.

Who is this? I wrote back, finger shakily typing. I waited a few minutes for a response, but none came. Maybe the message wasn't intended for me. I exited the app and inhaled a long breath, pressing my back into the driver's seat. I'd show the message to Mark later. He'd know what to do.

Remembering what I'd been doing before receiving the creepy message, I backed out of my parking space and followed the directions toward the address. A former bread shop would be the perfect space for my cake business, even if it was a pipe dream. I had already come up with a potential name: Inked Cakes. A sign reminiscent of a tattoo parlor with Gothic black lettering against a red background materialized in my mind.

I left the parking lot and drove through our suburb's quaint downtown area, scanning the storefronts, cafés, and restaurants. There was another bakery on Main Street, but it was more of a coffee shop bakery, serving muffins and scones along with hot beverages. It wasn't competition for a novelty cake concept like mine.

A few minutes later, I reached the Oak View strip mall entrance. The lot was about half filled with cars. A dentist's office, a tutoring service, a cell phone shop, and a boutique shoe store filled the spaces closest to me. Next door to a vision center sat a small storefront with a brown sign with *Baked* written on it. The lights were off, and a commercial realty company had affixed a *For Lease* sign to the window. My foot pressed the accelerator as my car crept around the edge of the lot, closer to the empty store. I stared at the front of the vacant shop, envisioning my edgy sign above the store and myself inside, wearing a tailored apron and finishing up the final details on a wedding cake. My imaginary masterpiece featured white chocolate icing with a show-stopping tattoo design across the top—the word "forever" and a fiery arrow piercing into a red heart. Another woman would stroll toward the counter to pick up her birthday cake order. My mind floated away on the warm waters of my idyllic vision. I felt as if I'd swallowed a gulp of sunshine, as if lightness radiated from my core, and out through my fingertips.

My phone buzzed, slicing through my daydream. I blinked, remembering the cake shop wasn't real. This bread shop sat vacant because it had gone out of business just like Mark had predicted. I fumbled to accept the call. Baking was only a hobby. Mom's name flashed on the screen. She didn't usually call when she was with Isabelle, but maybe she needed something from the store. I swerved left into an open spot.

"Hi. What's u—"

"Jessica, don't panic, but there's been an accident." Isabelle's wails nearly drowned out Mom's voice. "I'm taking Isabelle to the emergency room now."

My daughter had been in an accident. My hands went cold, and I felt as if all the blood was draining from my body. "What happened? Is she okay?"

"She fell out of the booster seat in the kitchen. I can't believe it. I only left her for a minute to find my glasses. The seat slipped right off the chair, and she landed on her head. There's some blood. We're in my car right now headed to Old Memorial on Jefferson." I could barely hear my mom over the screams. The seat of the car seemed to disintegrate beneath me.

"I'll meet you there."

Panic rose in me, hot tears stinging my eyes as I sped from the parking lot and rushed to the emergency room. What an idiot I'd been. Sophie had warned me about the booster seat, and I hadn't bothered to remove it and order a new one. My daughter's safety should have been my top priority. I'd been too consumed with my silly dreams and made-up murder mysteries to focus on my daughter's well-being. Mark, Sophie, and Bree had suggested I stop living in my fantasy world of what-ifs and live in the here and now. I hadn't listened. If anything happened to Isabelle, it was all my fault. The strange message I'd received minutes earlier suddenly seemed more relevant as it reverberated through my mind:

Enjoy your perfect family.

SEVEN

Mark tightened the nylon strap around the base of the kitchen chair and jiggled the new booster seat. "There we go. That sucker isn't going anywhere."

Isabelle hopped. "Yeah!"

"Yeah!" Mark joined her, pumping his fist.

I pulled Isabelle into my lap and kissed the top of her head, appreciating the feel of her silky hair against my skin. She was okay, although yesterday's fall had left a cut near her hairline that required four stitches. After Isabelle's treatment at the hospital, I'd immediately driven to the closest baby store and purchased a new booster seat. By the time I'd thought to show Mark the mysterious message I'd received through The Neighbor List, someone had deleted it altogether. I couldn't locate any users named Admin1.

Mark slurped down the last of his coffee. "I've got to go to work."

The clock on the wall read 8 a.m. I tipped my head toward the seat. "Thanks for installing that."

"Sure thing."

I slid Isabelle to her feet and raised myself from the chair. "I'm still creeped out by that message. *Enjoy your perfect family.* Who would say that? It sounds threatening. Doesn't it?"

Mark exhaled, shaking his head. "Or like advice from a fortune cookie." He smirked, but I didn't laugh. "Maybe the app has a virus," he said. "You said yourself there is no user by the sender's name. The message probably wasn't even meant for you, which was why someone deleted it."

"Yeah. Maybe."

Mark set down his mug and turned to Isabelle, a smile competing with the angst in his eyes. "Hey, can you get me a fruit salad from your kitchen?"

Isabelle nodded and bolted toward her play kitchen in the living room.

Mark stepped closer to me. "Listen, I was thinking about your mom." His voice was a lower pitch than usual.

"What about her?"

"Maybe she isn't the best person to watch Isabelle anymore. You know, she's getting older. More forgetful. Not to mention, she acts like she still lives here half the time."

My muscles constricted. Mark frequently got away with offhand comments when it came to my mom but blaming her for Isabelle's fall wasn't fair. "The accident wasn't Mom's fault. I told you already. I should have replaced the booster seat as soon as Sophie warned me about the recall. It's my fault Isabelle fell."

"Yeah. But your mom wasn't even in the room when it happened."

"She misplaced her glasses. She went into the other room for a split second. It could have happened to any of us."

Mark touched his clean-shaven face as he gazed toward the window. "I guess."

"Anyway, you should have seen how devastated Mom was. Isabelle means everything to her."

"Yeah. I know." Mark turned away, shoulders slumping.

"And I haven't found a good time to bring up the unannounced visits yet. But I will."

"Daddy! Here's your fwuit salad." Isabelle stared at Mark with her butter-soft gaze, shoving a blue bowl brimming with wooden fruits in front of him. He pretended to gobble it up like all good dads did and then kissed us goodbye before he left through the garage. I hoped I'd put his concerns about my mom to rest.

Several hours later, I added the final details to the top of my almost-famous double-chocolate pudding cake. I'd gone with a "Home Sweet Home" design, featuring a log house with roots growing below it and intertwining into a heart. It was freshly baked and ready to deliver to Bree's most recent love interest, Rick.

First, I retrieved my sketchpad from the kitchen table, eager to replace it to its secure spot in the desk drawer of our first-floor study. The notepad was a piece of myself, the place where I recorded all my design and recipe ideas, including detailed, colored mock-ups of what my future Inked Cakes sign might look like. Since the dinner at Frederick's, I'd decided it was important to have a dream, even if it never became a reality. I carried the pad through the living room and into the wood-paneled study, my eye catching on something amiss. I stepped toward the spot where my favorite family photo usually sat on an upper shelf. It was the picture Mom had snapped of me, Mark, and Isabelle on the beach last August. In it, Isabelle grasped our hands, head thrown back in laughter, as we swung her between us with the Lake Michigan surf in the background. That had been a fun weekend. I touched the frame, which now lay face down. An inexplicable shiver skittered across my skin. I righted the frame and gasped at the crack running across the glass. The object had fallen with such force that the protective layer of glass had shattered. I looked around, realizing Mark left the window in here open sometimes. A gust of wind must have blown it over. Either that or Roo had knocked himself into the shelf while chasing a ball or barking at a squirrel. I noted the size of the image—five by seven inches—and added "buy new picture frame" to my to-do list.

"Mommy!" Isabelle said.

I tucked my notepad into the drawer and returned to the

kitchen where Isabelle perched over a mini table in the corner, making pretend cakes with Play-Doh. I winced every time I caught sight of the medical tape covering the stitches on her head.

I wiped a speck of frosting on my apron. "Okay, darling. Are we ready to deliver this cake to our new neighbor?"

"Yeah. And this one." Isabelle pointed to the mound of Play-Doh on a plastic plate.

"Oh. You made a cake, too?"

"Yeah."

We dropped a treat in Roo's dish and left him dozing near the door. Our overgrown grass brushed my ankles as we cut across the yard. Mark had skipped mowing this week because of his long hours at the office, and I'd campaigned to hire a lawn-care service. When Mark suggested I cut the grass in my free time, it felt like another brick piled on my shoulders, another gaffe opening between us caused by a complete lack of understanding. There was no free time, other than the few hours on Thursday mornings when Sophie helped out, and I didn't want to spend it mowing the lawn. On a matter of principle, I'd resisted.

Isabelle and I made our way down the street, crossing Maple-view Lane to avoid the Drapers' house. I carried my cake in a large tote while Isabelle held hers out in front of her. She took method-ical steps as if she were navigating a balance beam rather than a sidewalk.

"Here we are." We'd reached the destination at last. I pointed to the nondescript ranch-style house that had recently changed owners and registered its condition, noticing a greater degree of neglect up close. Overgrown vines scaled the beige brick, trapping the house in their sprawling webs. The worn siding and shutters practically screamed for a coat of paint. The moss-covered roof dipped in a spot over the garage. The previous owner, Greta Wash-burn, had let the place go. Rick had a huge project awaiting him.

We climbed two cement steps, and I rang the doorbell. There was no movement. I half expected to hear demolition going on inside or to see contractors' trucks parked in the driveway, but the house lay quiet. I worried we'd have to repeat our welcome wagon later in the day.

I knocked.

"Cake delivewy!" Isabelle yelled.

I began to turn back toward our side of the street when a deep voice called from beyond the fenced-in backyard. "Be right there." A broad-shouldered man battled with a misaligned latch on the gate but forced his way through. He smiled as he strode around the house toward us with a confident posture. His hair shone gold in the sun, and he wore it chin-length, the ends barely staying tucked behind his ears. My gaze traveled from his muscular build to the rugged crinkles around his eyes. I could see why Bree was attracted to him.

I raised my hand in a wave as he approached. "Hi. I'm Jessica Millstone from across the street and two doors down. This is my daughter, Isabelle. I hope we're not intruding, but we wanted to welcome you to the neighborhood."

"Well, hello. It's a pleasure." His words stretched with a slow southern drawl. His calloused hand closed around my smooth one. "I'm Rick Smith." As he extended his arm, I noticed a swirling tattoo extending past his elbow. It was the wing of a bird, probably a hawk or an eagle, etched in intricate detail. The top of the design was covered by his short-sleeved shirt.

"We made cakes for you." Isabelle held up her mound of clay.

The man's honey-brown eyes widened in delight. He took Isabelle's creation first, then the bag from me, peeking inside. "Wow. These look delicious." He did a double take at mine. "What a cool design. I truly appreciate it."

"I've been practicing a new recipe. The designs are tattoo-inspired." I nodded toward his bicep.

"I can see that." He raised his inked arm. "I got this one about ten years ago. Think about getting another one every once in a while, but I chicken out every time." He smiled. The smooth twang of his accent made me feel like I was lounging on a veranda sipping lemonade on a hot summer day. Maybe Bree was on to something here.

I steadied my feet. "Whereabouts are you from? If you don't mind me asking."

"Just outside Atlanta, originally. I've lived in the Detroit area for about five years now, although I move about once a year. I own a house-flipping business. It's more cost-effective if I live where I work." He thumbed toward the house. "This place was a strong candidate for renovation."

I chuckled. "We're glad you're fixing it up. I'm a friend of Bree's. She told me a little about you."

"Hopefully only good things." He winked.

"Of course. Bree knows her stuff."

"She sure does." He turned, stretching his chin toward our house. "Bree mentioned you, too. Said a friend of hers grew up in that house and then bought it from her mom a couple of years ago. That's really something."

"Yeah. It's kind of weird, I know."

"Not at all. It must be nice to have such strong roots."

"It is, but we have plenty of home improvement projects to do ourselves."

"I bet." Rick flashed a smile. "I look forward to eating these beautiful cakes. In fact, I'm going to eat this one right now." He pretended to take several large bites out of the Play-Doh cake. "Mm, hmm! That is good. Thank you so much, Miss Isabelle."

Isabelle hopped up and down, her wide eyes entranced by our new neighbor.

Rick eyed Isabelle's lopsided bandage. "I see you have an injury on your head. That's what I look like half the time too. My hammer swings back when I least expect it and bonks me in the head." Rick swooped his arm through the air and hit himself in the forehead with his palm before going cross-eyed.

Isabelle doubled over with laughter, and I couldn't help chuckling myself.

He handed the plastic plate back to Isabelle. "I'm going to put this other piece of art your mom made inside for later. Then I best get back to repairing the pool. It's in bad shape."

"We won't hold you up." I stretched my neck to the side and tried to glimpse beyond the privacy fence. I'd almost forgotten Mrs. Washburn had a pool hidden back there. I vaguely remembered swimming in it once or twice as a child. My parents had joined the woman occasionally for cocktails on her patio, and I'd gotten to tag along. I doubted anyone had used the pool in years.

"It's usually a lot quieter around here," I added, nodding toward the Draper house. "This hasn't been a typical few days by any means."

Rick exhaled and wiped his palm on his shirt, eyes flickering across the street. "Yeah. It was quite a welcome to the neighborhood. I couldn't believe the sirens and police cars the other morning, but Bree stopped by and filled me in on the details. I understand Barbara Draper wasn't going to invite me to any tea parties anyway."

"No. Probably not. She was a little... abrasive."

Rick sighed, shaking his head. "Accidents happen everywhere, I guess. Even in nice neighborhoods like this."

"Yeah." I hooked my thumb in my pocket, not sure how to respond. Phil's statement cycled through my head: *It wasn't an accident.* Of course, I wouldn't reveal my suspicions to Rick. I didn't want to scare him away or do anything else to prevent him from fixing up the pile of bricks he'd purchased. A flip of Greta Washburn's house would help everyone's property values.

"I'm sure the drama will have blown over by the time I go to list it for sale again. This house needs several months of work." He made a face. "More than I realized."

"Well, good luck with everything." My feet shuffled backward. "We'll get out of your hair."

"Thanks again for the cakes." Rick tipped his head. "It's been a pleasure, ladies."

"For us too." I looked at Isabelle. "Can you say goodbye to Mr. Smith?"

Isabelle waved her sticky hand. "Bye, Mr. Smith."

I smiled at him and gripped Isabelle's fingers. She clutched her ball of dough and plastic plate in the other hand and traipsed next to me. I couldn't help noticing Rick had mowed his lawn in an attractive pattern of diagonal lines. I considered pointing it out to Mark later but worried my passive-aggressive tactic could backfire.

As we crossed the street, the warm feeling in my chest dissipated as I eyed the line of hedges stretching along the Drapers' fence, remembering the rustling noises I'd heard a few nights before. The upstairs window reflected in the sun, more like a mirror than a piece of glass. I couldn't shake the feeling something sinister had taken place inside those walls. There was no view into the house, only the imprint in my mind of Barbara's staring eyes, only her muted scream echoing in my ears. I squeezed my daughter's hand more tightly and hurried home.

THE NEIGHBOR LIST

Username: AMoreno

Subject: Lawn Mowing in Ridgeview Pines Neighborhood

Hi Neighbors! My teenage sons are earning money for their college funds by mowing lawns in the neighborhood this summer. Please message me if you'd like a quote.

StephPeale: Good for them! It's nice to see teens doing honest work.

Coach58: I could use some help. I'll message you.

Click to view thirteen more comments

EIGHT

Thirty minutes later, heavy breathing crackled through the baby monitor, broadcasting the sounds from Isabelle's room upstairs. Her chattering and singing had finally faded, and I knew she was asleep. I melted into the couch cushion and clicked off the job search site I'd been browsing, finding only one lukewarm lead—a marketing position with a local bank that barely paid enough to cover the cost of full-time day care. I tipped my head back and massaged my temples, unsure where my future would lead. My planned six-month maternity leave had already morphed into three years. The longer I waited, the weaker my résumé would appear to a potential employer. Still, the thought of locking myself inside a sterile office from nine to five every day filled me with dread. Many other people did it, though. Why did I expect to be different? Then again, we could survive on Mark's paycheck. We'd been doing it for three years now, although we had little left over for family vacations or other extravagances.

I wanted my child to view me as a modern woman who could balance a career, family, and social life. And Isabelle would be starting Kindergarten in a couple of years. Then what would I do? A persistent thought continued to force its way into my head. Baking and art—two things I was good at. The idea of combining them both into a business lit a fire inside my belly. Sometimes I popped awake in bed at night thinking about ways to change up an old recipe—a tablespoon of lemon zest here or a dash of peppermint extract there—and picturing the perfect tattoo to go along with a certain flavor or occasion. My lime-coconut cake would feature an image of a palm tree with the words "Life is a Vacation" inked in a swirling ribbon around the trunk. My strawberries and cream layered cake would showcase my take on the classic Mom tattoo with a heart and an arrow, making the perfect Mother's Day surprise.

But Mark was right. Opening my own business was too risky. There was too much to lose. My eyes wandered across the safe and familiar walls of my childhood home, more evidence that I wasn't the risk-taker I'd made myself out to be.

I picked up my phone to check The Neighbor List, telling myself I was merely checking for new job leads. It was a relief to find no more messages from unidentified people waiting in my inbox. Before I realized what I was doing, I'd typed Barbara's name into the search bar, pulling up a list of her most recent posts. There were dozens of them from the last month alone. I scanned the headings.

WHERE CAN I GET A DECENT CUP OF COFFEE IN THIS TOWN?

PLEASE! Control your screaming kids when shopping!

What IDIOT added a four-way stop at the Riverwood Intersection???

Horrible Service from Glenn Hills Heating and Cooling!

Taxpayer dollars WASTED on new bike lane!

Another heading containing Barbara's name caught my eye. It

was an obituary for Barbara Draper. The Neighbor List had never
seemed like the most appropriate outlet for death notices, but
people posted those things on the app from time to time.

> *Barbara Draper, a lifelong resident of Glenn Hills, died in her*
> *home on May 7th at the age of 68. She leaves behind a son, Phillip,*
> *a sister, Kathryn Lancaster, a brother-in-law, Joseph Lancaster,*
> *and two nephews, William and Oliver, who reside in California.*
> *Barbara and her late husband, Edward Draper, were graduates of*
> *Oakland University. They married at the age of 22 and settled in*
> *Glenn Hills. Barbara was well known by locals for her vocal and*
> *robust opinions. She will be remembered by her family as a loving*
> *wife and mother, a patron of The First Methodist Church of Glenn*
> *Hills, and an occasional volunteer at the Suburban Detroit*
> *Women's Shelter.*

The obituary had been posted by a user on The Neighbor List
named Ellen Hardy. A thumbnail of a woman with pale skin and
chin-length gray hair appeared next to Ellen's name. I was
surprised this Ellen person had posted the news of Barbara's death,
rather than Barbara's son. I clicked on Ellen's profile, finding her
employer listed as The First Methodist Church of Glenn Hills.
Maybe they did this for all of their parishioners.

Several comments under the obituary drew my eye downward:

BPerkins: *On the bright side, everyone's business ratings should*
go up by at least two stars now.

CHall: *I hope she's happier in death than she was in life.*

HHammill: *She was miserable. Always yelling at my kids.*

LNeueson: *Have some respect people! This woman has a*
family!

UChung: *These comments are shameful. I've notified the administrator.*

I coughed out a breath, remembering why I usually avoided reading the comments under anyone's posts. Barbara had pissed off a lot of people. I recalled how Phil had been so distraught that he'd passed out on his front lawn. The thought of him reading these horrible comments about his mom made my heart sink. My fingers rushed to type in his name in the app's search bar. There were zero results for Phil Draper or Phillip Draper. At least he wasn't active on The Neighbor List.

Returning to the obituary, I noticed seven people had liked each of the first three comments, while over twenty people had liked each of the last two entries reprimanding. I clicked on the likes next to the first post, finding a list of names. My gaze snagged on the fourth name down—AMoreno. Avery Moreno. I checked the people who liked the second and third comments, finding Avery Moreno again. I'd seen her walking her golden retriever past me the night Barbara died. The golden retriever was the dog the Morenos adopted to replace the other who had suddenly died the day after Barbara had been yelling at it to shut up. The other night, Avery had cast a nervous glance toward the Draper house as Roo and I approached her. Why had she looked so apprehensive that evening? It seemed Avery was happy to be rid of the neighbor who shared her backyard fence.

A motor zoomed down the street from beyond our windows. I dug my heels into the floor and pulled my eyes from the screen, recognizing my imagination was spiraling. My new theory was a wild one, backed by zero evidence. Why would a presumably intelligent person like Avery Moreno like these offensive comments on The Neighbor List if she had been involved in Barbara's death? The clicks would only draw attention to her. Besides, the Morenos' other dog had died over a year ago, and no one had ever proven that Barbara had anything to do with its death. Still, a woman hitting her head as she fell into a full bathtub and then drowning was also unlikely, even if the medical examiner had found otherwise.

Isabelle's even breathing huffed through the baby monitor. I closed my laptop, forgetting about my job search and replaying Phil Draper's statement in my mind: *It wasn't an accident.* I tended to agree with him. The branch of our maple tree wavered on the other side of the living room window, its leaves shifting in the wind. The movement pulled my eyes in the direction of the Drapers' house. I didn't know what Phil knew about his mom's death, but he must know more than I did. Barbara may have been a total monster to everyone else, but she'd been kind to me once. And Phil seemed like someone who needed a friend.

I stood up and glanced up the stairs, listening again to the soft puffs of air leaving Isabelle's mouth. I could take the baby monitor with me and run over to talk to Phil while Isabelle was still asleep. I'd tell him I was checking in to make sure he was okay after the incident the other night. Then I could ask him what he meant when he said, "It wasn't an accident."

I roused Roo from his dog bed, clicked on his leash, and slipped on my shoes. My hands wriggled through the sleeves of a zip-up sweatshirt. I grabbed the monitor and placed it inside my sweatshirt pocket. Leaving a sleeping toddler alone in the house wasn't going to win me any parenting awards, but I was only going two doors down, still within the monitor's range, and I wouldn't be away for more than five minutes, tops. Isabelle usually slept for another forty-five minutes.

I slipped out the front door, locking it behind me and hoping Stephanie wasn't out for a stroll, her prying eyes searching for my absent daughter. My feet moved in double time as I hurried down our stone walkway and along the sidewalk. Roo stopped at his favorite shrub in front of the Delaney's house, but I pulled him along, listening to the crackling monitor. A gate closed across the street. Rick strode out from his backyard wearing a tool belt over his work pants and clutching a measuring tape in his hand. I nodded toward him.

He gave a quick wave. "Delivering more cakes?" he yelled.

"I'm all out of cakes today." I smiled and kept walking as Rick disappeared around the far side of his house. I needed to text Bree and tell her that I approved of him.

The Draper house rose before me with the same silent and foreboding vibe as a haunted house or a mausoleum. I decided to use Roo as an excuse not to have to go inside. I edged toward the wood-planked front door and grasped the brass door knocker, clanging it four times. My muscles tensed as I waited. I wasn't sure how much of the other night Phil would remember. There was a chance my visit would upset or anger him. I shifted my weight from foot to foot, hearing no movement inside. I rang the doorbell and waited another minute. Only the crackling of the baby monitor and a faint groan of the old house met my ears. I stepped toward the backyard, surveying the shrubs and peering over the fence. No one was back there as far as I could tell. Phil either wasn't home, or he was holed up inside, ignoring me or passed out. I craned my neck upward, finding opaque windows staring like gaping eyes. There was no sign of life behind them, although I couldn't shake the feeling someone was watching me.

NINE

I shuffled back to the sidewalk, hoping the Drapers' front door would swing open, but it didn't. Movement further down the block caused me to turn my head. Avery Moreno approached from the opposite direction again, walking her dog toward the corner. My fingers tightened on the leash, and I pulled Roo along, almost at a jog. If I hurried, I could meet my neighbor at the intersection of Mapleview Lane and Birch Run in an "accidental" run-in. The timing was tight, but I hurried past four more front yards, out for a pretend jog. Roo ran alongside me, flashing confused sideways glances because I'd never taken him running before. We met at the corner, me huffing and puffing. Avery strolled in an expensive-looking jogging suit with her black hair pulled back in a shiny ponytail and her fluffy golden retriever trotting dutifully beside her. I didn't know Avery well, but she carried herself like she was the former president of her sorority or perhaps the current head of the PTO. Her boys were much older than Isabelle. Despite the proximity of our houses, we ran in different circles.

"Oh, hi," I said as we met at the corner. I kept my words light and breathless as I feigned surprise.

She smiled and dipped her head in a silent greeting. The dogs sniffed each other.

"I'm Jessica, from down the street."

Avery nodded in recognition.

I motioned in the direction of my house. "I saw you walking out here the other night. It's crazy about Barbara, isn't it?"

The woman's smile faded. "I guess."

"I mean, not many people die in their bathtub."

She shortened her dog's leash, features hardening. "Maybe so. There weren't any tears shed at our house. Barbara Draper got what she deserved." Her words flung from her mouth like a slap. It took a second for me to compose myself.

"I'm sure she was a difficult person to share a fence with."

"Ha. That's the understatement of the century." A storm brewed in Avery's dark irises.

"What do you mean?"

"Barbara screamed at my dog—both of my dogs. I mean, dogs bark sometimes. That's what they DO. Any normal person would know that yelling at a dog only makes them bark more. She berated my boys every time they raised their voices above a whisper." Avery narrowed her eyes and leaned closer to me. "They lost a soccer ball over the fence once, and she grabbed it and threw it in her garbage can. Said it was on her property, and they couldn't have it back. I mean, what kind of person does that? We didn't feel comfortable being in our own backyard because we never knew when that crazy hag would start screaming at us to be quiet! It's a relief to have her gone."

"Wow." It took a second for Avery's harsh words to filter through me. "I can understand why you would feel that way." Barbara's actions had been even more horrible than I realized. I was thankful my family and I had been invisible to the abusive woman. Barbara had never so much as acknowledged me since we moved back, at least until the night she died.

"Her son is weird, but at least he keeps to himself. Hopefully he'll sell the place." The wind dislodged a lock of Avery's hair from her ponytail, and she smoothed it back. She pinched her lips together and crossed her arms as if recognizing she'd said too much.

My fingertips touched the monitor in my pocket. The crackling had stopped, and I realized I'd traveled out of range. I cut to the chase so that I could head back home. "Did you happen to notice anything strange that night? When you were out for your walk? I'm only asking because I heard a rustling in the bushes when I passed Barbara's house. And then I saw her staring out the window and struggling to open it. I thought I heard a scream. It was kind of creepy, to be honest. Now I'm wondering if someone might have been hiding behind the shrubs."

Avery made a disapproving face. "It was probably a raccoon. They're active at night, and we have tons of them. Besides, the police said Barbara died in an accident. She slipped on a wet bathroom floor and hit her head. I don't even have anyone to thank for it."

Her statement caught me off guard, but I forced a smile and pulled Roo closer. Perhaps if Barbara had ever threatened Roo or berated Isabelle, I would have felt the same hot hatred boiling over. "Okay. I'll let you go. Enjoy your backyard."

"Yeah. We will." She gathered the leash but paused, refocusing on me. "Oh, Jessica, I've been meaning to tell you that my boys have started up their own lawn-mowing business. It's only for people in the neighborhood because Luke can't quite drive yet. I'm helping them spread the word."

I wondered if she'd noticed our unkempt lawn and I tried to keep my face still, hiding my mortification. It was during moments like this when I missed city living. "We could use their help. I'll talk to Mark about it and let you know."

Avery dipped her chin, satisfied. "Great. See you later."

I turned away but spun back around, remembering how the older son, whose name I'd just been reminded was Luke, had suddenly materialized in front of our car. "Oh, Avery. Luke should put a light on his bike. We almost didn't see him on the street on Saturday night when we were driving home from dinner."

"I didn't know he was out." The smile on Avery's face faded as she pulled her chin into her neck. "He was grounded. I'll have a word with him."

"Oh." *Oops.* I shrugged. "Teenagers. Right? Well, bye."

Avery didn't smile but tugged her dog to attention and continued on her path. I did a U-turn with Roo and power walked toward home, hoping Isabelle was still fast asleep. Avery's revelations about her hatred for Barbara weighed down my thoughts. The photo I'd glimpsed on the wall of the Drapers' living room—the one of Barbara in her wedding dress laughing with a young Mr. Draper—flashed in my mind. The contrasting image of the widely hated woman was difficult to reconcile. Barbara's outlook must have darkened after her husband died, her pain snowballing into anger. As I walked, I noticed a sedan pulling into our driveway. It was Sophie's dented Ford Focus, but today wasn't Thursday.

The baby monitor came back to life as I reached the edge of the Drapers' house. Frantic screams ripped through the speakers. *Isabelle.* They were the cries of a frightened child who had been left alone and gone unheard. Isabelle had worked herself up. She couldn't catch her breath. My feet picked up speed, a layer of cold sweat prickling across my forehead. This couldn't be happening. I'd been careless and stupid to wander outside of the monitor's range. I shouldn't have left Isabelle alone in the first place. And what was Sophie doing at our house? It wasn't her day to come over. The timing couldn't have been worse. My daughter's screams blasted through the monitor. I switched it off as I ran.

Now Sophie was at the front door, knocking and peering through the narrow window beside the entryway. She turned toward my pounding footsteps as I neared, her face twisting in confusion. "Jessica?" She looked at me, then Roo. "Where's Isabelle?"

"I had to run over to the Drapers' house. Isabelle was sleeping, so I thought it would be okay." I fumbled for my house key. "But she woke up, as you can hear." I jammed the key into the hole and barged into the house, running up the stairs for Isabelle's room.

"You left her alone?" A note of judgment weighed in Sophie's voice. Her footsteps quickened behind me.

I flung open Isabelle's door. My daughter stood on her toddler bed, red-faced and wailing. Snot dripped from her nose. Her body was hot against mine as I scooped her into my arms. "It's okay. You're okay. Mommy is here now."

"Where were yooouuu?" Isabelle howled.

"I was checking on our neighbor. I thought you were asleep."

Sophie stood near the doorway motionless, as if I'd shot her with a Taser gun.

"It was only for two minutes," I said to the horrified nanny. "I thought I'd be back before she woke up."

"But that's not..." Sophie started to say but stopped herself. She stepped closer. "Oh my gosh. What happened to Isabelle's head?"

"Oh," I said over Isabelle's sobs. "She fell off the booster seat when my mom was watching her. She's fine, but she needed four stitches."

Isabelle twisted her neck around to see Sophie. Her crying quieted, and she hiccupped. "I got ice cweam."

"Oh, wonderful, sweetie." Sophie's face changed when she focused on me. "Was it a new seat?"

I felt my cheeks redden. "No. Actually, I hadn't gotten around to switching out the old seat. We have a new one now, though."

Sophie's eyelashes blinked in rapid succession as if she couldn't understand what I'd told her, that I hadn't heeded her warning about the recall.

My jaw tightened at the judgment that darkened her face. Sophie was single and childless. Someday she'd understand that it was impossible to be a faultless parent. The learning curve was steep, the pitfalls perilous. I squared my shoulders at her. "I didn't get rid of the old one immediately. I made a mistake. No one is perfect." My voice was defensive and more forceful than I intended, like a rock accidentally flung across the room.

Sophie's eyes bulged, and she pivoted away from me.

"I'm sorry," I said, softening my tone. "I didn't mean to yell.

I've been under some stress. I kind of feel like I'm failing at everything right now." I kissed Isabelle's downy hair, feeling the edge of the bandage against my nose.

"No. It's okay." Sophie waved her arm toward Isabelle and me. "This is the most difficult job of all, being a mom. I don't know what it's like. Accidents happen. I didn't mean to sound judgy."

"Thanks." I studied Sophie for a moment, noticing how frail and breakable she looked with her cornsilk hair, her twig-like arms crossed in front of her, and skin so pale I could see her blue veins. She was a sweet young woman who had a gift with children and a knack for staying on my good side. "How did I luck out finding a babysitter like you?"

She offered her charming, gap-toothed smile. "The Neighbor List."

I chuckled as I set Isabelle down. "Why are you here, anyway? It's not your day."

"Oh." Sophie touched her ear. "I left a pair of earrings here last time. I'm going out with some friends tonight, and I wanted to wear them. They should be on the shelf downstairs. I put them up high so Isabelle wouldn't get them, but then I totally forgot about them. I was hoping I'd catch you at home."

"Let's go find them." I waved Sophie ahead of me. Isabelle traipsed between us, hopping a little to keep up with Sophie.

"Let's pway hide-and-seek, Sophie," Isabelle said.

"She's not here to play with—" I started to say.

"I might have time for just one game." Sophie swiveled her head toward me and winked as Isabelle released a gleeful squeal.

Sophie and Isabelle headed to the living room to collect the earrings while I disappeared into the kitchen to unload the dishwasher. Their loud counting and laughter floated into the kitchen. A few minutes later, the game had ended, and Sophie told me she was on her way. "I'm happy to take on a few more hours every week if that helps."

I hesitated at the offer as I opened the door. I didn't understand why I was so preoccupied with Barbara Draper's death when no

one else seemed to give it another thought. Maybe it was because
my eyes had connected with hers that night, and I'd seen something vague and unidentifiable in them. Or maybe it was the
memory of her helping me that day when I was just a child and I'd
fallen off my bike, or the possibility she hadn't been opening the
window to yell *at* me but to yell *to* me for help. I hadn't stuck
around long enough to hear her cries. The never-ending questions
were beginning to interfere with my life.

"That's nice of you," I said to Sophie as I snapped myself out of
my reverie, "but between your help on Thursday mornings and my
mom's frequent visits, I think I'm all set."

"Okay."

"Have fun with your friends tonight."

"Thanks." Sophie clutched her earrings in her hand and
headed toward the front walkway as I closed the door. I watched
her through the narrow window as she strolled toward her car with
steps so light she almost bounced. It wasn't too long ago that I'd
been just as carefree. My friends and I used to hit the neighborhood bar after work and sneak occasional cigarettes while making
jokes about our co-workers and tossing seductive glances toward
attractive men. I'd stayed out until the wee hours of the morning,
drinking and laughing until my belly ached, flashing the tattoo on
my hip and savoring the taste of tobacco on my tongue. I used to let
myself dream about things out of reach and imagine endings so
wonderful that they didn't seem possible. I'd never felt guilty about
any of it. Then again, people always remembered old times better
than they were. After meeting Mark, I'd quit smoking, bought
longer shirts, and taken the safe route into my thirties.

And really, I had no right to complain. I was married to a good
man with a stable career. He wasn't perfect, but we had an
adorable, healthy daughter and a charming house, albeit with a
mortgage that pushed the boundaries of a single income. We
contributed the correct percentage to retirement funds and had
opened a college savings account for Isabelle. Still, it wasn't lost on
me that Mark and I got excited about things like installing energy-

saving appliances and resealing our driveway. The chains of responsibility weighed on every decision I made. Dreams were no longer for me but for my daughter. I wondered if not everyone could handle being an adult. Maybe Barbara Draper had lost a dream. Maybe that's what had led her down the thorny path from a gleeful bride to a miserable woman.

A rush of unwanted thoughts whipped through my mind. Mark had left in such a rush this morning; he hadn't bothered to kiss me. Then, I'd gotten the uneasy feeling of someone watching me as I knocked on the door of the Tudor house two doors down. I'd witnessed Avery Moreno's unabashed hatred for her deceased neighbor, followed by Isabelle's screams crackling through the monitor. Finally, I'd seen the judgment flickering behind Sophie's eyelashes when I'd confessed that I ignored her warning about the recall.

I leaned my back against the door and closed my eyes, reminding myself no one was perfect. I would try again to be a good mother, a good wife. The police were handling Barbara's death, and I needed to step aside, get my priorities straight, and trust the process. Despite my internal pep talk, emotion crackled through me, making my legs unsteady. I might have burst into tears if Isabelle hadn't been standing a few feet away, the white bandage on her head pointing at me like an accusatory finger.

TEN

I sat across from Bree with two cardboard coffee cups between us, mine a decaf. A full day had passed, but my insides still jittered whenever I recalled the incident of having left Isabelle home alone. When my mom had appeared at our door less than an hour ago for another pop-in visit, I seized the opportunity and texted Bree to meet me at a nearby café. My friend had already heard some details of the ordeal, including Sophie's ill-timed visit to our house. The hiss of an espresso machine sounded from behind the counter, and several people sat alone at nearby tables, entranced in their laptops.

Bree studied her phone, her eyelids flickering. "These people on The Neighbor List are out of control. How can so many people be this upset about the new bike lane on Jefferson Boulevard? If anything, we need *more* bike lanes."

I shook my head, having read the same "New Bike Lane" post on the app a few minutes earlier. There'd been dozens of angry comments from people who couldn't cope with the altered road configuration. "People have way too much time on their hands. Don't they have jobs? Or kids?"

Bree chuckled. I told her about the mysterious message from Admin1. She agreed with Mark that it probably wasn't meant for me and that *Enjoy your perfect family* didn't sound like much of a threat. She set down her phone and tapped a manicured nail against the lip of her cup. "What did you want with Phil Draper anyway?"

I lowered my voice. "I can't stop thinking about Phil saying that it wasn't an accident. I mean, so many people hated Barbara. Like, *really* hated her. I was reading the comments under her obituary on The Neighbor List. And guess who liked all the nasty comments?"

"I have no idea."

"Avery Moreno."

"So."

"So, I also saw Avery in front of Barbara's house the night she died. Avery was walking her dog. The new one."

"She lives around the corner. Besides, weren't you walking your dog that night too?"

"Yeah."

"So maybe Avery thinks you killed Barbara." Bree narrowed her eyes.

I ignored her. "Anyway, Avery is the reason I went out of the monitor's range yesterday. I saw her heading toward the corner, and I jogged to catch up. I thought she might have noticed something unusual the night Barbara died, like a clue."

Bree tipped her head down. "Oh, no. That woman is strung too tight. You didn't ask her for clues, did you?"

I swirled my coffee around, secretly thinking that Avery was a better friend match for Bree than me. The two of them were so confident and polished. Opposites attracted, I guessed. I was glad Bree had chosen me. "I only asked if she had noticed anything. Avery was happy Barbara was dead. She told me all these horrible things Barbara had yelled at her boys. The Morenos were afraid to use their backyard."

"Yeah. Barbara complained about them when I was discussing property values with her. She always cited the noisy neighbors behind her as one of the reasons she was thinking about selling."

"I guess there are two sides to every story."

Bree huffed out a breath. "Hardly a motive for murder."

Bree wasn't willing to humor my neighborhood murderer conspiracy theories. I leaned toward her and stifled a grin. "Okay, back to today's cake delivery. Rick is a catch. I think you found a good one." The air smelled like coffee beans with a whiff of caramel cutting through it. I couldn't help wondering how to make the combination into cake form.

"He makes a strong first impression, that's for sure." Flecks of green surfaced in Bree's blue irises. She sipped her latte and set down the cup. "I've learned not to jump in too fast, though. Sometimes the most charming men can be the biggest jackasses in the end."

I could tell by the way Bree's eyes dimmed that her thoughts had shifted toward her ex-husband. I remembered her telling me about their whirlwind romance and the marriage that followed. Their relationship had ended a year later, with Alex cheating on her.

"Just give Rick a fair chance. That's all I'm saying. He was so good with Isabelle too. You should have seen it. He's a natural." I failed to stifle my smile.

"You're getting way too far ahead of yourself. Besides, I don't know if I'll ever be cut out for motherhood." Despite Bree's words, a smile pulled at the corners of her lips. She wore her long, honey-blonde hair down today, showing off its natural waves; her casual, beachy look suited her. "I'll give you an update after our dinner tonight."

"A realtor and a house flipper. Who could ask for a better pairing?"

Bree's eyes rolled back in her head. "Be thankful you don't have to go through this dating bullshit anymore. You're so lucky to have found Mark. You really should enjoy your perfect family, like the message said." Bree winked.

"Yeah. I know." My hands cradled the coffee cup, but the painful truth twinged in my gut. There'd been a distance between

Mark and me recently. He'd been returning home later and later from work. I couldn't deny the seed of resentment that had been growing since our dinner at Frederick's when my husband had discounted my dream of opening a cake shop. He might have been correct about it being reckless to start a new business, but he could have handled it differently. He could have been more hopeful and less dismissive. And even before that conversation, I'd felt the same resentful energy from him. His discontent was with my mom's lack of boundaries. Really, it was with me for not dealing with my mom. And then there was his suggestion that I take over the lawn mowing as if I sat around eating bonbons all day instead of caring for our daughter. But these were mere annoyances, surmountable issues as far as marriage went. We'd made it through worse. I forced a smile at Bree and asked her about real estate.

An hour later, I was back at the kitchen table with Mom as Isabelle sat at her play table and stirred a bowl of bubbly water with a giant spoon. A bottle of dish soap sat nearby. Mom was always coming up with creative new ways to play.

"Thanks for watching Isabelle. It was nice to go out for coffee with Bree."

"I'm glad the two of you have become such good friends. It's funny how some people find their way back into your life." Mom had a faraway look in her eyes and I wondered if she was thinking about my younger sister, Chelsea, who moved to Seattle for graduate school five years ago and never returned, except for the occasional holiday. "Will Mark be home soon?"

"Usually around 6:15." The clock on the wall ticked toward 5:30. "Sometimes later," I added, remembering Mark's unusually late return last night. It had already been after 10 p.m. when he'd arrived through the back door. I'd been asleep by the time he'd climbed into bed.

"I saw Barbara's obituary in the *Glenn Hills Yodler*." Mom

pressed her lips into a thin line as she shook her head. "What a shame." Something close to nostalgia flickered in her eyes.

"Yeah." It seemed Mom was one of the few people saddened by our neighbor's death. "You know, when we were helping Phil the other night, I saw a photo of Barbara on her living room wall. It was from her wedding day. She looked so happy."

Mom rubbed her chin.

"Did she used to be different?"

"She was happier once. It seems like a million years ago, now. Believe it or not, Barbara used to go all out with the holiday decor—Halloween, Christmas, Birthdays—it didn't matter. You were too young to remember, but that house was always the most festive on the block. And that was back when we had to make homemade decorations. None of this pre-ordered stuff on Amazon. She had a soft spot for kids."

"Really?" The scene Mom had described seemed impossible, especially after hearing Avery's horror stories. I could feel my mouth gaping open. "What happened to her?"

"Well, I don't know the whole story. We were never close friends, but Barbara had been friendly enough. Phil was older than you and Chelsea. But I'd run into Barbara outside once in a while, on the sidewalk or at the park. We chatted about neighborhood issues. I suppose things changed after her husband, Ed, died."

"How did he die?"

Mom gritted her teeth and looked at the floor. "It was a horrible accident. Barbara found him at the bottom of the stairs with a broken neck."

My spine straightened. "An accident?"

"Yes. Ed tripped over a laundry basket and fell down that long flight of stairs. Poor Phil was only about ten years old. He's had a rough time of it."

I remembered the steep wooden staircase at the back of the Drapers' living room. Phil's sunken features and scarecrow body floated before my eyes, the man's morose demeanor and drug addiction suddenly making more sense.

Mom continued, "At least Ed had taken out a hefty life insurance policy, so Barbara and Phil were taken care of in that sense."

My fingers gripped the edge of my chair as new suspicions took hold of my thoughts. "What are the odds of two freak accidents in one family? Two deaths?"

"I don't know, honey. It's been nearly thirty years since Ed died. The two accidents are hardly connected."

I eyed Mom. "Phil was at home for both of them."

Mom waved her hand in the air. "Oh, honestly, Jessica. Don't be ridiculous! Do you really think a ten-year-old boy would murder his own father? And then take out his mother almost thirty years later? She was the only person who has stuck by his side through all of his troubles."

I shrugged. "Stranger things have happened. And you have to admit, Phil is a little off."

"Stop. I'm not having this conversation." A vein bulged in Mom's neck as she shook her head. She wasn't a person who angered easily, and the iciness in her usually tender voice made me slide back in my chair. "That poor boy has been through enough. You don't need to spread your wild theories to any neighbors."

"But, you have to admit—"

"No. I don't admit anything. Ed died in an accident. Then, twenty-eight years passed, and Barbara died in another accident. The police said so themselves." She raised her chin. "Now, don't be a gossip and leave it be."

"Okay." I pressed my palms into my thighs, feeling like I was five years old again, and Mom had sent me to sit in the corner.

Mom's body lost its rigidity as her gaze drifted past me toward Isabelle. "What are you making over there, Izzie?"

"Wemonade and cupcakes."

Mom clasped her hands together and smiled. "That's just wonderful."

I pretended to praise my daughter's bubbly water creations but couldn't dislodge the wariness lurking in a dark corner of my mind. A few months earlier, I'd watched a detective interviewed on a real-life crime show. Something the man had said had stuck in my head; he could blame one accidental death on an unfortunate set of coincidental circumstances. But two untimely deaths in the same family suggested something more sinister at play. Too many coincidences pointed to murder.

There'd been two deadly "accidents" at the Drapers' house. A warning bristled deep in my core, whispering to me that the similar manner of the deaths was more than a mere coincidence.

ELEVEN

Mark didn't come home at 6:15 p.m. like I'd told Mom. For the second night in a row, he'd called and said he had to stay late to finish a report for a client. When he finally rolled in at almost 9 p.m., Isabelle was in bed, and I was bursting to tell him the news from the last two days. I started by describing the cake delivery to Rick and my approval of him as a match for Bree. Then, I reported my run-in with Avery Moreno and her insight into Barbara's unneighborly behavior, skipping the part about leaving Isabelle home alone. Next, I mentioned my coffee with Bree, followed by detailing Mom's bombshell that Ed Draper had died in an accidental fall down the stairs twenty-eight years earlier.

"Wow. Sounds like a lot of excitement." He edged toward the wet bar built into the far wall of our living room and poured himself a vodka on the rocks. Then he flopped on the couch. There was an edge to his voice, but I ignored it.

I perched next to him, eager to share my suspicions. "What are the odds that both Barbara and her husband would die in freak accidents inside their house?"

Mark's phone buzzed with a message. He looked at it, angling the screen away from me.

I scooted closer to him. "Who was that? George?"

"Uh, no. A different client. I'll deal with it tomorrow." He gulped his vodka and let out a long sigh.

I nudged Mark's arm. "Anyway, don't you think that two unlikely deaths are suspicious?"

"It's kind of weird. But twenty-eight years is a long time. Barbara was a frail woman, so a slip-and-fall makes the most sense. Accidents happen." His phone buzzed again, and he turned it off. "You shouldn't spend any time worrying about it, especially if the police aren't pursuing it."

I eyed his phone, which he'd turned upside down. "Someone is persistent."

"You said your mom came over today? Did you invite her?"

The way Mark jutted out his chin told me he was preparing for a confrontation. I should have known he would fixate on the mention of my mom, but I'd already omitted the drama I'd caused by leaving Isabelle home alone. I didn't want to turn my dishonesty into a habit. The air deflated out of me. "No, I didn't invite her. It was fine, though. I used the time to grab coffee with Bree."

"It's not fine, Jess. You need to tell her this isn't her house anymore. She can't swing by whenever the mood strikes her. I don't understand why you won't talk to her about it." He ran his fingers through his thick hair, leaving it standing on end. "Why can't we set some boundaries?"

My jaw tightened. Boundaries probably worked for someone like Mark. His parents lived several states away on Hilton Head Island and called exactly once a month for a fifteen-minute check-in. We only saw them in person about once a year, sometimes less. My mom was cut from a different cloth. My sister had ripped Mom's heart out when she moved to the west coast and rarely visited. Now Mom lived and breathed for every minute she could spend with Isabelle.

"I will talk to her."

"You've been saying that for months. If anything, your mom's visits are only becoming more frequent."

"It's not that easy. You know how emotional she is. She still feels terrible about Isabelle's fall from the booster seat. She was probably only trying to make up for it by giving me some time for myself. Which I appreciated, by the way."

Mark jiggled the ice in his glass. "Look, I'm glad she can help you out once in a while but schedule the visits with her in advance. We pay a hefty mortgage for this house, and she lives somewhere else now. It doesn't seem like she understands that she doesn't own this place anymore."

I rested the back of my head against the couch cushion and thought about Mark's sentiments. As much as I hated to admit it, he was right. Mom's behavior had become a little smothering. It was up to me to draw a line. "Okay. I'll talk to her about planning visits with us instead of stopping by unannounced all the time."

"Thank you." He slipped his arm behind me and squeezed as a light kiss landed on the top of my head.

"By the way, Avery mentioned her boys started a lawn business in the neighborhood. I think we should hire them. I'm sure it's cheap."

"The kid on the bike who I almost hit?"

"Yeah. And his brother."

Mark made a face. "Nah. I can do it."

"Really? When? It looks pretty bad."

"This weekend."

I bit my tongue, not wanting to argue.

Mark stretched his arms up and yawned. "Man, it's been a long day. Do you mind if I turn on the Tigers game?"

"Sure."

We watched baseball together for a while, but all meaningful discussion ceased. I headed to bed earlier than usual. The pages of a mystery novel distracted me for a few minutes, but I couldn't focus. I set it aside and turned out the light. Although I was exhausted, my body buzzed with unsettling sensations as if it was a taut rubber band about to snap or a wild animal was clawing at my insides. My thoughts spun. I wondered if the barista had accidentally poured me a regular coffee instead of a decaf. But the jittery

feeling was more than too much caffeine. Thick dread spread from
my core and into my limbs. I tried to pinpoint the origin of my trepidation, to assign some order to it or contain it, but I found my fear
had several sources. It was the apprehension of hurting Mom's feelings. It was the way Mark had hidden his phone at the incoming
texts.

His secretive behavior brought back painful memories of a low
point in our marriage. On the surface, we'd moved past his "friendship" with Sharon, the woman who lived across the hall from us in
Detroit. But I'd never forgotten the obvious attraction between
them, and the way Mark's lengthy, animated conversations with
her in the hallway and secretive, late-night texts had rocked my
confidence and left a permanent scar on me. The mugging had
been months behind me then, but I'd been a new mother, sleep-
deprived and not feeling particularly sexy. Sharon was young and
shiny and oh-so-happy all the fucking time. Mark's flirtations with
her had escalated after Isabelle was born, at least that's the way I'd
perceived it. He was quick to offer to help her fix her squeaky door
or put air in her car tires. There was one night when Mark said
he'd been out with friends and had never come home, claiming he'd
crashed at his buddy's pad. I'd never had any proof, I'd never
caught Mark and Sharon doing anything, but I'd seen the looks
pass between them, observed the body language. Although I often
cited the mugging as the reason I was so anxious to move back to
Glenn Hills, my suspicion about an affair between Sharon and
Mark was the real catalyst for our relocation. I wanted to put as
much space between them as possible. Mark insisted over and over
that he'd never cheated on me, he'd even gone to several weeks of
couples therapy with me, until I felt comfortable putting the ordeal
behind us. But I wasn't entirely sure he'd always told the truth.
Maybe I didn't really want to know.

On top of my other worries, news of the accidental deaths of
both Barbara and Ed Draper reeled through me. I understood that
relatively few people died by falling down the stairs or hitting their
heads on the way into the tub. The disturbing thoughts kept

coming, reshuffling themselves into different scenarios. My arms hugged my pillow against my face. I didn't sleep all night.

* * *

I chopped the melon into cubes and placed the fruit into an air-tight snack container. Sophie could use it for one of Isabelle's snacks if they went for a walk or to the park. *Dora the Explorer* played from the TV in the next room, the animated voices of the cartoon characters slicing through the kitchen and into my eardrums. It was Thursday morning, and Sophie would be here any minute. My eyelids weighed heavily, and my thoughts unfurled in slow motion. I hoped my lack of sleep wouldn't affect my morning plans.

A few soft knocks sounded from the front door.

"Sophie's here!" Isabelle jumped from foot to foot and clapped her hands.

"Yay," I said, opening the door.

Sophie wavered in the entryway, fresh-faced and bright-eyed in her cropped jeans and flowered shirt. Unlike me, she looked like a breath of spring air. She extended her arms toward Isabelle as she stepped inside. "Hi, girl. Are you ready to have some fun?"

"Yeah!"

"How are you, Sophie?" I asked. "Did you have a good time with your friends last night?"

"I'm good. Thanks. Yeah, we had fun. Thanks for letting me pick up those earrings." She flashed her signature grin.

"Of course," I said, thankful she hadn't mentioned yesterday's lapse in my parenting judgment. "I left a fruit cup in the fridge for a snack. The usual lunch choices are in there too. And don't let Isabelle mess with the bandage on her stitches. She'll get that off in a few days."

"Sounds good." She refocused on Isabelle. "Maybe we'll head to the park before the rain hits."

I glanced through the front window, where gray clouds gathered to the west. In my sleepy haze, it hadn't occurred to me to check the weather report. A part of me wanted to cancel Sophie altogether and stay home and nap on the couch while Isabelle played or watched a Disney movie. But Sophie was already here and—after reading numerous books on how to be a happy, successful mother—I'd committed to taking an hour or two to do something for myself once a week. I'd already skipped the Thursday morning yoga class at the YMCA two weeks in a row to run errands. I needed to stick to my plan. "I'm headed to yoga and then to run some errands. I'll probably be back around one."

"Sounds good. I can stay later if you need me to."

"Thanks." I swallowed, wondering if Sophie's offer was because of the debacle she'd witnessed yesterday.

I kissed my daughter goodbye. It would be a relief to have the yoga instructor order me to focus on nothing but my breathing for an hour, especially considering what I had to do afterward. My stomach churned at the thought of setting boundaries with Mom, but I couldn't put it off any longer.

With my yoga mat under my arm, I left through the back door, opened the garage door, and walked around to the back of my car to load my things. That's when I noticed something on the ground. My pulse raced as I stepped onto the driveway, reading words scrawled with Isabelle's pink chalk across the black asphalt:

Mind your own fucking business!

My feet stumbled backward as my gaze flicked from the words to the empty street. Only Isabelle's car was parked at the curb. The babysitter had taken the front walkway and, thankfully, must not have seen the message on the far side of the driveway. My breath felt thick in my throat as visions of Barbara Draper drowning in the bathtub floated to the top of my mind. *Did someone know how much I wanted to know what happened to Barbara?* I reread the words, admitting that I'd ignored similar advice from Mark, Mom, and Bree.

I closed my eyes, inhaling and leaning my weight against my car's back bumper. This was the second message left for me in forty-eight hours. But the two messages—*Enjoy your perfect family* and *Mind your own fucking business*—seemed unrelated. My eyelids widened, and I took in our overgrown grass, which sprouted in clumps across the lawn, realizing the answer was probably not nearly as dramatic as the scenario spinning through my head.

Luke Moreno had been weeding one of Mr. Delaney's flower beds last night. I'd seen him kneeling down with his back turned toward me as I pulled in the driveway. I remembered the way the teenager had glared at Mark and me through the windshield Saturday night when we almost hit him. Then there was the way Avery's face had soured when I'd told her we'd encountered Luke on his bike. The boy had obviously sneaked out and I'd inadvertently ratted him out to his mom. Even my thirty-three-year-old self knew that wasn't cool. This chalk message was likely nothing more than a teenage prank Luke had played on his walk to school this morning. I might have done the same at his age. I walked to the side of the house, turned on the hose, and sprayed the words away.

TWELVE

An hour-and-a-half later, a mist of rain dampened my cheek as I crossed the YMCA parking lot. I hoped Sophie and Isabelle had gone to the park already. My yoga class was complete, and I should have felt more relaxed. There had been moments during the exercises when I'd experienced some calming effects, like when I stayed in child's pose for several minutes and almost fell asleep. But the angry chalk message had knocked me off-kilter, making me feel strangely violated. Now the thought of talking to Mom about a sensitive subject caused a familiar strain to return to my chest.

I closed myself inside my car and drove to the Main Street café to pick up two almond milk vanilla lattes to go. The drink was Mom's favorite, and I hoped it would help soften the blow. Plus, I needed another jolt of caffeine to make it through the day.

My clammy fingers squeezed the life out of the steering wheel as I drove another ten minutes to Mom's condo on the north edge of town. I scolded myself for the ridiculous reaction. I was merely going to suggest that she make a phone call or send a text an hour or two before stopping over. I wasn't banishing her from our lives. Still, the conversation would offend her. With Dad gone and Chelsea having moved as far away as possible, Mark, Isabelle, and I were all Mom had left.

I turned my SUV onto her street, passing rows of identical beige-and-white townhomes with treeless patches of grass in front. I found the lack of character and color in this new construction development depressing, providing additional insight into why perhaps Mom felt the urge to return to her old house so often. An oversized flowerpot filled with purple and white pansies sat on one front porch, differentiating Mom's condo from the others. I took a deep breath and pulled into her driveway.

I traversed the walkway with a coffee in each hand, using my elbow to ring the doorbell. The sky was dark, even though the rain had lightened. The calm in the air felt temporary, like a held breath. I forced a smile onto my face and waited for Mom to open the door, but nothing happened. Setting the cups down, I knocked a few times and closed my bleary eyes, hoping Mom wouldn't comment on the bags underneath. Still, no movement sounded from inside. Maybe she'd gone to the grocery store or one of her garden club activities. The irony hit me that I was engaging in the same behavior that I wanted Mom to stop—I'd dropped by with no forewarning. I chuckled to myself, remembering one of Mom's favorite phrases: The apple doesn't fall far from the tree.

A quick phone call would sort everything out. Maybe I could pin down a time to return later, although it would be more difficult to talk things through with Isabelle in tow. I swung my purse forward and rummaged inside to remove my phone. A notification glowed on my screen. It was a text from Sophie. Sophie had never contacted me while watching Isabelle before. My pulse accelerated as I assumed the worst. Reading her message extinguished my fear but ignited a different rage within me:

> *Hi Jessica. Your mom is here and wants to watch Isabelle. She offered to pay me and said I could leave. Just wanted to check with you first.*

Another message sent ten minutes later:

Your mom said again I should leave. I'm not sure what to do. I don't want to offend her. Call me?

Five minutes after that:

Hi. Your mom said she cleared it with you, so I am leaving now.

Anger boiled through me, my vision blurring at the edges. I gripped my phone so tightly I thought it might crack. Mark was right, Mom didn't have any boundaries. *How could she be so oblivious?* I should have put an end to her overstepping before it got out of control. My feet stumbled sideways, knocking over one of the coffee cups. The latte spilled into a puddle and trickled off the porch. "Shit." I picked up the cups but left the mess for Mom to hose off later. A scream of frustration gathered in my throat, but I held it back, reminding myself that Mom's heart was in the right place. I closed myself inside my car and messaged Sophie back, knowing I was about thirty minutes too late:

I'm so sorry! I had no idea my mom was coming over. No problem about leaving.

A second later, a message popped back from her:

Okay. Thanks! She paid me BTW.

I released a breath, amazed Sophie hadn't quit yet. I'd ignored her recall warning. Then she'd been witness to my out-of-range monitor screw-up, and now Mom's aggressive takeover of our comfortable Thursday morning routine. I hoped the events wouldn't tempt our treasured babysitter to leave us for another less dramatic family.

I tapped the side of my phone, trying to decide what kind of message to text to Mom. A phone call was probably in order, but I wouldn't be able to hide the resentment in my voice. I tipped my head back against the upholstered seat as I scanned the street of cookie-cutter condos. A sky the color of bruises loomed above the rooftops, creating an oppressive backdrop. The longer I stared at the sky thinking about Mom's solitary life, the more guilt seeped through me, tempering my annoyance. Mom had her friends and her garden club, but she must have been lonely in this silent, sterile neighborhood, at least in comparison to the full and vibrant life she'd lived in her younger years in the Ridgeview Pines neighborhood. Chelsea had escaped to Seattle only two years after Dad died of a sudden heart attack. He'd been gone for over seven years now. So, of course Mom would cling to me and Isabelle and Mark. I eyed the empty coffee cup, another wave of guilt tugging at my gut. I heaved myself out of the vehicle with a sigh and trekked back to Mom's front porch, where her hose lay nearby in a neat coil. I sprayed the mud-colored puddle off her porch, being careful not to spray any coffee onto the pristine flowerpot.

I called Mark when I returned to my car. He didn't pick up, so I left a vague message about having another eventful morning. Next, I texted Bree, who responded immediately. She was at her real estate office, preparing a mass mailing of marketing materials, and said I could come by to vent. I bit my lip as I debated whether to drive home and air out the situation with Mom, but a mixture of emotions swam through my veins. Today was supposed to have been my morning off. Mom could have her time with Isabelle before I confronted her.

THE NEIGHBOR LIST

POSTED MAY 13

Username: BreeSells4U

Subject: Price Reduction on Fourth Street Condo!

Ten-thousand-dollar price reduction on modern two-bed, two-bath condo with garage parking! Private balcony. Steps from Main Street. Message Bree Bradley for a showing.

JonHolmes: I used to rent in that building. Horrible construction. Buyer beware!

Aroberts75: Realtors are only allowed to only post in the real estate section of this app.

Click to view four more comments

THIRTEEN

Ten minutes after I'd left Mom's condo, I dodged through the sprinkling rain and entered the double glass doors of the Eastside Real Estate Group. The lofty space held the aroma of new carpeting and fresh paint. Floor-to-ceiling windows made up the front wall, making me feel like I'd wandered into an atrium or a fishbowl.

"Welcome to Eastside. How can I help you today?" a woman with a plastic smile and a sing-song voice stared me up and down. Her gaze traveled upwards from my sneakers, yoga pants, and zip-up hoody to my damp face.

I pulled my shoulders back. "Hi. I'm Jessica Millstone. I'm here for Bree Bradley. She's expecting me."

"Go on back. She's in the fourth row of cubicles, on the right."

I hesitated for a moment. *Cubicles?* Bree used to occupy a private office bordering the wall of windows.

"It's that way. You can't miss her." The receptionist motioned to the aisleway behind her, probably noticing that my feet were cemented to the floor.

"Sure." I forced my legs forward, counting the rows until I reached the fourth aisle. A smattering of voices—realtors on phone calls—echoed through the open space, but more cubicles were empty than filled. I found Bree three cubicles in, drowning in stacks of fliers. She wore tennis shoes, jeans, and a casual T-shirt. "Hi."

Bree turned her make-up-free face toward me, an unusual lack of effort for my polished friend. I almost didn't recognize her without mascara, liner, and eyeshadow, even though she didn't need it. "Oh, hi. I've got to approve these and get them out. What do you think?" She held up a shiny ad that featured her million-dollar smile and a small colonial with beige siding and black shutters.

"Looks good. Don't you usually do digital ads?" I asked, envisioning her regular posts about available properties on The Neighbor List.

"Yeah, but sometimes I get old-school clients who want to double down on paper." Her lips pulled down. "I'm going to lose this listing if I don't get an offer soon."

"Can I help?"

"Thanks, but not really. I'm ready for a break." Bree rolled over a chair from the vacant cubicle next door and motioned for me to sit down. "How was yoga?"

"Oh, fine." I lowered myself, trying not to stare at Bree's naked face and wondering how a person could look so good without any hint of make-up. "Didn't your office used to be over there?" I pointed toward the windows.

She nodded, but her mouth sagged. "Sales have been down this year. Those offices are for the top producers."

I'd seen Bree's "top producer" claim on her fliers from previous years. I hadn't realized she'd lost that status. I hadn't meant to pour acid on her wound.

"Oh. I'm sure it's only a dip. You'll be back on top soon." I motioned toward her jeans. "No showings today?"

"Nope. I'm taking the day to do some housekeeping and get caught up."

I scratched an imaginary itch on my arm. I'd been planning on venting to Bree about my mom, but it seemed my friend had enough on her plate. I steered the conversation toward a happier subject.

"How did your dinner with Rick go?"

"It was fine." Her voice lacked the spark I'd expected to hear.

"Fine?"

"Yeah. It started out great. Good food. Good conversation. The guy knows how to turn on the charm." She stopped talking and touched her chin like she was afraid of saying more.

"Then what happened?"

"I don't know. About midway through the meal, things got a little weird."

"Weird. How?"

"I can't describe it. Rick was trying too hard to impress me, I guess. He bragged about how much money he made on a couple of his flips. Then he went on and on about how picky he was when it came to who he dated, like I'd won some kind of prize by eating dinner with him or something." Bree scrunched up her face like she'd stepped too close to a dumpster.

"Maybe he meant his selectiveness as a compliment. And to be fair, you can be picky too. Remember when you broke up with that guy because he didn't pause long enough at stop signs?"

Bree lowered her eyelids and chuckled. "There was more to the story."

"I'm shocked about Rick," I said, uncrossing my legs. "I bet he was nervous. I mean, look at you. You should cut him some slack."

"It wasn't just Rick's bravado. He asked way too many questions, but not really about me." Bree folded her arms in front of her chest, shielding herself from something unidentifiable. I waited for her to continue, but she stopped talking.

"Like what?" I leaned closer, feeling a little like I was extracting teeth.

"I don't know." Bree's voice was so low I could barely hear her. "He asked a lot of questions about you."

"Me?" The shock of Bree's statement knocked me sideways. I steadied myself against the chair.

"Yeah. About our friendship and what you were like back in our school days. He wanted to know how you met Mark, how you ended up living back in your childhood home, and where you learned to bake. It was so strange. Like he was more interested in you than me."

"Oh my God. I'm sorry. I barely spoke to him. I don't know why he would have done that." I searched Bree's face for any sign of resentment but found nothing. "Maybe he didn't want to be too direct with you, so he deflected toward me. Because he knows we're friends." Now I was rambling. I couldn't begin to imagine how a single, handsome bachelor like Rick could focus on a sleep-deprived, married mother like me when gorgeous and confident Bree had been sitting across the table.

"I've been on a lot of dates, and that's not normal first date conversation." She rested a slender hand on her hip, a faraway look on her face. "Do you know Rick from somewhere? Maybe you met him at college?"

My fingers instinctively raked through my ponytail as I thought of the men I'd dated in college, the people in my art classes and my study groups, the other students who flung dough at the pizzeria where I'd worked part-time. "No. I've never met him before. I have a good memory for faces. Rick isn't familiar at all. Plus, I would have remembered that southern drawl."

Bree fiddled with her necklace. "Anyway, I told him in no uncertain terms that you'd already found the perfect man, and he took the hint. After that, we talked about the local real estate market and shows we like to watch on Netflix. But I was already out by then, to be honest."

"How did it end?"

"He invited me back to his house to eat a slice of the cake you made, but I said I was tired." She patted my arm. "As much as I wanted to eat your delicious cake."

I made a face. "How dare you?"

"Ha." A warm smile spread across her face and lifted her features.

I was relieved by the lightened mood, but my insides churned with an odd sort of guilt. I felt somehow responsible for the failed date.

Bree tilted her head. "On the bright side, I guess if things don't work out with Mark, you already have another man lined up."

I dismissed her with a shake of my head, but I couldn't deny the sensation of butterfly wings flapping in my chest. I was flattered someone as handsome as Rick had noticed me. Indulging in an extra-marital romance wasn't an option though. Mark wasn't perfect, but neither was I. My husband made butterfly wings flap in my chest from time to time too, even still. Despite some bumps in the road, we loved each other. We had a beautiful daughter. We'd built a life together.

The sky unleashed a torrent of angry rain outside. The downfall hammered like nails against the wall of glass, causing me to cower away from the windows.

"Wow. It's really coming down." Bree raised her voice over the noise.

We sat for a minute, just staring at the deluge. I hoped Mom hadn't taken Isabelle anywhere. After a while, the rain lightened, but dark clouds lingered over nearby buildings. The storm wasn't over yet.

I refocused on Bree. "Do you ever dream of doing something else? Something crazy. Like moving to Costa Rica and selling timeshares?"

"Um. Yeah. I dream about escaping this shitshow all the time." She flashed a wry grin. "I'm joking. I like real estate. It just doesn't like me back right now."

The fast-moving clouds drew my eyes outside, pulling my thoughts along with them.

Bree inched closer. "Why? Do you dream about a different life?"

"No. Not really. I've just been feeling a little like a caged lion lately. I've had this crazy idea that I can't get out of my head. I've been dreaming about opening a cake shop featuring my tattoo designs. It would be called Inked Cakes."

A smile tugged at the corner of Bree's mouth, and I couldn't tell if she was happy or struggling not to laugh. "Not to bring up Rick again. But he went on and on about how cool the design was on your cake."

"He was probably just trying to lure you back to his place so he could make his move."

Bree handed me a look that said to cut the crap. "Have you been baking a lot recently?"

I shrugged. "I've been messing with some new flavors. I came up with a coconut-lime cake that's pretty unique. And I'm creating a vegan line. I've even designed the sign for my imaginary shop."

Bree's face lit up. "Plant-based foods are the way of the future, and people still rave about that cake you made for my birthday party. I don't think anyone's ever seen anything like it. They would pay good money for your creations. Do you know how much Alex and I paid for our wedding cake? Over $2,000." The sparkle in Bree's eyes fizzled out. "What a waste that was."

"Well, the cake shop is a dream for another day. I mentioned it to Mark, and he's not on board. It's too risky, financially speaking. I'm supposed to be looking for a marketing job, but I've been dragging my feet."

"I say follow your passion." Bree looked around and softened her voice. "Then again, maybe if I had a responsible person like Mark in my life, I wouldn't have led myself down this road of ruin." She waved toward the stacks of fliers, but I got the feeling she was talking about more than just her stalled listing.

"So, you think Mark is right?"

"Probably. Not that you need to go back to marketing, but it's not fun to be stressed financially. And you have a daughter to consider. Anyway, don't take advice from me. Every decision I make seems to be the wrong one." Her lip quivered as she spoke the last sentence, and I could see she was overwhelmed.

"Things are going to get better for you, Bree." I stood up and hugged her, deciding not to share more about my growing resentment toward Mark ever since he shot down my dream, or how going back to work at a meaningless office job, sounded about as appealing as digging my own grave.

My phone buzzed from within my purse. I pulled away from Bree and dug it out. Mom's name flashed on the screen. "Hi, Mom."

"Jessica. I'm with Isabelle."

"I know. Sophie told me."

"I don't know how this happened. She was right next to me."

There was a quiver in her voice that caused my knees to weaken.

"What? What happened."

"Isabelle's had another accident."

FOURTEEN

Isabelle's pudgy feet hung from the table inside the examination room. Pink blotches appeared across her skin, and a spot of fresh blood seeped through the medical tape on her head. Her tears had matted her feathery hair against her face. A man with ruddy cheeks who looked too young to be a doctor leaned toward her, shining a penlight into my daughter's eyes.

"I don't see any sign of a concussion, not to say she couldn't have suffered a minor one. Sometimes there's no solid evidence."

Mom clapped her hands together. "Oh, thank goodness."

The young doctor flicked off his light and stepped back. "The more pressing issue for us is to redo those stitches. It looks like the fall broke them open."

"Can we do that here?" I asked, eager to get us out of the sterile emergency room and back home.

"Yes. I'll be back with a nurse in a few minutes, and we'll get Isabelle patched up again. In the meantime," he turned toward the wall and rummaged through a stack of multi-colored fliers, "here's some literature on home safety protocols for parents of toddlers. Be sure to check the latch on your stair gate for any defects. She was lucky her injuries weren't worse."

I took the paper and nodded, but my cheeks burned as he left

the room. It felt as if he'd scolded me for being a negligent parent. I
hadn't even been home at the time! The accident was my mom's
fault. I placed my hand on Isabelle's leg so she wouldn't topple off
the table, but my eyes found Mom's as I envisioned the long, open
stairway leading down to the basement door.

"Did you unlatch the gate to the basement stairs, Mom? Maybe
you went down there for something earlier?" I fought to keep my
voice light and non-accusatory. We had plans to renovate one day
but for now our basement was nothing more than a glorified cellar
with a large storage area. It was damp, dreary, and crawling with
spiders. I avoided it at all costs. But Mom still stored several boxes
down there that she claimed she didn't have room to keep at her
new place.

"No. I didn't go downstairs." She pursed her lips. "We were
playing in the living room. Then I went into the kitchen for a
couple of minutes to make lunch."

"Okay," I said, doubting she'd only left Isabelle for a couple of
minutes. I didn't question whether her heart was in the right place,
but I noticed how her eyes didn't meet mine when she answered
my question. An uncomfortable sensation traveled over my skin.
Mom would do anything to protect her time with Isabelle, and I
wondered if she was lying.

Several hours later, Mark and I sat on the couch while Isabelle
huddled on the other side of the room, wearing pink headphones
and playing a game on my iPad. The rain had passed, and the sky
had turned inky and black outside.

Mark heaved out a breath as he leaned forward and perched
his elbows on his knees. "So you still haven't talked to your mom
about not coming over whenever the mood hits?"

"I couldn't. She was so upset by the fall. The timing wasn't
right."

"Jess, you know your mom is the only one who would have
opened that gate, much less have left it unlocked."

I pulled my knees to my chest, hugging them close to my body. "Sophie was here before Mom showed up."

"Has Sophie ever gone down into our basement before?"

I stared straight ahead. The question didn't require an answer. Sophie was the most safety-conscious person I knew, especially when it came to baby and toddler equipment. The odds of her venturing down the stairs and into our creepy, cave-like basement were slim. She had no reason to go down there. The chance she'd carelessly left the gate unlocked was even more minuscule. I turned to face my husband. "Have you gone down to the storage room recently? Maybe one of us forgot to latch it."

"No. I haven't been down there since I changed the filter on the furnace last month. I checked the gate a day or two ago. It was locked."

"I haven't been down those stairs in weeks."

Mark's eyebrows furrowed. "Your mom had a reason to go down there. She's storing five or six boxes on that bottom shelf. She probably went to find something and forgot to lock the gate. I bet Isabelle tried to follow her."

My head felt like it weighed a thousand pounds, and I let it fall back into the cushion. The scenario Mark had just described sounded like the most plausible explanation. "You might be right. I can see why she wouldn't want to admit it."

"I'm wondering if, while you're setting boundaries with her, you can also mention that we're not comfortable with her watching Isabelle on her own anymore. Only if one of us is also around."

My stomach sucked in on itself as if it had been wrapped in plastic and vacuum-sealed. It took me a few seconds to speak. Telling Mom to call before she visited was one thing but telling her we didn't trust her with Isabelle would kill her. "She'll be offended. There's no way she won't take that personally. I mean, I'd basically be accusing her of lying. And then to say she can't be alone with Isabelle on top of that—"

Mark rubbed his temples. "I can live with offending your mom. What I can't live with is our daughter suffering any more injuries.

Think about how terrible we feel now and how scary it was after Isabelle fell from the chair. Can you imagine the pain of something even worse happening?"

There was a grain of truth to what Mark was saying. Still, the restriction felt extreme. "We're all human, Mark. We all make mistakes, even when it comes to Isabelle." I thought of my lapse in judgment in leaving Isabelle home alone while I chatted with Avery. Something terrible might have happened if our curious three-year-old had wandered out of her room. Part of me wanted to confess my own negligence to him, but I could feel his anger building. I tightened my jaw.

He crossed his arms. "Yes. We're all human. But some of us are more capable than others."

"I know she's not as sharp as she used to be. I'm just not sure I can take away her time with Isabelle."

"She can still have the same amount of time, but one of us will be around."

"I don't know." Hot tears built behind my eyes. I tried to blink them back, but they leaked down my face. Mom had lost so much. Now I was taking this from her too. At the same time, if something else happened to Isabelle while she was in Mom's care, Mark would never forgive me. I'd never forgive myself.

Mark reached across the middle cushion and held my hand. "Jessica, this is too important. I'm not compromising. My goal isn't to hurt your mom's feelings. It's to keep Isabelle safe." His eyes searched mine and I could see the worry in them. It was the same way he looked at me for days after the mugging in the parking garage, like my well-being was the only thing in the world he cared about. Still, he was putting me in an impossible situation. "If you don't want to have the conversation with your mom, then I will. But I think she'd take it better coming from you."

I released the gulp of air I'd been holding and wiped the wetness from my eyes. "Okay. I'll talk to her about it. You need to give me a couple of days, though."

He squeezed my hand. "Yeah. Okay."

Mark's phone buzzed, one text followed by another. He dropped my hand and swiped the phone off the coffee table. He barely glanced at the screen before shoving the phone into his pocket.

"Who's that?"

"Oh, it's work stuff. George is on my case about getting the financial projections finished."

"Why does he think it's okay to text you at eight o'clock at night?"

Mark shrugged. "Because he's my boss, and he doesn't have a life."

"Maybe you should set some boundaries with him." My voice carried more venom than I'd intended. Resentment expanded inside me, whether my feeling was warranted or not.

"Maybe I will." Mark eyed me. "Sorry, but I need to look up some numbers for him. It will just take a minute."

I stood up and noticed Isabelle was still involved in her iPad game. "I'm taking Roo out for a walk."

Roo's dog tags jingled as I stepped in a puddle on the sidewalk. Inside the house next door, a baseball game flashed across Mr. Delaney's flat screen. A dim light glowed from somewhere deep within Rick's fixer-upper on the other side of the street. With everything that happened with Isabelle, I hadn't even had a chance to mention Bree's first date story to Mark. Rick's apparent interest in me was strange, but something stirred in my chest at the thought of him. And it seemed the feeling was mutual. It had been a long time since anyone other than Mark noticed me in a romantic way or vice versa. Rick was a good-looking, charismatic man, and anyone would be flattered by his attention. I decided the invisible connection between the new neighbor and me would be my secret. Maybe a meaningless flirtation was just the kind of harmless diversion I needed to give my confidence a boost. I wouldn't act on it, of course. Mark and I trusted each other. We'd worked hard to over-

come the damage caused by his overly friendly relationship with
Sharon, who, as far as I knew, he hadn't had any contact with since
we'd moved to Glenn Hills.

Roo pulled me ahead, sniffing a patch of tall grass. The day had
left me empty and drained as if the rain had poured right through
me and washed away my convictions. The deep breath in my lungs
felt restorative. The breeze held the mountain-meadow freshness
that comes after a rainstorm. My feet splashed along the sidewalk.
A bird squawked somewhere in the distance. I tightened the leash
and paused in front of the Drapers' house, where a sliver of light
flickered from a downstairs window. I wondered if Phil was
watching TV in the dark.

It must have been horrible for him these past few days. He
didn't appear to have any close friends. His mom must have been
his only confidant, the only one who saw past her son's strange
mannerisms and quirks. I wondered if Phil might have passed out
inside that somber house. That could explain why no lights were
on. What if he had overdosed? Maybe his grief—or guilt?—had
gotten the better of him. There would be no one to find him. We
had helped Phil the other night. Maybe he needed my help again.

My anxiety got the better of me. I looked over my shoulder,
confirming no one was approaching from either direction. The
street was devoid of cars, not even the faint hum of a motor or a
distant gleam of headlights. I inched forward, following the Drapers' brick walkway at first but then veering across the lawn toward
the front window. My rain boots sank into the grass with each step.
Roo lifted his front paw and shook the droplets from it, but I
tugged him along. The window offered a view into the living room.

My muscles tensed as I neared the glass, hearing the woosh of
my breath in my ears and feeling my heart thump against my
ribcage. I leaned forward, eyes searching. The leash strained
against my palm as I made out a couch and then a table through the
dim light. No one was there.

"What are you doing?"

I spun around at the sound of the stern voice, feeling like my heart was exploding. A man loomed behind me. Too close. His silhouette shifted in the shadows as a flashlight in his hand flicked on, illuminating our faces. It was Phil. His features looked grotesque in the beam's uplighting. He'd appeared from nowhere like a ghost; his colorless lips pulled back. Roo strained toward him, sniffing. I fluttered my eyelids and forced a smile as I tried to think of what to say.

"I was just... out for a walk... with my dog." I motioned toward Roo. "I thought I'd check in on you."

"Why didn't you knock on the door then?" His eyes bulged, never blinking.

"I don't..." I stared at the toes of my rain boots, "I didn't want to bother you."

Phil stabbed a finger at me, invading my space. "I know who you are." His breath was hot and rank.

I stumbled backward. *Had Phil slurred his words?*

"Jessica. Right? You've never talked to me before. Why now?"

I anchored my weight in my heels and found my voice. "Actually. You're right. I'm Jessica Millstone from two doors down. My husband and I saw you out here on the lawn the other night. We helped you inside and got you some water. Do you remember?"

He blinked, and his shoulders seemed to loosen. His hand lowered ever so slightly, the new angle of the light casting different shapes across his face.

He didn't speak, so I continued, "You were in a pretty bad state the other night. Are you feeling better?"

"Yes. Thank you for helping me. I don't remember things too clearly."

"I'm sorry about your mom."

Phil swallowed and creased his eyes like he wasn't sure if he believed me.

"You said it wasn't an accident."

He tilted his head. "What?"

"When I was about to leave the other night, you said, 'It wasn't an accident.'" I tugged at the hem of my shirt, not sure how far to push. It could be dangerous if I knew too much.

"I didn't kill my mom."

My gaze slipped past his bulging eyeballs. I thought about the accidental death of Phil's dad so many years ago. I didn't know what to think. "What did you mean by it, then?"

More shadows morphed across Phil's face. "There was someone else in our house that night."

I rocked backward and opened my mouth, stunned by the revelation. I heard the sound of the hedges rustling in my mind. The rattling window. The muted scream. Phil was bolstering my fears that someone really had murdered his mother. Right here, in this safe, suburban neighborhood, where I'd grown up and where we just wanted to raise our daughter in peace.

"Did you see someone?"

"No. I heard footsteps. At the time, I assumed it was my mom. I didn't think too much about it. I thought she was wandering around the bathroom getting ready for her bath. But it was noisier than normal. Someone stomped a couple of times. I didn't realize until the next morning what had happened. The coffee maker wasn't on. She always turned it on first thing." Phil shifted his weight. His eyes flickered toward the house, then back to me. "But also the back door was unlocked. Mom always locked it before she went to sleep. I think whoever came into the house left out the back."

"Oh my God." I turned Phil's statements over in my head, terrified that his theory was correct. "Was there anything else?"

"That realtor, Bree Bradley, had been to our house earlier. She made me anxious."

"She did?"

"Yeah." Phil rubbed his palm on the side of his jeans. "She's so pretty and smart and nice. And to hear her talking to Mom about selling the house. It made me feel all wound up. You know? I made a mistake and took a couple of pills to take the edge off."

"Okay." I bit my lip, determined to stay non-judgmental. I

wondered if the slow delivery of Phil's words was the result of his years of chemical addiction.

"A few minutes after Bree left, I found her cardholder in-between the couch cushions. It was one of those nice silver ones. It must have slipped out of her purse when she was talking to Mom. I thought she might come back for it, so I went outside, hoping she'd run into me. The pills had calmed me down by then, and I wanted an excuse to talk to her."

I remembered Bree searching her purse for her cardholder the morning we were at the park.

"Anyway, while I was outside, I heard a weird noise in the backyard, like a branch cracking. I wandered around back to check it out. I thought it was the Moreno boys. They're always messing around out there. That's when I saw someone running away."

"You did?"

"Yeah. It was dark. I couldn't see who it was."

"Which direction were they running?"

"That way." Phil motioned toward Mr. Delaney's backyard. "I only glimpsed the figure for a second."

"And you didn't find your mom in the bathroom later?"

"No. There's a second bathroom upstairs. That's the one that I use. I'd already said goodnight to her before she went up for her bath."

"Did you tell the police all this?"

"Yeah. I told them everything. I thought they would look into it, but the detective ignored me after I admitted to taking a few pills. He probably thought I was unreliable." Phil made air quotes with his free hand. "The medical examiner had already decided Mom's death was consistent with an accidental fall. I guess they didn't want to bother with anything that went against his findings."

"Are they going to press charges? For the drugs, I mean?"

"No." Phil raised his chin, releasing a breath of laughter. "Their search was a joke. It's easy enough to hide pills away in an old shoe or a hollowed-out book. They didn't even look."

"I heard something in your bushes that night too. Over there by the fence." I pointed in the direction of the shrubs. "I was walking the dog. It was probably around the same time, shortly after Bree left. I must have been there just before you came outside."

Phil leaned closer. "Did you see anything else?"

"No." I remembered how everyone else had discounted my suspicions about the rustling bushes. "It could have been a raccoon for all I know."

"Huh." Phil paced a few steps away and then back, his nervous energy demanding an outlet.

"But I saw your mom in the window up there." I pointed to the spot where Barbara had stared out at me.

Phil stopped moving. "That's the bathroom."

"She looked like she was trying to open the window. I ran because I thought she was going to yell at me." I paused, not wanting to say too much. "Did you hear your mom scream?"

"I heard her talking and yelling upstairs, but I didn't give it much thought. That was her normal behavior." Phil hung his head. "She threw tantrums sometimes when she was alone, complaining to herself about whatever had gotten under her skin that day. I wish I'd gone up to check on her. Instead, I was annoyed by the screaming and stomping. I went outside with the cardholder to wait for Bree."

I noticed the way Phil's mouth pulled down and twitched in the corners. He looked like someone who needed a hug, but it wasn't appropriate, so I patted the top of Roo's head instead. "You couldn't have known that night was any different than the others." I studied Phil's shadowy face. "Who would want to kill your mom?"

Disbelief stretched across Phil's face. "Who wouldn't want to kill her? My mom wasn't very well liked, in case you didn't know."

I glanced away, not sure how to respond.

"Let's see. The Morenos, behind us, are pretty good suspects. Avery would have pushed Mom in front of a moving train if she'd had the chance. There was the contractor who repainted all the bedrooms two months ago. Mom called his work 'shoddy' in an online review and refused to pay him. Dozens of small business owners in Glenn Hills probably weren't too happy with her one-star reviews. Or it could have been someone from church."

"Church?"

"Yeah. Mom really pissed off a lot of people on the soup kitchen committee." Phil shook his head, a chuckle escaping his mouth. "She showed up to every meeting and tried to divert the funds to new hymnals. It got ugly at one point."

I nudged my toe into the ground, remembering the obituary posted by a woman from The First Methodist Church. The web of people who disliked Barbara spread far and wide.

"Or it could have been the man, Leo, who she dated about six months ago. He was actually a nice guy. She dumped him. I mean, she left him cold, waiting at a restaurant on Valentine's Day."

"Really? Your mom was dating?"

"Yeah. She used a dating app for a while." Phil grunted. "It could have been the doctor she sued for malpractice last year. I told the police all this. They don't care. They hated her too."

"They did?"

"Yeah. Do you know how many times she called in complaints about people shoveling their snow incorrectly or putting their yard waste in the wrong-colored bin? She reported a kid's lemonade stand once for not having a permit. She must have called the station a few times a week with little things like that. They are obligated to go and check on every single call that comes in."

"Wow. I had no idea." I fiddled with Roo's leash, contemplating the complicated relationship Phil must have had with his mom, not to mention the incredible drain on resources Barbara must have caused. No wonder the police didn't want to spend too much time on her now. "That must have been difficult for you. I'm sorry the police aren't taking your concerns seriously."

Phil dipped his head. "Yeah."

I wondered if I should offer to make a statement to the police about the noise I'd heard in the bushes. Maybe my account would help corroborate Phil's claims. Then again, I hadn't witnessed anything of real significance. I glanced toward the upstairs window, where Barbara had peered down at me the night she died. After talking to Phil, I attributed a new meaning to the unsettling look on her face. I thought she'd been furious when Roo's barking interrupted her peaceful night. But now I knew for sure that I'd gotten it wrong. Barbara Draper hadn't been angry. She'd known someone was inside her house about to attack her. She'd been scared.

FIFTEEN

My stomach groaned, reminding me lunchtime was near. I flipped over a blue-and-white checkered card.

Isabelle squealed with delight. "Wong again!" She bounced in place as we leaned over the coffee table, a game of memory spread out between us. The natural light dimmed and lightened from outside. It was Monday, one of those turbulent days when broken clouds flew past the sun. I placed my cards face down and gave Isabelle a chance to make a match.

Three days had passed since my conversation with Phil, but the details of the encounter still rolled around in my mind. I'd given him my number and asked him to text me if he needed anything.

Isabelle studied the grid of cards, turning over a pink duck and a yellow dog. "Oh, no!"

The ring of the doorbell pulled my focus from our game. I stood up and paced toward the door. The lock turned when I was a few feet away, but I grasped the handle and pulled, already knowing who I'd find on the other side.

"Hi, Mom."

"Hi, Jessica." She looked over her shoulder. "You really need to cut the grass."

"I know."

Mom wore khaki pedal pushers and a bright pink shirt. She held up a reusable grocery bag. "I thought I'd surprise you with some lunch. How's Isabelle doing?" She stretched her head around me.

"Oh, thanks. She's fine." Isabelle's feet padded behind me.

Mom spread her arms. "There's my angel."

My insides twisted as they hugged. I'd hoped to put off my conversation with Mom for another few days, but Mark would be annoyed if he found out she'd turned up unannounced yet again and I didn't say anything. She was forcing my hand.

Mom strode into the kitchen. "I brought tuna fish salad. We can make sandwiches."

"Thanks." My mouth had gone dry, my appetite all but vanished. I encouraged Mom to play with Isabelle while I assembled the sandwiches and made grilled cheese for Isabelle. I didn't know how to bring up the subject, especially with Isabelle nearby. I felt the unspoken conversation ticking between us like an undetonated bomb.

Five minutes later, I called them into the kitchen, where we gathered around the table—Isabelle securely fastened into her booster chair—and ate our lunch. Mom rambled on about a long line she'd encountered at the grocery store and the seven-day weather forecast while I chewed. The bread tasted thick and gummy in my mouth, and I worried I might choke.

"Is everything fine with you?" Mom tilted her head and asked me for the second time.

"Yeah." I nodded and sipped my water, avoiding her eyes.

Mom glanced toward the window. "I saw some activity over at Greta Washburn's house. I'm glad Bree finally got that commission."

"Yeah. A guy who flips houses bought it. His name is Rick." I felt my cheeks redden as I said his name, my eyes finding my plate. My shame was ridiculous. I'd practically sewn a scarlet letter to my shirt for noticing that my new neighbor was handsome. I should have been more embarrassed about my over-the-top welcome cake.

"He'll have his hands full." Mom chuckled. "I don't think Greta did one speck of maintenance in all the years she lived there." Mom stood up. "I'll do the dishes."

"No. Leave them."

Mom paused, eyeing me. "Okay." She began unbuckling Isabelle from the chair, but she tugged at the wrong strap, loosening it several inches. "Oh, no. What did I do there?"

"It's okay." I cut in front of her. "It's the one over here, just like the old seat." I clicked the buckle and pulled Isabelle toward me, realizing Mark might have been right about Isabelle's first accident. I'd blamed myself for the spill because I'd ignored the recall, but Mom had just provided solid evidence that the fault could have been her user error. I pulled in a slow breath and steeled myself. I knew what I had to do. I turned on a cartoon for Isabelle in the living room and motioned Mom toward the kitchen. "I need to talk to you about something."

Mom's pallor increased, her eyes questioning. "Is everything all right? Is it something with Mark?" She looked small and frail as she took her seat at the table and hunched forward. I felt the strange sensation of a reversal of roles as if I was the mother and she was the child.

I lowered myself across from her. "No. It's nothing with Mark. It's more about Isabelle. And you."

"Is she okay?" I could see questions and fear swimming in Mom's eyes.

"Yes. She's fine. Thankfully." I squeezed my hands together, deciding to begin with the more comfortable subject. "Mark and I would like you to stop dropping by the house unannounced. I know you lived here for so long that it probably feels like this is still your house, in a way." I waved my hand toward the flowered kitchen wallpaper Mom had selected forty years earlier. "But it's not anymore. It's our house now. And we need some boundaries."

"Oh." Mom lowered her eyelids. Her mouth opened and

closed. "I'm sorry. I didn't realize you felt that way. I guess that wasn't very considerate of me."

"We still want to see you, but it would be best if you could call me an hour or two ahead of time and make sure it's okay. Sometimes we have other plans."

"Yes. I will. I will make an effort to do that." She clasped her hands in front of her.

"Thank you." I looked down, thankful she'd received my request so easily.

"What does that have to do with Isabelle?"

My throat was scratchy. This part would be more difficult. "There's one more thing." I hesitated but decided to rip off the Band-Aid and stop prolonging it. "The two accidents with Isabelle scared us. A lot. I know you'd never do anything intentionally to put her in harm's way, but both injuries happened while you were watching her. You weren't even supposed to be here the other day. Sophie watches Isabelle on Thursday mornings."

Mom sat forward. "Those accidents weren't my fault. I still don't know what happened."

"You weren't watching her closely enough, Mom."

"I'm sorry you feel that way." Mom released an exasperated sigh. "I think you're being a bit dramatic, but I promise to do a better job from now on."

"No. We can't risk anything else happening. Either Mark or I need to be home when you're with Isabelle."

Mom's mouth fell open and she blinked. "What? You don't trust me to watch my own granddaughter?"

"Of course we do, just not without one of us around too. It's because of everything that's happened. I think you might have gotten distracted the other day and not realized you left the gate unlocked. Same with the booster seat."

Mom pressed her lips together and shook her head. "No. No. I didn't touch that gate. I only left the room for a minute. And you said yourself that booster seat was defective."

"Yes. It was, but we've had it for six months and never had a problem."

Mom's chair scraped across the floor as she stood up. "Well, I guess I'm useless. Past my expiration date. Is that what you think?" The sharpness in her voice didn't match her watery eyes.

"No. Of course that's not what I think." I stood too, but my legs were unsteady. "We're only thinking of Isabelle's safety right now. You would do the same in my position."

"No. Actually, I wouldn't." Mom turned away from me and marched into the living room. Her back rose and fell as she hugged Isabelle for several seconds.

"Bye, Gwamma."

Mom released her hold on Isabelle and turned around, tears reflecting on her face. "I'll get out of your hair. I don't want to put my granddaughter in any danger," she said without meeting my eyes.

"Mom, wait. Let's talk about this."

She strode past me toward the foyer. "I hope you enjoyed the sandwiches." The front door opened and closed with a thud.

I followed a step behind and yanked the door open again. "Mom!"

She refused to look in my direction as she set a path toward her car. The keys fumbled in her fingers and fell to the ground. She picked them up before ducking into her car and backing out of the driveway.

I stood, shocked, in the doorway. I'd been anticipating a difficult conversation, but that had gone even more horribly than I imagined. I'd hurt my mom's feelings. But what was I to have done? I'd faced an impossible situation, forced to choose between being a good daughter or a good mother. I'd chosen the latter, and now it felt like a gut punch to the stomach.

Isabelle sidled next to me. "Why did Gwamma leave?"

A rush of hot emotion surged through me, and I felt a little like I might throw up. I closed my eyes and inhaled, struggling to keep myself together. "I don't know."

SIXTEEN

I flipped over another non-matching pair of cards, fingers shaky. I wouldn't have been able to find a match even if I'd been trying to win the game of Memory with Isabelle. My thoughts had left the house with Mom. A few half-hearted rounds later, Isabelle had accumulated all the pairs. I set her up with some watercolor paints at her play table in the kitchen and called Mark.

"Hey. What's up?"

"I talked to Mom." My voice quivered as I spoke. "It didn't go well."

"Oh, I'm sorry. I guess it might take her a day or two to get used to the new arrangement, but she'll come around."

"I don't know. She was so angry and hurt. I feel terrible. What if the accidents weren't her fault?"

"They were. She was in charge. She should have been watching Isabelle more closely. You did the right thing, Jessica. Maybe we can invite her over this weekend. She'll see that things aren't really any different."

"I don't know if she'll want to come over. She stormed out of here." I bit my lip to keep from crying. "Can you come home?"

Mark sighed. "No. I can't. I've got a conference call at 3:30."

My shoulders slumped against the wall. "Okay."

"I'll be home by 6:30 as usual, though. Hang in there."

"Okay. Bye." I ended the call, loneliness tunneling through me. I found Bree's name and called her next, but it went to voicemail. My finger hovered over Mom's name, but I pulled it away, deciding to give her some time.

Liquid splashed as Isabelle's paintbrush cup tumbled across the linoleum floor. Roo trotted toward the mess to investigate.

"Uh-oh." Isabelle trudged through the brownish water to retrieve the cup as Roo's muddied paw prints followed.

The air inside the kitchen was thick and warm. I could feel that caged lion inside me, pacing, gnashing its teeth. I needed to get out of the house before I screamed.

"How about we go outside for a walk?" I held my breath, grabbing a wad of paper towels and mopping up some of the mess.

"The park! The park!" Isabelle hopped from one foot to the other.

"Okay. We'll go to the park. We'll have to leave Roo here." In addition to being fenced and secured with a locked gate, the Ridgeview Pines playground had a strict "no dogs" policy. Barbara Draper had surely approved of the rules.

A couple of minutes later, we walked down our front path. Mr. Delaney stood near the side of his house pruning a forsythia bush. "Afternoon," he said with a wave and a nod, which I returned. We continued down the sidewalk as sunlight filtered through the fast-moving clouds. The wind against my face made it easier to breathe. I adjusted the strap of the canvas bag hanging from my shoulder and gripped Isabelle's hand. My eyes veered toward Rick's house as we approached. I almost missed him there, kneeling among the bushes below the front window. He was jiggling something, maybe testing the rot level of the window frame.

He turned toward us, perhaps feeling my eyes on him. He stood up, pulling off his work gloves and striding toward us with a broad smile. "Hi, there!" He strolled toward the edge of his lawn.

Isabelle and I crossed the street to meet him.

The sunlight creased Rick's eyes, and the wind tousled his hair. "I just wanted to let you know how delicious that cake was. I'm not kidding. I've already eaten the whole thing."

My skin tingled as I smiled back at him. "I'm so glad you enjoyed it."

Isabelle jumped. "We're going to the park!"

"No kidding. What park?"

"Down there!" Isabelle pointed down the street.

A wrinkle formed on Rick's forehead. "I didn't know there was a park down there. I always come in from that direction." He pointed to the main road beyond the far side of our house.

"There's a neighborhood playground. It's a good place to meet people for picnics. And the subdivision holds a block party there every August. We'll show you." I squeezed my daughter's hand. "Unless you're busy."

Rick shook his head. "I was just taking a break. I've got an architect stopping by in about forty minutes, but I'm free until then. If you don't mind letting me tag along to the park, that is."

Isabelle bobbed her head in an exaggerated nod.

"Of course. We'll give you the tour."

"How's your head, Miss Isabelle?" Rick asked as we continued in the direction of the park.

"Good."

"Happy to hear it." Rick whistled as we walked, and Isabelle laughed. "This is fun," he said. "Is this what happy families do every day?"

"Sometimes," I said, steering my thoughts from the pain I'd recently caused Mom. "I heard you and Bree had a nice dinner the other night."

"Really?" Rick gave me a sideways glance. "I got more of an 'I'm just not that into you' vibe."

"Bree went through a bad divorce recently. She's a little gun-shy."

"Nah. She's not interested. It's fine."

"Well, it's her loss."

Rick swung his head toward me, a hint of a smile showing itself. I had the feeling I'd said too much, crossed a line. We walked in silence for a minute.

Two blocks later, we arrived at the park. I motioned toward the fenced-in area. "Here it is, the Ridgeview Pines neighborhood playground."

Isabelle made a beeline for the entryway. I retrieved the key and unlocked the secured gate to let her through. I held up the oversized key with the neighborhood emblem and the words *Do not duplicate* etched on one side. "These keys are worth more than gold. Didn't Bree give you one at your closing? Everyone in the subdivision has access to the park."

More lines formed on Rick's forehead. "Hmm. Bree must have forgotten mine. Maybe she thought I didn't need it because I don't have kids."

"She probably sold it to someone in the next neighborhood to make some extra money." I smiled to show I was joking.

"I'll have to ask her for my cut." Rick and I chuckled as we stepped through the gate. Isabelle skipped over the sandbox and grabbed a shovel. Rick surveyed the park, where about a dozen kids with their parents or nannies were spread out, enjoying their day. Rick let out a low whistle. "Wow. This is one heck of a park. I wish I'd had somewhere like this to hang out when I was a kid."

"It's nice enough." I surveyed the swing set, curvy slide, monkey bars, the picnic tables, and the cement tunnel that held my teenage secrets. I'd never thought of the worn playground as anything extraordinary, but it was convenient to have it so close, and because of the limited access, it was never very crowded. "Where did you grow up again?"

"A small town on the outskirts of Atlanta. I thought swinging a stick in an empty field was as good as it got."

I was about to take a seat on my usual bench when I heard someone call my name from behind the swings. I looked up to find Stephanie striding toward me, her boys trailing a few steps behind.

"Hi, Jessica." The shifting sunlight reflected off her fiery curls.

I raised my hand, my stomach sinking as she eyed Rick.

"Who's your friend?"

"This is our new neighbor, Rick Smith. He bought the Washburn house. He's fixing it up."

Stephanie reached her hand toward Rick. "Oh! Welcome to the neighborhood. I think you'll like it here. We've been in our house four years already."

"Stephanie and her husband, Sean, live behind us," I said to Rick as he shook her hand and nodded along.

The twins joined Isabelle in the sandbox, and the three of us found seats on the bench overlooking the children. I was both thankful and annoyed that Stephanie had inserted herself between Rick and me.

"Do you have kids?" Stephanie asked Rick.

"No. Not yet, anyway."

"Stephanie has a parenting blog," I said, explaining the eagerness in her voice.

"That's cool."

Stephanie gasped. "Oh my gosh! Is that a bandage on Isabelle's head?"

"Yeah. She fell off a chair when my mom was over the other day. She had to get four stitches, but she's fine." I left out the part about how I ignored the recall, knowing a perfect mom like Stephanie would never forgive that mistake. And, of course, I didn't mention the second fall down the basement stairs.

"Poor thing. How scary! Did they check for a concussion?" Now Stephanie rummaged through her bag, removing two wax paper baggies filled with a variety of snacks, which I would bet my life were organic and gluten-free.

"Yes. Isabelle's fine. Thank God." I readjusted my position on the bench, deciding to steer toward a new subject. "The neighborhood has been turning over lately, huh?"

Stephanie nodded. "I wonder if the Drapers' house will go up for sale next."

"I don't think so," I said. "Phil still lives there."

Stephanie lowered her body toward Rick. "You heard what happened, right? Death by falling into the bathtub. Watch out for Phil Draper. He's a strange bird. Best to keep your distance. And be thankful you never had to meet his mother." She paused before adding, "God rest her soul."

I pinned my lip under my teeth to keep from commenting. I didn't know how Stephanie failed to recognize her husband was just as strange as Phil, although in a different way. Maybe she was too close to Sean to see it.

Rick rubbed his chin. "I haven't had much free time to meet anyone yet, except these two lovely ladies." He stretched his neck around Stephanie to catch my gaze. His eyes traveled to Isabelle and back to me.

Stephanie cleared her throat. "I see."

I straightened my back, hearing the note of suspicion in Stephanie's voice. "How's Sean's run for City Council going?" I asked, changing the subject.

"It's fine. It seems he's neck and neck with a few others."

Rick's eyebrows raised. "Oh, there's a politician in the neighborhood."

"My husband is a podiatrist, but he has future political aspirations. He likes to stay involved in the community, and it just so happens there's an open City Council seat. I'll leave a flier in your mailbox." Stephanie extended her arms and jiggled the unbleached baggies. "Ben! Braydon! Come get your snacks."

Rick stood and faced us. "Well, I better head back in case my architect is early. Thanks for the walk and for showing me the park. Nice to meet you, Stephanie."

"You too. Hope to see you again soon."

"Bye, Rick." My chest weighed with disappointment as he strolled away. I'd hoped to learn a little more about his plans for the house.

Stephanie's sharp elbow poked my arm, the corners of her lips twitching. "Well, well. Isn't he a dreamy southern gentleman? Does Mark know you made a new friend?"

"Stop." I waved her off, but my cheeks burned. "I'm only being neighborly. Mark and Rick haven't even met yet."

"Right."

"Rick and Bree went on a date, but I guess it wasn't a love connection."

"Huh. Too bad for Bree."

The kids scampered toward us to claim their snacks. I handed Isabelle a granola bar and she followed the boys toward the slide.

I caught Stephanie staring at me, her eyes glittering like I'd just confessed to robbing a bank or stabbing my mother. She scooted closer, smelling like dish soap and baby powder, her breath hot in my ear, "Don't worry, Jessica. I'm good at keeping secrets."

SEVENTEEN

I perched on the corner of the bed as Isabelle splashed in her soapy bath. The open bathroom door offered a pathway for her babbling voice and a clear view of her wet head sticking up from the bubbles. I turned a shiny leaflet over in my hand, having found it shoved into the crack of our front door—another professionally printed promotional piece advertising Dr. Sean Peale's run for the open City Council seat. I winced at his lopsided grin and "family values first" platform. In my experience, the people who screamed the loudest about morality were usually the ones hiding the most skeletons. My buzzing phone pulled my attention away from the image of Sean Peale's probing eyes. Mark's name flashed across my phone below the time: 6:32 p.m. I picked up the call.

"Hi."

"How are things?"

"Good. It's bath time."

"Ah." A few deep breaths sounded on the other side of the line.

"Will you be home soon? I fed Isabelle already, but I thought I'd make us tortellini and salad for dinner."

Mark sighed. "That's why I'm calling. I'm stuck here for a while longer. George wants me to finalize these projections before the meeting tomorrow morning."

My shoulders suddenly felt heavy. "Oh."

"I'm sorry. Go ahead and eat without me. I'll pick up a quick sandwich somewhere."

"Okay. Hope it doesn't take as long as you think."

"Yeah. Me too. I should be home by nine, at the latest."

We said goodbye. I slumped forward, about to set down the phone, when I noticed a new job notification on The Neighbor List. I clicked on the app's icon, finding another entry-level position that wasn't worth my time. Isabelle hummed to herself from the bathroom as she piled a tower of bubbles into a cup. My finger flicked at the screen, scrolling through the app's most recent community forum posts. I didn't have to travel far before a heading grabbed my eyes, my pulse accelerating.

Subject: Barbara Draper

TYuno: *Does anyone know if there's been an arrest in the death of Barbara Draper?*

TheDude: *No. My brother works in the police department. They said her death was an accident (slip and fall).*

Motowner1: *It's so obvious her son killed her. I bet he'll be arrested soon.*

WaterLilly: *It might have been suicide.*

JBleeker: *A middle-aged man living with his mother? It was totally her son!*

I gasped at the allegations but kept reading.

Aroberts75: *Nothing like accusing innocent people without any evidence. I'm contacting the administrator.*

I swallowed, sinking my weight into the mattress. Apparently, I wasn't the only one doubting the cause of my neighbor's death. I felt an inexplicable need to defend Phil against the accusations, although I'd had similar suspicions about him only a few days ago. Thankfully, Aroberts75 was keeping everyone in line.

My finger hovered over the "new comment" bubble as I debated whether to defend Phil's innocence or spout my unsubstantiated theory that an outsider had murdered Barbara. I read through the comments again, finding the last one had been posted only twenty minutes earlier. Accusing people of crimes was most definitely against the app's rules, and I guessed the entire post would soon disappear.

Don't be a gossip, Jessica. Mom's disapproving words rattled through my mind. I exhaled and placed my phone face down on the quilt without joining the online conversation.

"I want to get out now." Isabelle stood in the tub, stretching one bubble-covered leg up toward the ledge.

"Wait! Sit down. Let Mommy help you." I bounded off the bed toward her, terrified she would slip and fall just like the authorities claimed Barbara Draper had. Isabelle lowered her foot back into the water. I scooped her out, placed her on the bath mat, and wrapped a towel around her before unplugging the drain.

The white medical tape near Isabelle's hairline was soaked, despite my best efforts to keep it dry when I'd shampooed her hair. The tape slid off into the towel, revealing four stitches in its place. A few beads of fresh blood seeped past the knots of thread. The nurse had warned me some bleeding might happen as a normal part of the healing process, so I didn't panic. Still, the glistening drops forming on my daughter's head were unsettling.

"Careful. Don't touch your stitches. We need to get some fresh gauze and tape to cover those." I retrieved the supplies from the medicine cabinet and pulled a length of tape, finding the roll all but empty.

"Oh, no." I dipped my head, feeling the relaxing night I'd envisioned earlier in the day completely slipping away from me. I thought about asking Mark to collect some tape on the way home but remembered the drugstore closed at eight. "We need to go to the store to get some more tape. Hold this on your head."

Isabelle pressed the gauze to her wound while I pulled on her jammies and gently tugged a comb through her hair. I temporarily secured the gauze with a couple of Band-Aids, grabbed my purse, and loaded her into the car.

We traveled the familiar ten-minute route toward downtown Glenn Hills. The spring days had gotten longer, and at 6:50 p.m., it was still bright outside. A red light halted our progress, and my car idled near the busy intersection of Main Street and Washington. As I waited for the light to change, my gaze wandered past the trees, people, and cars around me. I did a double take on one flashy vehicle in particular—Bree's shiny Mercedes. It was parked at a meter on the side of the street. I craned my neck to see if she was still in the driver's seat, but the car was empty. I wondered if she was getting in some evening showings or merely enjoying a night out. I scanned the sidewalk through my window, spotting her red four-inch heels striding away from me. A black skirt hugged the curve of her hips, and a cream silk blouse rippled in the wind. She'd pinned her hair into a loose bun. I was about to roll down the window and shout, "Hi, Bree!" when I caught sight of the person she was meeting.

Mark stepped toward Bree, all smiles and not a spreadsheet or a financial projection in sight. He wrapped an arm around her and kissed her cheek. They continued walking side-by-side past Frederick's and another half-block down. They paused in front of a casual diner, a place where I'd never eaten with Mark, but occasionally met Mom for a salad or a sandwich. Mark opened the door and waved Bree in front of him. His hand hovered near the small of her back as she passed through the doorway.

I closed my eyes, stars exploding behind my eyelids. A sob formed in my throat. I swallowed back my emotion and clutched the steering wheel, aware of Isabelle sleeping in the back seat. Was my husband cheating on me with one of my best friends? Mark said he had to stay late at work, but he'd lied. I'd just seen him entering a restaurant with Bree.

A car honked behind me. I jerked my head up, no longer sure how I'd arrived at this location. The light was green. An empty road loomed in front of me. I slammed my foot against the accelerator and sped down the rest of the block toward the drugstore, parking in the first open spot. I buried my face in my hands, feeling like I might throw up.

Was this really happening? Maybe Mark had grown tired of me, tired of my dawdling around my job search and my inaction in dealing with Mom. Maybe he wanted to be with a self-made woman, someone more career-oriented than me. But having an affair was hardly the answer. Still, Mark had a history of crossing the line from friendship to flirtation—and maybe more. I thought of bubbly, fake Sharon. I believed she was history, but now I realized that she and Bree bore a vague resemblance. Maybe Mark had a type, a type who looked nothing like me. Bree's presence was difficult to ignore. Her curvy figure, sun-drenched hair, and high cheekbones turned heads. Unlike me, she made an effort to dress in nice clothes and make herself up. Since Isabelle had been born, luxuries like that had become low priorities. I'd never thought of Bree as a threat before. I assumed I was safe with Mark, especially since we'd moved to Glenn Hills.

The double betrayal stung like two slaps to the face.

How long had this thing between Mark and Bree been going on? My breath turned jagged as red flags popped in my mind. I remembered Mark's statement from the other night. *Bree likes to play the field, that's for sure.* Had there been a glint in his eye when he said it? Suddenly, his words took on a new meaning, some sort of sick private joke. The secretive texts he'd hidden on his phone must have been from Bree, not George. And Bree's frequent comments about how lucky I was to have found the perfect man and her quick dismissal of Rick, the most eligible bachelor she'd met in a while. Had she tired of the dating pool and decided to steal my husband for herself? I remembered the nights Mark claimed he had to work late. *How many times had he lied?* I pressed my palms into the seat. I thought of the cryptic message:

Enjoy your perfect family.

That message had appeared on my phone just before I'd found our family photo smashed on the shelf. Bree had been Mom's realtor for a couple of weeks and probably still had a key to our house. *What if she'd smashed our photo? Or worse, what if Mark had done it?* I couldn't stop the unwanted theories from spinning through my head.

"Are we here?" Isabelle's voice made me jump.

"Yes." I glanced at her in the rearview mirror, struggling to keep my voice steady. I exited the car and led Isabelle into the store, focusing only on my breathing and the feel of her warm hand inside my cold one. The ground seemed to fall away beneath my feet as I walked. The bright lights inside the store disoriented me, and the elevator music warped through my ears in slow motion. Somehow, I found my way to the correct aisle and grabbed the tape. Now I was at the counter, paying for it. My fingers fumbled to press in my debit card's four-digit code. The checkout guy looked at me, perhaps noticing my altered state. Did I have the look of someone whose world had just shattered?

"Have a nice night," he said, and I forced myself to nod back. I squeezed Isabelle's hand as we headed out to the parking lot. My insides were hollow and shaky, and I didn't know if I had the strength to drive us home.

I tried to read a book, but the words rearranged themselves and jumbled into nonsensical sentences. Mark brushed his teeth in the bathroom. It was earlier than I usually headed to bed—only 9:15 p.m.—but the last two hours had drained me. I'd gotten home and fixed up Isabelle. Once I'd tucked her into bed, I'd closed myself in the bathroom and sobbed. I'd debated calling Mom but decided against it. Instead, I splashed my face with cold water and told myself to pull it together.

When Mark had stepped through the door a few minutes earlier, I fought the urge to attack him and call him a selfish asshole. I made myself wait. I wasn't ready for my marriage to fall apart tonight. I yearned for some other explanation.

Now Mark stood near the bed, but I couldn't look at him.

"Sorry I was late again."

My teeth clenched. I didn't know how to play my cards, how much to reveal. I decided to give him a chance to come clean. "Did you eat anything?"

"Yeah. I picked up a salad from Panera."

I closed my eyes. Another surge of nausea rose in my throat. I took a breath.

"What kind of salad?" I asked, wondering how far he'd take the lie.

"The Asian chicken one."

"I hope they gave you enough dressing this time."

Mark eyed me, maybe detecting the cold distrust in my eyes, the hint of poison in my voice. He stepped closer. "Everything okay?"

I wanted to scream at him and call him a liar, but I didn't have any energy left. I needed some time to figure out what to do before he discovered that I knew about his massive betrayal. "It's been a long day. I thought Mom might reach out to me, but she didn't." I angled my face toward the opposite wall so Mark couldn't see the tears building.

"She'll come around." He squeezed my shoulder. "I'm going to watch TV for a few minutes. I'll be back." He leaned forward and kissed my head. I watched him leave the room, wondering if things would ever be the same.

EIGHTEEN

I'd spent the early morning hours retreating to my happy place, beating the life out of eggs, smothering softened butter with the back of a spoon, and diving up to my elbows in flour. I lost myself in baking, the same way other people escaped reality by running marathons, meditating, or popping painkillers. I plopped another half-cup of butter in a saucepan and set it over a flame, watching the yellow rectangle shrink and spread into a hazy liquid. I mixed in brown sugar and cinnamon to create the sauce that would become the sweet veins running through the cinnamon-cappuccino coffee cakes. There'd be enough for two cakes when it was all done—one for Mom and one for me and Isabelle. My lying husband wouldn't get any of it.

Mark had left earlier than usual, citing preparations for his big Wednesday morning meeting. I hadn't responded with anything more than one syllable as he rushed out the door. Now Roo wove around my ankles, waiting for a speck of anything to drop as I pulled the first cake out of the oven to let it cool. I checked the time —8:05 a.m.—less than two hours until Sophie arrived. She'd happily agreed to add a second morning to our usual schedule. I hadn't told her the reason, but I needed to see Mom and make amends. Because Mom would know what to do about Mark.

I glanced at my phone, noticing a new notification on The Neighbor List app. I wiped my hands on a dish towel and clicked it. A new message waited in my inbox. I opened it, my eyes tumbling over the words:

You will pay.

This time, the sender's username was RVenge. I stepped backward, reading it again and putting the pieces together. *Revenge. You will pay.* I swung my head around the kitchen, confused. What was this all about? I had no idea who would want to seek revenge on me. Even if Bree was playing the role of jealous mistress, what could she possibly believe I owed her? It didn't make sense.

Who is this?

I wrote in response. I stared in disbelief at the phone in my shaking hand. As I waited, the message from a few days earlier stirred through my mind again.

Enjoy your perfect family.

Now I knew for sure that first mysterious message had also been a threat. The chalk message on the driveway suddenly seemed more relevant.

Mind your own fucking business.

I'd assumed the scrawling across the driveway was from Luke Moreno. Maybe the angsty teen was more upset about me ratting him out than I realized and had decided to double down on his threats, finding a more high-tech method to mess with me.

I tapped the app's search bar, typing in RVenge to find information on the sender. But no user by that name was found. My head dropped as I returned to my inbox. It was empty. Whoever sent the message had already gone back in and deleted it.

I steadied myself against the counter, wondering what to do next. On a normal day, I'd call Mark, but after last night, that no longer felt like an option. The message was gone anyway. I'd seen cyberbullying in the news and on social media but had never been a victim until now. This person had rattled me, but I didn't know why I'd be anyone's target. I decided to contact the app's administrator later to report the incident and find out how to block messages.

Nearly an hour later, the cakes had cooled but I realized Mom wouldn't want one. She'd been following a new diet on the advice of her doctor that limited her carb and sugar intake, and I didn't want her to think I was sabotaging her. I remembered the way Rick had raved about my first cake, and I decided to give it to him instead. At least, it would go to someone who appreciated it. I'd showered, blown out my hair, and applied my make-up. The extra mascara didn't hide the pink marbling in my eyes, but I thought I looked pretty good, considering. I rallied Isabelle. "We're going to deliver another cake to Mr. Smith."

"Yay!"

I placed the warm cake on a plate and lowered it into a reusable grocery bag. Isabelle skipped next to me as we trampled over our jungle-like grass. In contrast, Mr. Delaney's lawn sat freshly mowed next door, no doubt the work of the Moreno boys. The handles cut into my arm as I crossed the street and headed toward Rick's house.

I rang the doorbell, followed by a knock when there was no response. I wavered for a second, considering leaving the goods on the doorstep and turning back, but Rick opened the door, eyes widening with delight. He wore black athletic pants and a T-shirt, different from the jeans and work shirts he usually dressed in.

He leaned back. "To what do I owe this honor?"

"My mom made you a cake!" Isabelle jumped up and down.

I blushed and looked at my painted toes. "It's a coffee cake. Cinnamon-cappuccino flavored. I hope you like it."

Our fingers brushed as he took the bag from me. The electric charge from his touch almost made me cry. I wondered how long it had been since Mark felt that excitement from me.

Rick peeked into the bag, then shook his sandy-blonde hair out of his face. "It looks delicious. I'm going to have to work out more if you keep bringing me all these cakes."

I smiled, admiring the blue-and-black inked design clinging to his bicep muscle. "It doesn't look like you have anything to worry about." I bit my lip, heat surging up my neck. *Did I just say that?*

A grin flickered across Rick's mouth. I sensed I'd treaded too close to dangerous waters. He motioned toward the door. "I'd invite you inside, but it's such a mess right now. I'm getting ready to demo a wall or two."

"Oh, that's okay. We don't want to take up any of your time, and Isabelle's sitter will be here soon."

"Maybe I'll walk to the park with you again sometime. That was fun."

I felt my shoulders lift. "That would be great."

"Thanks again for the coffee cake," he said.

"You're welcome."

"Bye, Mr. Smith." Isabelle waved.

My heart pounded as we re-crossed the street. Rick had stared at me for a moment too long. There was something magnetic between us, and I was sure he felt it too. No matter how wrong it was, a furious, jealous part of me screamed for a balm for my pain. I needed the distraction more than ever.

A few soft knocks rapped against the front door, and I knew it was Sophie. She always knocked lightly as if not wanting to disturb anyone more than necessary. I opened the door and found her standing in a beam of sunlight, smiling toward me.

I waved her forward. "Good morning. Thanks for helping out last minute like this." Roo stood next to me, wagging his tail as Isabelle bounded from the living room.

"No problem." Sophie slipped past me with her backpack slung over her delicate shoulder. "I hope everything is okay?"

"Yes," I said, lying. "I need to visit my mom and maybe run an errand or two." My phone buzzed with a text, and I did a double take at the sender's name: Phil Draper. Sophie and Isabelle were already crouched over a half-completed puzzle on the floor. I clicked on the message, holding the screen close to my face as I read:

I found evidence of an intruder. Can you take it to the police? They don't believe me.

My fingers fumbled to respond:

What is it?

A key to the park. It's not ours. And I know it wasn't there the day my mom died. I was doing yard work in the same spot near the back door that afternoon. I would have seen it.

More bubbles appeared as I waited to see what else Phil wrote. A second later, his words popped on the screen.

I think someone from the neighborhood murdered my mom.

NINETEEN

"Are you okay?" Sophie raised herself off the floor and stepped toward me with her head cocked.

I must have let out an audible gasp as I stared at Phil's message on my phone.

I think someone from the neighborhood murdered my mom.

Vivid memories from the night Barbara died tumbled through me: the rustling bushes and Barbara's strange expression staring down at me from behind the glass, her struggle to unlock the latches, the muted scream as I ran away from her. *How close had I been to a run-in with the killer? Was it someone I knew?*

Sophie inched closer. "Jessica? You look like you've seen a ghost."

"I just got a message from Phil Draper. He found a key to the neighborhood park near his back door. He thinks it might be evidence relating to his mom's death."

"Maybe it was his key?"

"He says it wasn't."

"But I thought your neighbor's death was an accident?"

"Maybe. But the police disliked Barbara. Some of us think they were a little too fast in drawing that conclusion. This might be enough to get them to take another look."

"Wow. That's crazy." Sophie bit her lip, and I hoped I hadn't scared her.

I wrote back to Phil, thinking about my schedule for the day. Mom was expecting me any minute. By the time I returned, it would be time for Isabelle's nap.

Can I stop by later?

Then I added:

Don't touch it. Might have fingerprints.

Phil replied:

It's in a ziplock bag now. I'm putting it in a safe place. Come over at 4 p.m.?

I gave his message a thumbs up and let out a sigh. "I'm going to stop by later and get it from him. I'll take it to the police and let them take care of the rest."

"Why doesn't he take it to them?"

"Phil thinks the police don't believe him. He's had a problem with painkillers. He's unreliable in their book."

"Oh." Sophie glanced furtively toward the front window.

"There's no need for alarm. It's probably nothing." I dug through my purse, relieved to find our own family's key to the neighborhood playground inside. The metal clanked against the ring as I handed it to Sophie. "Speaking of which though, here's ours. In case you want to take Isabelle over to the swings."

She smiled and took it from me. "Thanks. It would be nice to get outside, even if there is a murderer on the loose."

"I think you're safe." I forced myself to smile as I gathered my things and kissed Isabelle goodbye.

Troubling thoughts filled my mind as I drove to Mom's condo. The devastation of Mark's betrayal weakened me from the inside out. I was angry at Bree too. *Some friend she turned out to be.* Then there was the threatening message on The Neighbor List, sent directly to me before it disappeared. But Phil's text about a possible clue to Barbara's death had injected me with unexpected energy. Nerves about seeing Mom again swirled in a separate stripe in my disjointed feelings. I'd hurt her, and she likely hadn't forgiven me yet.

A few minutes later, I located the purple pot of flowers to confirm I'd parked in the correct driveway and paced toward my mom's door as my emotions built.

She opened the door before I had a chance to ring the bell, standing in the opening with one hand on her hip. "Hi, Jessica. To what do I owe this honor?"

I tried to speak, but no words came out. The sight of her caused something inside me to crack as my anguish swelled beyond my calm exterior. My hands flew to my face, and I burst into tears.

I felt Mom's bony hand on my shoulder as she urged me inside, toward her couch. "What on earth? Is this your way of apologizing to me?"

I shook my head. "No. There's something else. Something much worse." I coughed out another sob.

Mom handed me a tissue. "Are you sick?" Creases formed across her forehead. "Is Isabelle okay?"

"I think Mark's cheating on me."

"Oh. Dear." Her mouth stayed open.

"With Bree," I continued.

"No." Mom touched her fingertips to her face. "I can't believe it. Are you sure?"

"I saw them last night, going into the diner on Main Street together. Mark told me he had to work late to prepare for an important meeting. He said he grabbed a salad from Panera for dinner. Why would he lie about that?"

"Well, I don't know. Did you ask him?"

"No. I was too worked up." I sniffled as hot tears streamed down my cheeks. "I was afraid to hear the answer."

"Have you talked to Bree? Maybe you should tell her what you saw. There might be a harmless explanation."

"No. I was too angry."

"Why don't you call her now?" Mom nodded toward my purse. "It's not good to carry too much stress and worry around." She lifted her chin. "I should know."

Mom's comment sent a ripple of guilt through me as I thought of all the stress I must have caused her the last few days. I removed my phone and let it sit like a rock in my hand.

"I'll wait in the kitchen," she said, edging away from me.

I pressed Bree's name, feeling a little like someone else was controlling my body. She picked up after one ring.

"Hey! What's up?" Bree's voice was light and bubbly. I couldn't help wondering if it was all an act.

"Hi."

"Is everything okay?" she asked.

"Not exactly." The story spilled out of me, from Mark's long hours at work to Isabelle's medical tape running out, the trip to the drugstore, and the sighting in front of the restaurant. I cleared my throat before asking the next question. "Is there something going on between the two of you?"

Bree gasped. "What? No. Is that what you thought?"

I gulped for air, unable to speak.

"Oh my God. It's nothing like that. I'm so sorry if that's what it looked like."

"Why did you go out to dinner with my husband last night? Why did neither of you mention it to me?"

"It's my fault. I needed some financial advice. I'm in such bad shape. Mark said he'd be happy to advise me for no charge, but his boss isn't cool with that sort of thing. He had to meet outside of work hours. I suggested meeting at the diner because they have big, private booths, and I figured we'd both be hungry."

"Why did Mark lie to me about it?"

"Because I told him not to tell anyone. Not even you. I'm just so embarrassed about how far I've fallen. Clients won't want to work with me if they find out how desperate I am for a commission. I don't want to lose my condo." Bree's voice splintered. "I promise you there is nothing romantic between us. Not even a little bit. I would never do that to you. Neither would Mark."

"Oh." Although I felt terrible about Bree's financial situation, my body loosened at the realization that maybe my marriage wasn't imploding, and my friend and my husband hadn't betrayed me. I could hear the sincerity in Bree's voice and I felt like an idiot for suspecting her of anything more sinister. Although I disapproved of their secretive dinner, the reasoning was plausible. I'd have a heart-to-heart with Mark later and get everything out in the open, see if his version of events matched with hers. I hoped I'd simply misread the situation. Clearly Mark's former relationship with Sharon had left me paranoid.

Bree sighed. "Obviously, we didn't handle it the right way. I'm sorry."

"It's okay. I guess I shouldn't have jumped to any conclusions."

Mom stepped in from the kitchen, smiling at my statement. "I had a feeling."

"Is someone else there?" Bree asked.

"I'm at my mom's right now."

"Hi, Bree!" Mom yelled, taking a seat next to me and giving my arm a loving pat. The relief in her eyes mirrored my own feelings.

"Here. I'm going to put you on speaker because now that I know you and Mark haven't destroyed my world, I have some news. There's a new development in Barbara Draper's death. I have to tell someone."

"What is it?" Mom and Bree asked at the same time.

"Phil texted me this morning. Remember how he said that his mom's death wasn't an accident? He found a key to our neighborhood park in his yard. He said he'd been doing yard work in the same spot on the day his mom died and it hadn't been there. He thinks it might be proof that someone else was in the house the night his mom died."

Bree chuckled. "A lost key? It's not exactly a smoking gun."

"Oh boy. I agree with Bree. That's quite a stretch. I'm sure there's no lack of snooping neighbors trying to peek in windows. Someone probably dropped it." Mom straightened up her shoulders. "I don't know why you insist on complicating things. Barbara Draper slipped and fell. Unfortunately, she died as a result. That's the end of the story. Even the police have said so."

I heard papers rustling on the other end of the line. "Hey, guys. Sorry, but I have to run. A client is calling on the other line."

"Okay," Mom said. "Goodbye."

I ended the call, turning toward Mom with narrowed eyes. "I don't get it. You knew Barbara Draper for decades. There's something strange about her death. Even if you weren't best friends, wouldn't you want to know if someone murdered her?"

Mom's fingers gripped the piping on the edge of the couch. "You really need to stop dredging things up, Jessica. The police clearly closed the case."

"But if there's new evidence, that isn't dredging things up, Mom. It's called getting to the truth." The volume of my voice continued to rise. "There's something else going on here. Phil knows it, and so do I. Not to mention that Barbara's husband, Ed Draper, died in another supposed accident in that same house. There are too many unanswered questions. Too many coincidences. And who's next? What if we're not safe? Because now I'm getting scary messages from some creep on The Neighbor List, and what if it's me?"

"Jessica. You're sounding crazy. Stop it! And don't mention Ed Draper!" Mom's eyes fastened on mine as red splotches formed on her neck.

"Why? Why do I need to stop looking into my neighbor's suspicious death?"

Mom tipped her head forward and breathed in and out. When she raised her face, her expression had changed, her eyes bright and cold as she shot me a gaze that felt like it could shatter glass. "You need to stop stirring things up because twenty-eight years ago, I killed Ed Draper."

TWENTY

For the second time in twenty-four hours, my world tilted on its axis, leaving me dizzy and unhinged. I shrank away from Mom, my body cold with fear. But I had to make sure I'd heard her correctly. "What did you say?" I asked, barely hearing myself.

Mom's wild eyes darted toward the windows and the door before landing back on me. "I murdered Ed Draper." She spoke in a loud whisper. "His fall down that staircase wasn't an accident. I pushed him."

I stared at Mom as if seeing her for the first time—the contours of her face, the bottomless depth in her black pupils. "Why?"

"He was a wife beater. He abused Barbara. Badly. She hid it pretty well for a while. Ed always acted like the perfect gentlemen around the neighborhood." Mom puckered her lips and slid her palms down the front of her pants. "I heard screams one day as I walked past the house. The next day, I went back to check on her. I caught Barbara out in the backyard, and she rushed to pull on a sweatshirt as I approached, but I'd already spotted the bruises on her arms. I confronted her about her injuries, and she denied them at first. I kept pressing, telling her I'd heard the screams. I'd seen the bruises.

"Barbara finally invited me inside for some tea. She had more bruises and scrapes hidden under her shirt, even a cigarette burn on her stomach." Mom squeezed her eyes shut and exhaled. "Eventually, Barbara confided in me, probably out of desperation, about the years of abuse she'd endured. She said the first time Ed hit her was on their honeymoon. Can you imagine? Things only got worse as time passed. She was worried for Phil's safety, but at the same time that he might turn out like his dad."

"Oh my God."

"Ed came home unexpectedly that day while we were talking, barging through the back door like a man looking for a fight. He was angry about something Barbara had done to help some kids in the neighborhood." Mom clucked and shook her head. "Barbara panicked and told me to leave through the front door, but I didn't do what she said. I couldn't leave her there alone with him." Mom inhaled another deep breath and touched a quivering finger to her chin. "I hurried upstairs, looking for a bedroom to make a hushed call to 911, but I heard them getting closer and I slipped into a bathroom. It didn't take long for Ed to start yelling at Barbara, calling her all sorts of horrible names that you or I wouldn't call our worst enemy. It was scary, and I was safe behind the door as long as Ed couldn't see me. I couldn't imagine how terrifying it must have felt for Barbara."

I pressed my heels into the floor, feeling as if all the blood had drained from my body. "I had no idea."

Mom continued, "Anyway, I heard the first smack. I'll never forget the way that sound tore through me, so violent and sickening. Then there was a louder smack, and another thud as Barbara whimpered and yelped." Mom paused, closing her eyes and opening them again. "After a few minutes, Barbara must have gotten away. She raced up the stairs, and I didn't understand why at first. Then I realized young Phil must have been there, in his bedroom. I heard Barbara speak in a calm voice. She told him to stay in his room. Then a door clicked closed. Ed's heavy boots clomped up those stairs. I peered through the crack in the door, barely able to hear anything over my heart pounding in my ears. Ed had the coldest eyes I'd ever seen in a human before, like a reptile who'd just spotted his next meal. He lunged after Barbara again, but she fought back this time. Ed dropped his hands for a second. Then he went for her throat. Her eyes bulged as he tightened his grip. I thought he was going to kill her, so I jumped out of the bathroom and yelled, 'Stop it!'" Mom shook her head, a hint of a smile showing on her lips, although her eyes watered. "Well, I just about scared the life out of him. Ed stumbled backward, toward the top of the stairs but facing me. I ran toward him, and, using every ounce of strength in my body, I shoved with both hands."

My fingers flew to my mouth but couldn't silence my gasp. Mom paused and then continued.

"Ed fell backward down those stairs, toppling over himself. I heard the crack of his neck before he landed in a heap on the floor."

I clenched my molars together, absorbing every word.

Mom balled her hands into fists as she continued the lurid tale. "Barbara and I stood there, stunned. She began to sob. I didn't understand her grief. I thought she would have been happy that son of a bitch was dead. But I guess her emotions were all tangled up. We retreated to the basement so Phil wouldn't see me. Barbara said she didn't want me to take any blame." Mom cleared her throat and placed her hand on the cushion. "Women didn't report domestic abuse back then. Not the way they're encouraged to do now. We made up a story that Ed tripped over a laundry basket and fell down the stairs. We vowed never to share what happened to anyone. Barbara even lied to Phil about the real cause of his dad's death, although I suspect Phil may have figured out as he got older that his dad hadn't accidentally tripped."

I gasped as slivers of facts rearranged themselves in my head. Phil's addiction to painkillers made more sense now. He'd grown up with a physically abusive father. He believed his mom had killed his dad in self-defense.

Mom stood up and paced in front of me. "I helped Barbara get cleaned up. We stopped her nose from bleeding and covered her bruises with make-up and long sleeves. I went home and showered and changed my clothes. She called 911 to report the fall. No one questioned her story. A few weeks later, she collected a hefty life insurance policy. We never talked about Ed's death again."

I studied Mom's features, seeing a strength behind the jut of her chin that I hadn't noticed before. How had I never known any of this? "Did Dad know?"

"No. Only me and Barbara. And now you."

I sucked in a breath, wondering how Mom had carried this secret around for so long. It must have been a terrible burden, even given the circumstances. "Is that why Barbara never yelled at me all these years?"

"I'm sure." Mom leaned back with a faraway look. "Her attitude changed in the years that followed Ed's death. It was like she had so much anger inside, but instead of dealing with it, she turned her rage outward toward others. It seemed our family was the only one she spared."

"Wow." The happy photo of Barbara and Ed on their wedding day flashed in my mind, and I wondered if she'd only kept it on the wall for show. Barbara's life had taken a tragic turn shortly after marrying Ed, and she'd never recovered from the tailspin. I recalled the obituary posted on The Neighbor List. There'd been a mention of her volunteer work at a women's shelter. So many things that had baffled me previously now made sense. Still, my chest heaved with grief. Perhaps Barbara had been so quick to help me that day I'd skinned my knee because she'd suffered through years of similar injuries. The woman's situation had not been anything close to the way I'd imagined.

Mom placed her hand on mine. "So, you can understand why I need you to stop looking into Barbara's death. It might stir up a new investigation into Ed's death."

I stared at my lap, realizing I'd unwittingly been poking around the edges of Mom's guarded secret. But Ed's case was long since closed. I shook my head. "So much time has passed. I doubt they'd bother with that. There's no evidence left."

Mom sat silent, tense.

"Wait. Did Phil know you were in their house that day?"

"I don't think so. He was in his bedroom and the door was closed. But I can't be certain he didn't see or hear something. That's the problem."

I rolled my shoulders back and took a breath. The threatening messages from The Neighbor List scrolled through my mind:

Enjoy your perfect family.

You will pay.

What if Phil had discovered that Mom had killed his dad and was now out for revenge? Perhaps Phil was luring me to his house to harm me. What if it was a trap?

I swallowed, shaking my head. Ed Draper was a violent and abusive man. Probably a horrible father. Phil must have kept quiet all these years because he believed his own mom was responsible for pushing his dad down the stairs. That was the only scenario that made sense. "Are you sure no one else knows?" I asked Mom.

She looked at the ceiling. "I'm certain. Not unless Barbara told someone, and I can't imagine she would have." She paused. "There is one thing that's always nagged at me, though."

"What?"

"Jim Delaney was out working in his yard that day. He saw me hurrying past his house right after it happened. He yelled hello. I smiled and waved, but I must have looked a mess. I always wondered if he'd seen me leave through the Drapers' back door, if he'd put two and two together."

I leaned toward Mom, forcing her to look at me. "But he's never said anything to you about it?"

"No. Not a word. And I'm sure if Mr. Delaney suspected anything, he would have come forward before now."

I looked away. Mom was right. It had been nearly thirty years since Ed Draper was discovered dead at the bottom of the stairs.

Mom squeezed my hand. "It's a lot to take in. I know. Would

you like some water?"

"Yes." I was paralyzed with shock as I watched Mom hobble into her kitchen, the new revelation whipping through my mind. Mom had killed someone. She had killed Phil's dad. Two of my neighbors might have had suspicions about what she'd done, although they'd never spoken about it.

I stayed at the condo for another hour as we talked through the events of long ago again. Our conversation circled back to how Barbara had fallen victim to domestic violence and how the general public was often willfully ignorant in identifying such things, not to mention holding the perpetrator accountable. Eventually, our talk found its way back to my sighting of Bree and Mark. Mom reassured me the situation was merely a misunderstanding, that I should go home and explain to Mark how his secret dinner with my friend had shaken me. I apologized to Mom for hurting her when it came to Isabelle, and she admitted she could understand our side of things. She agreed to give me and Mark a little more time to think about everything.

By the time I flopped into the driver's seat and backed out of her driveway, Mom and I had aired out our worries. My body should have lightened with the relief. Instead, I felt ripped and worn, like I'd been run over by a truck. I was less concerned with what Mom had said about Mr. Delaney. My next-door neighbor was a kind man who'd probably never thought twice about waving to Mom as she passed on the sidewalk that day. But I couldn't stop envisioning a ten-year-old Phil, fearful and holed up in his bedroom as his dad tumbled to his death. Phil had a mysterious way about him, as if he'd swallowed up others' secrets, hiding the skeletons somewhere deep inside. I couldn't help wondering how much he really knew.

* * *

"Here's your park key." A wisp of Sophie's fine hair had escaped her ponytail and hung over her face as she stood in the foyer and dropped the key in my hand. "We stayed at the playground for nearly an hour."

Isabelle tugged at my pants. "It was fun."

"That's great," I said, curling my fingers around the keychain and thinking about a similar key I was supposed to collect from Phil. "Thanks so much for helping out at the last minute."

Sophie smiled at Isabelle. "I can do it any time."

I opened the door to let the babysitter out, pausing in the opening at the sight of Rick. He strode along our front walkway toward me, a glass plate in his hand. He looked up, his welcoming eyes crinkling in the corners. "Hi, neighbor. I thought you might be running low on plates. This one is from the other day." He held up the dish.

Butterflies fluttered in my stomach, and I told myself to stop it. Mark wasn't cheating, and I wasn't going to flirt with danger either. I took the freshly washed plate. "Thank you. That's nice of you to return it."

Sophie stepped next to me. Rick's eyes popped as they landed on her, pausing for a second too long. "Hello." He extended his sturdy arm. Their hands clasped together, free of wedding bands.

"Hi. I'm Sophie. Isabelle's babysitter."

"Yeah. I saw you out walking with Isabelle earlier." Rick grinned as if confessing the true reason for his visit. "I live in the rundown place across the street."

"Rick flips houses," I said, stepping closer. But Rick and Sophie weren't paying attention to me. They locked their stares on each other, and I could see there was something between them. It was an attraction more appropriate than whatever nonsense Rick and I had been playing at.

Sophie pulled her eyes away and motioned toward the door. "Well, it was nice meeting you. I was just leaving."

"Can I walk you to your car?" Rick's voice dripped with southern hospitality.

I may as well have been invisible.

Sophie peeked toward her dented sedan, which sat only fifty

feet away.

He grinned. "It's a short walk. You won't be stuck with me for long."

Sophie giggled as she tucked her hair behind her ear. "Sure." She dipped her head toward me, cheeks flushing. "Bye, Jessica. Bye, Isabelle."

We said our goodbyes, and I closed the door. I spied through the narrow window as Rick and Sophie strolled side by side toward the car, glancing at each other with nervous smiles. They paused in front of the car, deep in conversation. Rick leaned closer, and Sophie nodded. He retrieved his phone from the pocket of his work pants and punched something into it, probably Sophie's phone number. I wondered if he'd asked her out to dinner. Despite the unwanted jealousy simmering beneath my skin, I had to admit they made a handsome couple.

Sophie deserved something good in her life. She was a smart, funny, attractive young woman. The first time we'd met, she'd confided that she'd postponed college initially due to financial issues, but now she was working to put herself through community college to fulfill her dream of becoming a teacher. She talked about her friends occasionally but had never mentioned a boyfriend. Sometimes I wondered if she was lonely. Rick had to be at least seven or eight years older than Sophie. Maybe an older man was just what Sophie needed. I hoped their date would go better than the one he'd had with Bree.

Sophie ducked into her car and reversed out to the road. Rick wavered near the street and raised his hand in a wave. He widened his solid stance as he watched her drive away, then headed toward his house.

I leaned my shoulder against the wall to support myself, still unable to pull my gaze from my handsome neighbor as he strode away. I couldn't help feeling I'd just lost something, but I scolded myself for my misplaced emotions. I turned my thoughts to my upcoming meeting with Phil, suddenly aware of the unsettling sensation draining through my body.

THE NEIGHBOR LIST

POSTED MAY 19

Username: Aroberts75

Subject: Slow Down!

I live on Astoria near Grand Ave. The speed limit on my residential street is 25mph, but most drivers go much faster. Yesterday, a reckless driver sped past my house and almost hit a woman on a bike. Please slow down before somebody gets killed!

JCooley: I agree. It seems everyone is in such a hurry and no one obeys the speed limits. More proof we need more bike lanes!

SarahP: Someone almost hit a little kid last week on Birch Run. Slow down!

Click to view forty-seven more comments

TWENTY-ONE

After Sophie left, I'd put Isabelle down for her nap, anxious for two or three hours to myself, an opportunity to wrangle my wild thoughts and emotions. First, I'd called Mark and revealed I'd seen him and Bree going into the diner. He stuttered for a second before saying, "It's not even close to whatever you're thinking. Bree asked for some financial advice." I interrupted and told him I knew he was only helping her sort out her money situation. I even thought it was kind of sweet. He apologized for not telling me about their meeting but said Bree had made him promise to keep it quiet because she'd been embarrassed. Mark's voice was earnest, his story matching the explanation Bree had offered earlier. I couldn't find a reason not to believe him. If anything, his reassuring words soothed me as we talked, tempering Mom's secret which bubbled inside me. I swallowed back any mention of the bombshell confession. I promised her I'd never tell anyone, and I would keep my word.

Instead, I told Mark about the second unsettling message I'd received from an unidentified person through The Neighbor List. He breathed heavily for a second or two before encouraging me to block the sender. Then George summoned him away to another task, ending our call.

After the heartfelt reassurances I'd received from both Bree and my husband, I felt at peace with my marriage again and was happy I had officially laid my juvenile attraction to Rick to rest. I lay on the couch, digesting the enormity of Mom's secret and debating whether I should still deliver Phil's evidence to the police or refuse to meet with him altogether. The odds of anyone digging into Ed Draper's accidental death after nearly thirty years seemed exceptionally slim. I didn't want to risk Mom's freedom, even though she had been acting in Barbara's defense. I had to put my family's well-being above a neighbor who I barely knew. Besides, if Phil knew what Mom had done, I could be putting her safety at risk.

A shadow passed by the back window, and I turned toward it, half expecting to find a fast-moving cloud flitting over the sun. But I caught a more defined shape just as it disappeared from view—the edge of a person's back, the heel of a shoe. My body bolted upright. Someone was in our backyard. I stood slowly, crouching low and slinking toward the wall as my heart thumped wildly. I made my way to the sliding glass door and peered beyond the edge into our fenced backyard. We always kept the gate closed. Someone would have had to let themselves through. Roo had been fast asleep on his dog bed a moment ago, but my awkward movements alerted him to potential danger. He ran to the window and barked. Gathering my courage, I inched to the center of the glass door, where I could now see a gangly person with short black hair rushing toward the gate. It was Luke Moreno. I released a breath and pulled open the slider. "Hey!" *You little shit*, I wanted to add but bit my tongue.

Luke halted just as he was about to slip into the side yard, his saucer eyes frozen in place.

"What are you doing?" I asked.

Roo raced past me and stopped short of the teenager, sniffing the air.

"Oh, sorry." Luke clasped his hands together and looked down. His voice was deeper than I expected. He seemed older than fifteen as he wiped his brow, the stubble of mustache shadowing his upper lip. A T-shirt hugged his shoulders, black athletic shorts and Nike sneakers completing the picture. "My mom said you might want a quote for grass cutting. I just needed to see how big your backyard was. Sorry. It looked like no one was home."

I shifted my feet. The threatening chalk message appeared in my mind, but I decided against hurling unfounded accusations. I'd done stupid things when I was a teenager too. It was more than a little presumptuous of Avery to send her son over, especially because I'd never followed up with her about the mowing. But I supposed our neglected yard hadn't gone unnoticed by the neighbors. "Oh. I'm not sure if we need any help this season."

"Okay." Luke's eyes flickered with confusion as they traveled across the waving clumps of crabgrass and sprouting dandelions.

Heat chased up my neck, into my cheeks. "Actually, I guess it would be good to know what you charge. We've been falling a little behind." I paused. "Shouldn't you be in school?"

"We had a half day. Your yard looks about the same as Mr. Delaney's, but I'll let you know." Luke put his head down and walked through the gate without telling me how much he charged Mr. Delaney.

I chuckled to myself as I went back inside, remembering that teenagers lived by their own rules. Maybe the boy didn't realize how inappropriate it was to barge into someone's private backyard without asking permission first. He'd scared the crap of out me, but Mom's story about Ed Draper and the threats from The Neighbor List had set me on edge. Still, I couldn't help wondering if Luke had been up to something else, another prank to show me he didn't appreciate me ratting him out to his mom. I headed to the kitchen to make myself some tea.

By four o'clock, the day had turned unseasonably warm, feeling more like July than May. My initial shock at Mom's revelation had dulled, but my feet weighed like concrete blocks as I approached

Phil's front door with Isabelle stomping next to me. The thought of facing the tortured man was almost unbearable, and I worried my newfound knowledge was tattooed across my face. *My mom had killed his dad.* What if Phil already knew?

Sweat prickled on my forehead as I adjusted my sunglasses, bracing myself to lie to Phil. I'd decided to take the key from him and hide it. Tomorrow, I'd tell him I tried to turn it over to the police, but they weren't interested. Maybe I'd say they thought the evidence was contaminated or they doubted how long the key had been lying there. In any case, I'd play dumb, telling Phil the investigation was closed and the medical examiner had been correct about his mom's cause of death. Then I'd keep my distance from him going forward.

"Can I knock?" Isabelle stretched her arms toward the brass door knocker. I held her up as she clanked the metal several times. I set her down, and we waited. After a minute or two, I banged the door knocker again, feeling a little like we were requesting entrance to a foreboding castle. Other than a light wind whistling through the gutters, only silence greeted us.

Isabelle frowned. "Nobody's home."

I retrieved my phone from my pocket and reread the text, confirming our plan to meet at Phil's house at four o'clock. "Let's check the backyard." We slunk around the house toward the backyard. The patio sat empty, with only a lonely lounge chair and a dirt-filled flowerpot baking in the sun. I cupped my hands around my mouth. "Phil? You home?" I yelled toward the upstairs windows. Still no answer.

The hum of a car drew my attention back to the front yard, my stomach churning as a police cruiser pulled into the driveway. My first thought was of Mom. *Had someone overheard her confession? Were the police here to question me?* I squeezed Isabelle's hand, shaking my head. No. That was ridiculous.

"Afternoon." A trim policewoman with olive skin and wispy bangs stepped from the car and nodded in my direction. "I'm Officer Lang."

"Hi." I looked around, surveying my surroundings. Maybe someone had spotted me lurking in Phil's yard and called the police. Although who robbed a house in the middle of the day with a toddler in tow? I produced my most non-threatening smile. "I'm Jessica Millstone. We live a couple of doors down. I was just looking for the man who lives here. Phil Draper."

Her eyes clouded with concern. "Are you a close friend?"

"What? Oh. Not really. More of an acquaintance."

The policewoman stared at me, pursing her lips.

"Why?" I asked.

The other woman looked from me to Isabelle. "Can we speak away from your daughter for a minute?"

"Oh. Sure." I looked around, spotting a ladybug crawling away from us down the stone path. "Isabelle, look at that ladybug. Can you follow it?"

"Yeah!" She crouched down and waddled a few feet away.

The police officer gave me a nod of approval as she leaned closer. "I'm afraid Phil Draper was killed this afternoon in a hit-and-run over near Elm Avenue. I came over here to see if there were any next of kin to notify."

"Oh my God. Phil's dead?" I steadied my feet, afraid I might topple. *Dead?* Despite the scorching sun, cold dread flushed through my veins.

She set her hands on her hips. "I'm afraid so."

"Who hit him?"

"Unfortunately, the perpetrator got away. There weren't any witnesses. At least, not that we've found. This was the address on his driver's license." She stepped toward the door to knock.

"Phil lived here alone," I said. "His mom was Barbara Draper. She died last week."

The officer turned toward me as a realization spread through her face. "Wait. The bathtub?"

I nodded.

She unhitched her phone and took a few steps in the opposite direction, turning her body away from me. "This hit-and-run near

Elm might be good for a suicide." The officer kept her voice low, but I could make out her words.

Suicide? I couldn't believe it.

The officer continued speaking into her phone. "Yeah. His mom died last week. Barbara Draper. We should have put it together before now. Right. I know. Okay. See you in ten." She strode toward me. "I thought that last name sounded familiar. I wasn't working on the other case. Any other family I should notify that you know of?"

"No. I don't think so." I inhaled and closed my eyes, struggling not to fall to my knees. "Wait, yes. Phil has an aunt in California. Barbara's obituary mentioned her."

The policewoman nodded at me as she was about to climb into the driver's seat. "Thank you for your assistance."

I forced my feet toward her. "Wait. I heard what you said just now about suicide. That can't be right. You don't have all the facts."

She paused behind her open car door, a slight tilt to her head. "There's a lot we've been learning about Phil. When we add in his mom's recent death, it sure starts to look like something he might have done intentionally."

"No." I shook my head. This woman had it all wrong. I had to make her see the facts through a different lens. Without thinking, I began spilling what I knew. "Phil believed his mom was murdered. He heard someone else in the house the night she died. I was walking my dog that night too, and I heard a rustling behind the bushes." I pointed toward the tall shrubs. "It sounded like someone was hiding. Phil told me he spotted a figure running through the yard a little after that. It was dark out, so he couldn't see who it was."

"He already came down to the station and reported this. Didn't he? The lead detective said Phil was under the influence of an illegal substance that night. There was no evidence of an intruder at the scene."

I squared my shoulders. "Phil didn't die by suicide. He was

supposed to meet me here at 4 p.m. He found a piece of evidence near the back door, and he wanted me to turn it over to the police because you guys didn't believe him."

"What kind of evidence?"

"It was a key to the neighborhood playground. Only people in the Ridgeview Pines subdivision have them. It wasn't his. He thought it must have fallen out of someone's pocket that night."

The officer lowered her chin, pity pulling down her features. "Look. I can see how every item Phil came across might have seemed like evidence, but something as small as a key could have been sitting there unnoticed for days or months, or it could have been dropped after his mother's death by a well-wisher. By all accounts, Phil was an extremely troubled person."

"But what if someone killed him on purpose? Why would the person who hit him drive away?"

She shrugged. "Fear. This is most likely a suicide or a hit-and-run. Maybe the driver was speeding. We'll find the driver and ask some questions. We'll continue searching for witnesses. The truth will come out, but premeditated murder is highly unlikely in cases like this."

I remembered all of the recent complaints on The Neighbor List about speeding drivers and realized she had a point. "Did Phil have the key on him?" I fumbled through my pocket, pulling out my oblong key with the Ridgeview Pines logo. "It looks like this."

Officer Lang pressed her lips into a line as she inspected my key. "The only things we found on him were his wallet, phone, and two other standard keys. A car key and a basic house key. Nothing like this one." She handed it back to me.

"Can we go inside the house and look for it?"

"I'm not authorized to do that, and even if I was..." she rubbed her temple, "a lost park key isn't real evidence of anything. Like I said, it could have been sitting there for weeks. Or a curious neighbor could have dropped it." She studied me as if measuring the disappointment on my face. "I'm sorry."

The police refused to acknowledge anything but the most

apparent theory of death for any member of the Draper family. Mom's dark secret burrowed inside me. I'd decided earlier I wasn't going to turn over the playground key, even if I'd had it in my possession, because it could stir up the past. Still, in a rush of emotion caused by the news of Phil's sudden death, it had felt wrong to not share all the facts with the officer. I had the safety of my family to consider. But now I could see by the officer's resistance that there was no point in arguing with her, that maybe she was correct about the cause of Phil's death, and there was no need to risk exposing Mom's secret. I needed to let things rest, even if my silence buried the truth forever.

As Officer Lang's police car disappeared down Mapleview Lane, something clawed at my gut, a seed of unrest that I wanted to ignore but couldn't. I gripped Isabelle's hand and peered up at the blackened window where Barbara Draper had locked eyes with me on the night she died. My skin bristled. I swung my head toward neighboring houses, finding so many windows staring at me from every direction. *What if someone knew Phil had discovered evidence of his mom's murder and wanted to stop him from sharing it? What if the same person who killed Barbara had also killed her son?*

TWENTY-TWO

I pinched a corner of the floral wallpaper and ripped it from the wall. Mark used a metal scraper to dislodge old glue on the other side of the kitchen. It was late morning on Saturday, and Sophie and Isabelle were upstairs, playing in Isabelle's room. We'd booked the babysitter for a few extra hours so that we could repaint the kitchen, but the project was already taking longer than anticipated. I checked my phone to see if The Neighbor List customer service had responded to my message detailing the threats I'd received. So far, only a guy named Tony had responded, confirming that no users by those names existed. He'd passed my complaint on to the tech team, who would supposedly get back to me within seven to fourteen days. So far, no word.

Mark had felt terrible about the misunderstanding over his secretive dinner with Bree and had returned home early that night with a bouquet of roses. Phil's untimely death had shaken me, but Mark held me close as he offered his condolences. Before I even mentioned Luke Moreno's surprise appearance in the backyard, Mark had gone outside and mowed the lawn. Later, after Isabelle was asleep, lots of sweet whispers led us into the bedroom. We'd both been eager to reconnect.

We'd woken early yesterday, thinking of activities to distract ourselves from the deaths two doors down. I knew how much Mark hated the flowered, mustard-yellow wallpaper, and I'd suggested repainting the kitchen as a temporary fix until we could afford a full remodel a year or two down the road. The commercials on TV always made painting a room look so fun—happy couples flicking glistening paint drops at each other as they magically transformed their space into a colorful oasis in a matter of minutes. We'd made a plan, selected a paint color, and bought supplies. So far, the experience was nothing like I'd seen on the commercials. The room was too hot, and my back and knees ached as I picked at the loose edges of wallpaper, only to watch it peel off into useless slivers.

Now three days had passed since Phil had died, and Mark had patiently listened to me rehash the string of events multiple times, including various interpretations of my conversation with Officer Lang. I shared my theory that someone had learned about Phil's discovery of the park key and wanted to stop him from taking it to the police. Mark agreed Phil's death was tragic but said I was getting ahead of myself. He thought the police were correct, that Phil most likely died by suicide—or was the victim of a reckless driver—and that the lost key probably had nothing to do with Barbara's death. He said I should keep my distance from the investigation and let the police do their jobs. I'd put my head down and agreed, not wanting to risk the exposure of mom's deadly secret from decades earlier.

Mark grunted, stepping away from the wall. "This stuff won't come off. What kind of glue did they use?" Sweat glistened across his face as he reached for the spray bottle and squirted glue-dissolver on the wall again.

I kept ripping shreds of brittle paper from the wall, my thoughts traveling back in time to when Mom and Dad had chosen the pattern. Had they adorned the walls before or after Mom shoved Ed Draper to his death? I think I'd been about five years old when the wallpaper went up, though it was a vague memory. My family history had always seemed so peaceful, my childhood ideal. But now, I examined my past in a different light. I wasn't sure what was true and what was merely a story I'd told myself so I could sleep at night.

Visions of a younger Phil Draper sifted through my mind—the skinny teenager who clattered along the sidewalks of the Ridgeview Pines subdivision on his rickety skateboard, crossing the street with his angular shoulders hunched forward to avoid making eye contact with others. His drab clothes had matched his somber face. Phil emanated a sour and secretive aura, causing people to avoid him, just as they avoided his mother. But now, my heart ached for ten-year-old Phil as he huddled in the corner of his bedroom while his dad beat his mom a floor below. He'd been a child who needed a friend. Instead, he'd isolated himself and retreated toward his hardened mother. Phil's dark, brooding eyes had never connected with anyone long enough to reveal the pain he must have held inside. It wasn't surprising he'd found a salve for his wound in prescription painkillers and alcohol. I'd barely scratched the surface of Phil's tragic story, and now he was gone.

As much as I tried to distract myself with vibrant paint colors and the pretty bouquet of roses on the counter, I couldn't escape the troubling fact that someone might have murdered two of my neighbors. Mom had killed the third member of the Draper family years earlier. Could the events somehow be connected? The timing of the threatening messages couldn't be a coincidence. I didn't know what had happened to the playground key Phil wanted to give me, but his text had said, *I put it in a safe place.* I guessed he'd hidden it somewhere in the house. The key might hold the fingerprint of someone who had been in or near the Drapers' home, possibly the night Barbara was murdered. I needed to find that key.

I pulled Roo along next to me, savoring the fresh air. Prepping the walls had been more than Mark and I had bargained for, and the hours had dwindled without us having completed any actual painting. My endless ideas about Phil's recent death continued to pour through me like acid spilling into a fresh cut. I felt jittery and jumpy as if I'd downed a few too many cups of coffee. The possibility that the same person had killed both Phil and Barbara—and might now be threatening me—had set me on edge.

I'd pulled and torn and crumpled and tossed the outdated wallpaper the entire day, but all the while, my mind spun. I needed to do something—soon—and I couldn't wait for a nighttime walk to make a plan. After I'd pried the last shred of wallpaper away from a crevice behind the refrigerator, I'd showered, changed, and left Mark and Isabelle at home to order pizza.

Now, the chemical scent of reconstituted glue clung to my nose and throat as I strode down Mapleview Lane, my sore fingertips gripping the taut leash. As I passed the Draper house, I let Roo sniff for longer than usual, my feet inching toward the edge of the sidewalk. My eyes traveled over the stucco exterior and the opaque windows, and I realized how attractive the prim exterior might appear to an outsider. I felt a sudden affinity for the silent house, for its ability to hold its secrets safe. The key was somewhere inside those walls. I could feel it.

My phone buzzed in my pocket, and I pulled it out, finding a message from Bree:

> *A tiny bit of a silver lining to all the tragedy on your street. Just got off the phone with Barbara Draper's sister. I got the listing for the Draper house.*

I reread the message as I looked from the screen to the house and back again. A breath lodged in my throat. I should have been happy for Bree, but something about her news felt wrong, rushed. Phil had barely been dead for three days. Someone might have murdered him. Everything was happening too fast. I gripped the phone, reminding myself not to ruin my friend's accomplishment.

Bree was desperate for money. Neither Barbara nor Phil had ever been going to sell their house, despite Barbara's pretenses, so this was nothing short of a windfall. I reconsidered my panicked reaction. Maybe Bree's listing was good news in more ways than one. As the realtor, she could let me into the house to search for the key. There might be other missed clues inside.

I responded:

Can you get me inside? Phil left something for me. I need to look for it ASAP.

Sorry. I don't have keys yet. Maybe in a week or so.

I dropped my head as more bubbles appeared on the screen.

It's not that park key, is it?

Bree followed her question with an emoji of a face with eyes rolling back in its head.

I grunted as heat gathered in my neck. Bree wasn't going to help, just like Mark, Mom, and the police weren't going to help. Apparently, I was the only one who believed something sinister had happened to both mother and son. Or maybe I was the only one who cared. I knew what it felt like to be attacked, to intersect with someone careening along a violent path, unable to get out of the way. I'd never forgotten the way the man in the parking garage strode toward me like he was going to eat me for dinner and spit out my bones. I'd been powerless, incapable of dialing 911 or screaming for help.

I shoved the phone back into my pocket and looked up and down the length of the street. A car turned the corner, and I waited, letting it pass. Kids screeched and laughed from a distant backyard, but no one else was nearby.

Inhaling a breath of courage, I ducked forward and hurried toward the privacy of the Drapers' backyard. Roo trotted next to me, foxlike. His jangling tags weren't ideal for the covert mission, but I didn't want to lose the opportunity to search for a way inside. Once I'd turned the corner, I pressed my back into the cold wall and scanned the area surrounding the back door. Two steps led to the entryway. A worn, bristled mat with a faded black "D" centered inside a gray rectangle sat below the bottom step. My pulse quickened as I lunged toward the mat, peeling up the corner and hoping to find a house key underneath. But my effort merely revealed a damp rectangle of concrete, a centipede recoiling at the light and wriggling toward the nearest crack.

I released the soggy covering and stepped toward the door, not willing to overlook the most straightforward option. I tightened my fingers around the metal handle and turned, but the knob stuck. Jiggling it served no use. I wasn't surprised to find that Phil had locked the door when he'd left. I backed away and moved toward the shrubs bordering the door. It was the spot where Phil said he'd found the park key.

I got down low and sifted through the woodchips, checking for anything out of place or a fake rock that might hide a key. But only a uniform layer of cedar chips covered the area beneath the shrubs. I rubbed my head, turning back toward the sparsely furnished patio. I'd been foolish to think it would be so easy to find a way into the house. The barren flowerpot languished next to a lounge chair. I stepped toward the pot and tipped it back, careful not to spill the dirt. A glint of metal met my eyes, and I coughed out a laugh. It was a single house key. I plucked it up and cupped it inside my hand, feeling dangerous and accomplished.

I hesitated, debating whether to go inside now or return later. A door slammed beyond the tall privacy fence, followed by talking and laughter.

"Let's set up the badminton net," a voice said, and I recognized it as belonging to Luke Moreno.

"Yeah. I'll get it," another boy responded.

"I'll throw the kabobs on the grill." It was Avery Moreno's husband, Paul.

I couldn't see them, but it sounded like the whole family was outside, enjoying their backyard. A low growl formed in Roo's throat. He barked toward the fence.

"Shh!" I tapped my dog with my foot, crouching low.

"Is there a dog over there?" a disembodied voice asked from beyond the fence.

Shit! Shit! Fear exploded through me. I bolted around the other side of the house, yanking Roo after me toward the street. I had to disappear before someone saw me and started asking questions. I slipped through an opening in the side yard and stumbled back onto the sidewalk, struggling to control my breathing. I straightened myself up, dropping the key into my pocket and smoothing down my shirt.

Someone coughed behind me. I spun toward the noise, heat prickling up my neck. Further down the sidewalk, Sean Peale pulled a red wagon in my direction, his toddler twins piled inside.

"Doggie!" one of them yelled.

I swallowed my nausea and offered a stiff smile.

Sean tilted his balding head at me with his crooked grin and strange, half-smiling eyes. "Hi, Jessica. Everything okay?" His eyes scanned over me as if he was cutting me into pieces and weighing my parts.

"Yes." I forced the word from my clenched throat. I wondered if he made his patients feel this uncomfortable when he examined their feet. "Have a nice walk." I nearly tripped over myself as I turned away and raced toward my house. Sean had likely seen me bolt out from the Drapers' side yard, a fact he'd surely mention to Stephanie. His wife's big mouth and love of neighborhood gossip were always a hazard, but were even more treacherous now that I needed to stay under the radar. I was running out of time to do what needed to be done.

TWENTY-THREE

I wasn't sure if my plan was crazy or dangerous or both, but some-times when I ruminated too long and too hard over an idea, it crys-tallized into something indestructible. I'd found an easy path into the Drapers' house with my earlier discovery underneath the flow-erpot. I needed to act before the eyes of the neighborhood were on me. The missing park key offered possible answers, an escape route from the harrowing questions that surrounded the deaths of Barbara and her son—and now the anonymous threats directed toward my family. I was convinced everything was somehow connected, although I had no idea how or why.

It was approaching 9 p.m. when I slipped out to our patio to plan exactly how I'd break into the Drapers' vacant house. I turned on the string of outdoor lights that crisscrossed above our patio—tiny lanterns that gave the space a festive look even as my neigh-bors dropped dead around me. Mark was upstairs reading picture books to Isabelle. Beyond our back fence, Stephanie's muffled voice echoed through a screen door. She rambled on and on about adding more "how-to" videos to her blog to cross-promote herself on YouTube and TikTok. No one responded to her, so I presumed she was on the phone with some unfortunate soul.

I cringed as I tuned out Stephanie's shrill diatribe and stared at an upstairs window, glowing yellow behind closed blinds. There'd been other nights when I'd gotten a clear view into that window, and I knew it was the Peales' master bedroom, complete with aqua-and-white striped wallpaper and a gold-framed mirror. Stephanie and Sean were such an odd couple, although I supposed they were both ambitious and unlikeable in their own ways. Despite Sean's "Family Values" platform in his run for City Council, their marriage didn't seem like a particularly happy one. I'd heard their shouting matches on occasion and witnessed their lack of warmth toward each other. Their toddler boys played well with Isabelle, though, and I reminded myself the state of the Peales' marriage was none of my business.

A gap opened in the blinds, and I nearly choked as Sean's face peeked through. His eyes connected with mine for a split second, and I looked away, pretending to adjust the string of lights. My gaze flickered up as the gap in the blinds closed again. I wondered what the man had been doing. A shiver blew across my skin, and I got a strange feeling that he'd known I was here. I pulled a chair closer to the fence and sat where Sean couldn't see me. The Peales' back door slammed shut, drowning out Stephanie's mind-numbing conversation. A car motor rumbled down the street, and dogs barked in the distance. Roo scratched at the glass door, asking to join me outside. To the side of me, an upstairs light glowed from Mr. Delaney's house. I inhaled the night air and closed my eyes, imagining how I'd accomplish the task ahead of me without anyone finding out.

Five hours later, I wrapped my arms around my pillow, squeezing fabric to my face and inhaling the lingering cotton-lavender scent of our household detergent. I stared through the darkness at the bright numbers on my bedside clock. 2:18 a.m. Mark snored softly next to me with the covers pulled up to his chin. My hands slid inside my pillowcase, fingers gripping the metal house key that would hopefully open the Drapers' back door.

I waited until 2:30 a.m., as I'd promised myself. Then I slipped out of bed and gathered the black leggings, sweatshirt, and socks I'd positioned under the bottom shelf of my nightstand before tiptoeing out to the hallway and gently closing the door behind me. I pulled the clothes on over my nightshirt, feeling the security of the tiny metal object in my pocket. The stairs creaked under my feet, so I stepped more slowly and lightly. Waking Mark or Isabelle would ruin my shot.

Roo lay curled in his dog bed near the bottom of the stairs, thumping his tail as I neared. His barking earlier in the evening had nearly exposed me to the Morenos. I tossed him a treat and then grabbed our flashlight from its spot in the console table drawer. My four-legged friend wasn't coming with me this time. I skimmed through the narrow opening of our front door, shutting it quietly behind me.

I felt like a criminal as I slunk along the sidewalk, my neck contracted above my hunched shoulders. I debated whether to turn on the flashlight. My vision acclimated to the blackness, and I decided against shining an unnecessary light. Even under the cover of night, I felt exposed. The sensation of someone else hovering nearby crawled up the back of my neck. Something ducked in the distance, near the dim outline of Mr. Delaney's house. I searched the shifting shadows, unable to discern any objects more than a few feet away. A breath huffed from my mouth. The movement must have been a trick of the eye—a tree branch wavering in the wind or a raccoon darting into the bushes.

My heart hammered against my ribs. I remembered feeling the same dangerous shot of adrenaline my senior year of high school when Annette James dared me to steal a soda from the Mobile station on the corner of 14th and Evergreen. *Fuck the oil industry.* That's what I'd thought to myself as I slipped the Coke can under my denim jacket and strode out of the gas station store, keeping my head down as I passed the security cameras without detection. But I was an adult now. And even as a teen, I'd never done anything on this level—breaking into someone else's house in the middle of the night—so, of course, my senses were on edge, my mind imagining things that weren't there. I wouldn't let my paranoia control me.

I forced my legs forward through the thick night air, following the sidewalk toward the Tudor two doors down and wondering if I'd officially gone mad. My eyes tracked the ground as I walked, my feet pausing on the one cement square that sat slightly off-kilter. It was the spot where I'd crashed my bike twenty-five years ago, the place where Barbara Draper had come to my aid, gently dabbing the warm washcloth on my bloody knee and giving me an orange popsicle to stop my tears. I knew a side of her—and now of her son —that no one else did, except, maybe, for Mom.

With renewed conviction, I dug my hand into my pocket and retrieved the key as I stepped forward, slinking across the Drapers' front lawn and turning the corner around the side of the house and into the backyard. A light wind brushed past me, sounding like a breath in my ear and sending a shiver through me. I'd gotten used to walking at night, but it had never been this dark or this quiet. There'd always been porch lights and dogs and an occasional passing car. I waited for a second, then I flipped on the flashlight, angling it down as I approached the back door. My plan was in motion. There was no time for second-guessing myself. The handle glowed under the beam, and I inserted the key. It slid in with a wiggle and turned, the door clicking open into a shadowy mudroom.

My heart pounded in my ears as I continued inside, closing the door behind me. I hurried forward, terrified that two hands would reach out and grab me from behind at any moment. Turning on the light would put me at ease, but I wasn't that stupid. Instead, I edged through the darkness, scanning the walls with the weak beam of light. A row of tiny hooks appeared near the door, an assortment of key rings hanging from them. I held my breath, spotting the oblong one that was bigger than the others with the plastic Ridgeview Pines logo attached to it. *Could it really be this easy?*

I touched the key, flipping it over, finding the word "DRAPER" printed in black, permanent marker on the reverse side. I released the object, watching it dangle as if laughing at me. This wasn't the secret evidence. The key in front of me had belonged to Barbara and Phil. Phil said he'd protected the park key he'd found by placing it inside a ziplock bag and hiding it in a safe place. I stepped away, realizing I had an entire house to search.

I spent at least five minutes pulling open drawers and peering under couch cushions as a vague memory surfaced in my mind. Phil had mentioned how easy it had been to hide addictions from people. He'd said something about burrowing drugs inside of an old shoe or a hollowed-out book. I assumed he'd been speaking in generalities at the time, but now I wondered if he'd unwittingly revealed the hiding place of his secret drug stash. My hunch was that he'd hidden the key in the same place. *But where?* I scanned the living room shelves for books, finding only half a dozen leather-bound classics resting near a clock. I opened each one, discovering all the pages were intact.

I craned my neck toward the stairway running up the far wall, its wooden steps steep and harrowing. I'd have to climb it to reach the obvious next target—Phil's bedroom. With trepidation, I made my way toward the stairs. The old house seized and moaned, almost as if its walls were whispering secrets. I stopped shy of the bottom step trying not to think about Ed Draper tumbling backward years earlier and cracking his neck. I blinked, banishing the vision of Mom perched above, her palms hot and shaking as she realized what she'd done, what she'd had no choice but to do. My eyes flickered toward the front door, but I refocused and scolded myself for even thinking about turning back. Now was not the time to allow the past to haunt me. I squared my jaw and marched through the twenty-eight-year-old murder scene, my shoes squeaking against each wooden step. The clock was ticking.

I passed a bathroom and couldn't help imagining Mom's eyes spying through the crack in the door. The master bedroom sat around a turn in the hallway. I bypassed it, landing at last on a room with beige walls and a navy bedspread. It must have been Phil's room. My beam of light swung wildly from wall to wall. A musty scent clung to the air, but I could see that Phil had taken pride in this space. He kept it tidy. The bed was made, the blanket smooth, and pillows fluffed. No clothes littered the floor. A sparse desk was positioned below double windows overlooking the back-yard. A queen-sized bed lay in front of me, flanked by nightstands. My light hovered over a glass of water sitting on the far nightstand; the glass was almost full. The sight of the glistening liquid caused me to choke on my breath. Phil never had a chance to drink the rest of his water.

I turned away from the glass and scanned my light over the far wall, finding a slatted closet door. Closets made good hiding places. I lunged toward the door and yanked it open, dropping to my knees and turning over every shoe I could find, even a smallish pair of leather cowboy boots that appeared to be left over from when Phil was a boy. Every single shoe was empty. I sifted through the sweaters on the top shelf, my eyes landing on a shoebox behind them. I stood on my tiptoes and pulled it toward me, removing the lid.

The circle of light from my flashlight revealed an award from a YMCA day camp. It appeared that Phil had played on a summer camp softball team, and they'd won the tournament for "Session 3". The paper was dated twenty-three years earlier, confirming my suspicions that this certificate was a relic from Phil's adolescence. I lifted the sheet, finding other awards from the same camp and dated within two years of the first one. A birthday card celebrating Phil's eleventh birthday and signed, *Love, Granny* lay below the others. Then, a "Student of the Week" award from Glenn Hills Middle School. I'd won the same award five years later. I skipped through a few more birthday cards, searching for a ziplock bag holding a key but coming up empty. A newspaper clipping at the bottom of the box caught my eye. I plucked it out, holding it under the light and gasping as Ed Draper's black-and-white photo smiled back at me.

Ed's obituary was barely two paragraphs long. The article outlined the man's upbringing. He'd been born in Muncie, Indiana, into a farming family. He'd graduated from Oakland University and had worked sixteen years in the insurance industry. His loving wife, Barbara, and his ten-year-old son, Phillip, had survived him. A breath of relief rushed from my lungs as I reached the end of the article. There was no mention of Ed's cause of death.

My shaking hands piled the papers back into the box and returned everything to the high shelf behind the sweaters. I closed the closet door, feeling my hope fizzle out of me. I paced the room, kneeling next to the bed and pressing my cheek to the woolly carpeting as I shone my light underneath. There was nothing under there. I raised myself off the floor with a sigh, questioning my sanity. How had I found myself in this strange house in the black of night, rummaging through the belongings of a dead man who I'd barely known? What if Mark woke up and wondered where I was? I hadn't even thought up a cover story.

Panic crept through me, and I debated giving up and running home empty-handed. But as I stood, the beam of my flashlight passed over something colorful next to the bed. I aimed the light at the bottom shelf of Phil's nightstand, finding a stack of hardcover science fiction books tucked toward the back. I inched toward them, pulling out the first one and flipping through it but failing to reveal any secret hollows within the pages. The second book produced the same result. The third book was lighter than the others and had a different feel. The moment I opened it, two plastic baggies fell out onto the bed.

"Holy crap." I spoke the words under my breath. My hunch about Phil's hiding place had been correct. My fingers pinched the corner of the first bag, and I examined its contents under the light. It was a key to the Ridgeview Pines playground, just like the one hanging near the Drapers' back door, except no last name was printed on this one. I stuffed the bag into the pocket of my sweatshirt, my eyelids still blinking in disbelief. I'd recovered the evidence.

Dozens of tiny white pills filled the second bag, which I lifted toward my face. The pills slid and tumbled over each other. It felt wrong to have them in front of me. Besides dabbling in marijuana in my younger days, drugs had never been one of my vices, and I didn't know what kind of pills these were. I presumed they were painkillers based on the rumors I'd heard about Phil. And based on their hiding place inside a book, I suspected they were also illegal. I stuffed the pills back into the book and replaced all three books on the shelf underneath the nightstand.

My feet spun beneath me as I hurried down the macabre stairs, clutching the railing so I wouldn't slip. A noise clicked from somewhere in the distance. I paused, crouching down and listening as my blood whooshed through my veins. After fifteen or twenty seconds of silence, I released my breath. My imagination had gotten the best of me. These old houses rattled and sputtered with every gust of wind. I straightened my shoulders and continued toward the door, toward home. In less than five minutes, I'd be back in my bed. Safe.

I made a beeline through the blackened living room, heading toward the kitchen and the mudroom and already planning how I'd sneak back into my house, tossing a treat to Roo and creeping into bed without anyone hearing me. The soles of my shoes skimmed over the rug and onto the linoleum kitchen floor. I grasped the handle of the back door, eager to leave the cursed house. But as I pulled the door open, a shadowy figure loomed in the opening, blocking my escape route.

A jolt of fear speared through me as I stumbled backward. I swallowed my scream and forced my shaking hand to raise the light toward the person's face. A whimper slipped from my lips when I saw his weird half-smile and the deadened look in his eyes. Sean Peale stepped closer, staring me down like a total psychopath.

TWENTY-FOUR

"What are you doing here, Jessica?" Sean's thin lips twitched.

My mouth opened, but no words came out. I thought about turning and running out the front door or hiding in the bathroom as Mom had done years earlier; only my feet wouldn't move. I lowered the flashlight.

"You shouldn't be here." His features were in shadows now, and I was glad I couldn't see the strange grin that never quite reached his eyes. "Should I alert the police to a home intrusion?"

My head jerked. "No. It's nothing like that. Phil had something for me, but he didn't have a chance to give it to me before he died. I came over to get it."

"In the middle of the night?" Sean's creepy, unfinished smile held steady. "I saw you lurking around here earlier. Is that when you took the key from under the flowerpot?"

I stared at the floor, at the wavering circle of light. *How did Sean know about the flowerpot?* Something tightened and bolstered within me, and I decided to fire back, "Why are *you* here?" Suddenly, I wondered if the playground key belonged to Sean. Maybe he was the one who'd bashed Barbara's head into the bathroom shelf and thrown her into the tub. I'd seen him wandering nearby the night Barbara died.

Sean released a long sigh as if exasperated by my stupidity. "Look. I'm going to make this easy for you. Hand over the drugs and I won't call the police. That way, no one gets hurt."

I rolled back on my heels, a new set of facts registering. Sean wasn't here for the playground key. An image of the tiny white pills in Phil's room spilled through my mind. Sean was a doctor. A foot doctor, but still a doctor. He must have been Phil's supplier. "I didn't come here for the pills." I squared my shoulders, realizing this newfound knowledge gave me the upper hand. "Phil found our key to the neighborhood playground," I lied. "I needed it back, but I didn't want anyone to see me coming into the house."

"Playground key?"

I slid the plastic baggie from my pocket and held it up, so my shifty neighbor could see I was telling the truth. "I take Isabelle there almost every day. I needed my key back."

My beam of light found Sean's face just as his features dropped. I detected something cold and dark brewing in his eyes, as if he'd realized his mistake and was considering what to do with me. One hand hovered near his pocket, his eyes narrowing. All at once, I feared he was going to reveal a knife or a gun. Instead, he reached forward and grabbed my arm. I pulled back. Sean's grip tightened as he gritted his teeth. "You can't ever repeat anything I just told you. I have a wife and kids to support. A story like this would ruin my career, not to mention my run for City Council."

I remembered Sean's shiny flier shoved in my front door preaching "Family Values" and I couldn't suppress my smile. But I also pictured the twins, Ben and Braydon, racing down the slide with Isabelle at the park, and Stephanie's quest to maintain a perfect family image. I didn't care about ruining Sean's political run, but the rest of his family didn't need to take the fall for his crooked actions. I yanked my arm away. "I won't say anything about the pills. As long as you don't tell anyone I was here. Not even Stephanie. Especially not Stephanie," I added.

He rubbed his temple and nodded.

I remembered Stephanie's words from a few days ago: *I'm good at keeping secrets.* "Does your wife know about your side business?"

"Shit." Sean exhaled another labored breath. "She found out accidentally a few months back, but I told her I'd stopped." He waved his hand toward the wall. "She doesn't know about my dealings with Phil. I was worried the police would discover his stash when Barbara died, but Phil said he hid them somewhere he knew no one would look." Sean touched his forehead. "But now Phil's dead too, and I can't risk anyone finding the drugs. I didn't know what evidence of our meetings Phil kept on his phone. There's always a chance they could lead back to me."

I glanced over my shoulder, almost feeling sorry for this horrible man and considering my next move. "I know where the pills are. I saw them when I found the key. I'll show you where Phil hid them. Then we can go our separate ways and pretend we never saw each other here tonight."

"No mention of this to Mark, either."

"Of course. Just us."

Sean dipped his head. "Okay. Deal."

I headed back through the living room and up the stairs, with Sean following a step behind. Although I didn't trust my shifty neighbor, the house didn't feel as scary now. The weak ray of light guided us back into Phil's bedroom, where I retrieved the book, removed the bag of pills, and returned the empty book to the shelf. Although it was too dark to see, I imagined a little color returning to Sean's pale face as he stuffed the bag of illegal drugs into his jacket pocket. We retraced our path, at last emerging from the house onto the outdoor mat. I locked the door behind me and returned the key to its resting place underneath the flowerpot.

"I'll go this way," Sean pointed toward Mr. Delaney's backyard. There was a cut-through to the house behind, which bordered the Peales' house. "You stick to the sidewalk."

"Okay," I said as a memory tingled my skin. Phil had seen a shadowy figure running away the night his mom died. He'd said the person ran away from his house, through Mr. Delaney's backyard, the same route Sean was about to take. "Okay," I said again, clenching my teeth and telling myself the route didn't prove anything. There was a one-in-four chance anyone would flee in that general direction. I turned toward the sidewalk, ready to hurry home before someone in my family awoke.

"Jessica." Sean spoke in a loud whisper.

I swung my head back toward him, unsettled by his twitching face.

"Why did Phil put your playground key in a ziplock bag and hide it next to drugs?"

I glanced away, thankful the night hid my lying face. "I have no idea."

He kicked something with his toe and flashed me his creepiest smile. "Huh."

"We've got to go." I motioned toward my house. Sean doubted my story, and I didn't want to answer any more questions. I lifted my chin in a half-hearted goodbye and jogged toward the sidewalk, feeling the weight of the man's stare following me as I ran.

TWENTY-FIVE

The sunlight burned through the morning mist as I hovered on the back patio. Roo wandered along our fence line, sniffing the fresh grass clippings. Mark had been snoring louder than ever when I returned in the wee hours of the morning, and I'd climbed back into bed without him suspecting a thing. I'd tucked the ziplock bag deep into the corner of my pillowcase before I made the bed in my usual fashion, piling more pillows on top.

Now I cupped my phone in my hand and searched for Officer Lang's number, at last locating it on the police department website. I called the main line before directing the call to her voicemail.

"Uh, hi, Officer Lang, this is Jessica Millstone." I paused and looked over my shoulder to make sure Mark wasn't approaching or that Sean Peale wasn't lurking beyond our backyard fence. "I met you the other day in front of the Drapers' house on Mapleview Lane. I wanted to let you know that I found that park key I was telling you about, the one that Phil Draper wanted to give me before he was hit by a car. It's in a ziplock bag." I paused again, leaving out the part about how I broke into my neighbor's house to retrieve the key and how I'd bumped into my other neighbor while I was there, a podiatrist who dealt drugs as a side hustle.

"Anyway, I know you've closed the case, but if someone did murder Barbara Draper, this key might belong to them, or even have a fingerprint on it. I thought you could take a look at it; run prints or whatever. I know it's Sunday, and maybe you're not working today, but please call me back when you get this. I'll bring the key to you."

I ended the call in a rush, noticing my racing heartbeat and dry mouth. Roo trotted toward me, and I sucked in the dewy air, attempting to pull myself together before I went back inside. The patio door slid open, and my dog darted in front of me. Mark and Isabelle sat at the living room table, crunching on cereal as the TV babbled in front of them.

"We're avoiding the kitchen," Mark said when he spotted me.

"I don't blame you." I peeked through the kitchen doorway, where Mark had unrolled plastic to cover the linoleum flooring. Painter's tape lined the edges of the ceiling. He'd gotten up early and had already been working.

A few minutes later, we changed into our work clothes and equipped Isabelle with a tiny paintbrush, a palette of watercolors, and a long spool of paper. The chemical smell of the paint cut through my grogginess and jolted me awake. I dipped my brush into the bucket's shimmering pool of paint, and the first splash of Tuscan Blue made it onto the wall.

Mark made a face. "Wow. That's bright!"

"This shade will look perfect next to the white cabinets. Trust me." I surveyed the mess of a room. "And someday soon, we'll replace this flooring with something more neutral."

"Okay. Let's go for it."

Mark used a roller, and I filled in the edges with a brush while also keeping tabs on Isabelle. We chatted about safe topics like home decor and newly released movies. It was a relief to skim along the surface of things for a while, not to plunge any deeper into the secrets of everyone around me.

"We should invite Mom over this week so she can see the transformation."

Mark stepped away from the wall, staring at the new color. "Do you think she'll be mad?"

"No. I think she'll like it," I said, although I felt a twinge of guilt in my gut. Each brushstroke of the bold new color felt a little like erasing a bit of my family history. There'd been so many meals shared in this room, birthday candles blown out, Mom's spaghetti twirled on forks, roasts pulled from the oven, veggies chopped, and strings of cheese stretching from pizza slices from Dad's favorite pizzeria. There'd been a lifetime of conversation, laughter, and tears accompanying those meals. A gulp of nostalgia formed in my throat, and I let it pass. People renovated their homes all the time. There was no reason to feel guilty.

The minutes morphed into hours. Slowly but surely, the fresh color expanded across the kitchen walls. I was thinking about what a good team Mark and I made when a series of beeps buzzed through his phone and interrupted my thoughts. I moved toward it.

"No. I got it." He leaped in front of me and snatched the device from the counter, angling the screen away from me. It was the same thing he'd done last week.

"Who is that?"

"It's George again." Mark pinched his lips together and shoved the phone in his back pocket. "He's relentless."

I fought the urge to yell, *For fuck's sake. Tell your needy boss to get a life.* But Isabelle stood next to me, humming a happy song as she mixed paint colors. I censored my response. "Seriously? It's Sunday."

"I know." Mark rubbed his forehead, leaving a smudge of blue paint on his eyebrow. "This Arlington portfolio is a nightmare. There's a good chance I'll have to stay late tomorrow night to make some adjustments. Just for an hour or so."

My jaw clenched as I shoved the brush into a crevice. Hopefully we could finish the painting today.

"I'll make sure to get this painting out of the way first," Mark said as if reading my mind.

I relaxed, realizing I didn't have any right to be annoyed with my husband. I was the one hiding the truth—about where I'd been in the middle of the night, about Sean Peale's drug dealing, about Mom's murderous history, and about my attempts at a juvenile flirtation with Rick. There was only one person keeping secrets in this marriage, and it was me.

TWENTY-SIX

At 9:30 on Monday morning, the dizzying fresh scent from the azure kitchen walls enveloped me. But the new color didn't have the desired soothing effect amid all the unanswered questions and recent discoveries about my neighbors' secrets. My eyes traveled over the bold shade of blue. I suddenly felt as if I was paddling through the rough waters of a foreign sea rather than standing on a worn linoleum floor in the suburbs. At least Mark and I had completed our weekend home improvement project. It might take a few days to get used to the kitchen's new aura. I leaned on the counter and rechecked my phone, confirming Officer Lang hadn't responded to my message.

My phone buzzed with the familiar sound of an incoming message. I lifted the screen, finding no new texts. My gaze paused on The Neighbor List app, a tiny "1" next to the app's icon indicating a new message was waiting for me. I clutched my stomach with my free hand, feeling the sensation of twisting intestines. I hesitated to check the message, afraid of what it would say. On the other hand, maybe someone from customer service was finally getting back to me, as promised. Maybe they'd uncovered who'd been behind the other messages. I held my breath and clicked the messages, eyelids blinking in defense of the new threat that greeted me:

I hope you sleep well tonight.

I stared in disbelief, reading the message again, my fingers going cold. This sender knew I hadn't slept last night. Whoever it was must have been watching me as I tiptoed out of my house, down the street, and through the Drapers' back door. It confirmed that none of the threats had been accidentally sent to the wrong person, as I'd hoped. This time, the sender's username was Isee-U666. *I see you*, followed by the devil's number. Someone was clearly trying to scare me, and it was working. My head whipped over my shoulder toward the kitchen window. I peered out to the side yard, spotting no one. I ran to the front window and closed the curtains, breathless. *Who would do this?* I tried again to think of someone I'd wronged but couldn't.

I pressed my back against the wall and refocused on my phone. Why would an anonymous person tell me to sleep well tonight? Was something going to happen tonight? Or was it merely a reference to my actions the night before? Sean Peale's rat-like eyes glistened in my mind. While he was surely a suspect, it was hard to imagine he'd want to draw any additional attention to himself. He could have just called or texted me since I'd already discovered his monstrous secret. Whoever this was, didn't want their identity known.

I dug into my purse, triple-checking the ziplock bag I'd tucked inside it the moment Mark had left for the office an hour ago. My fingers tightened around the metal object inside the bag. Officer Lang had been ignoring me, but I wouldn't give up so easily, especially in light of this newest threat.

I wriggled my arms into a lightweight jacket and helped Isabelle into her shoes, ushering her out to the car. Twenty minutes later, we parked in the lot of our county police department. Nerves rattled through me as I entered the brick building's glass doors and squeezed Isabelle's hand.

We bypassed a mostly empty waiting area and approached an unsmiling receptionist, her head of wiry hair propped above bony shoulders. A couple of uniformed officers hovered on the perimeter of the room; I couldn't help feeling they were watching me, that they had some special law enforcement X-ray vision that allowed them to discern every illegal thing I'd done in my life, from back in high school when I'd regularly smoked pot in Danny Lubock's basement, to last month when I'd accelerated through a traffic light as it turned red. And then there was that soda I'd stolen from the gas station, not to mention my most recent lawlessness—breaking and entering into the Drapers' house. There'd been other things too. Now that I thought about it, my rap sheet was longer than I realized. An irrational part of my brain suddenly felt guilty for ever causing any problems for anyone. I kept my head down and approached the desk, reminding myself that no one except Sean Peale knew about my midnight excursion. I took a breath.

"Can I help you?" The woman asked. The scowl on her colorless face suggested she'd prefer to do just about anything in the world rather than help me.

"Yes. I'd like to speak with Officer Lang. I'm Jessica Millstone. She knows me."

The woman's frown deepened. "What's it concerning?"

"I'd rather not say." I pinched my lips together, matching the receptionist's curt manner.

The receptionist eyed me as she lifted a receiver and punched in a few numbers. "Hi. There's a Jessica Millstone here to see you." She sharpened her eyes toward me. "She says you don't have an appointment."

"I called, but she didn't respond. Please tell her it will only take a minute or two of her time."

The woman angled herself away from me. "She says it will only take a minute." She huffed and hung up. "Officer Lang will be along shortly."

Before I could respond, the woman turned her back on me and rifled through a stack of folders on a nearby shelf.

A vague sense of dread trickled through me as I wavered under the lobby's fluorescent lights, my daughter at my side. A voice spoke nearby, piercing through my thoughts.

"Jessica?" Officer Lang stood near my side, her head cocked, her eyes darting from me to Isabelle, questioning.

I stepped toward her. "Hi. Thanks for seeing me."

"Let's go in here." She waved me down a side hallway and into a no-frills, empty room. Cinder blocks made up the walls and the scent of old sneakers hung in the air. The officer closed the door and sat at a metal table, motioning for me to sit across from her. "My shift starts in ten minutes, so I don't have much time." Her words were clipped, and I could tell she wasn't in the mood for small talk.

"Okay. This won't take long." I pulled the ziplock bag from my purse and placed it on the table between us. *The smoking gun.* "Here's the park key that Phil Draper found in his backyard. It didn't belong to his family. He said it wasn't there the day his mom died. He knew that because he'd been doing yard work in the same location earlier that day, and he would have seen it." I paused, trying to gauge Officer Lang's reaction, but she was stone-faced. "Only people in the Ridgeview Pines subdivision have these keys. See." I nudged the bag closer to her. "It says 'Do Not Duplicate,' and it has this plastic logo melded to the top. I know the medical examiner said Barbara's death was accidental, but this could prove that someone murdered her."

The officer held up the bag and inspected the key, her lips twisting to the side. "So, let me get this straight. Your theory is that someone who lives in the Ridgeview Pines subdivision murdered Barbara Draper by breaking into her house and pushing her into the bathtub while her thirty-eight-year-old son was home? And you think this key somehow proves that?"

"Yes." I nodded vigorously. "The killer could have dropped this key as they fled. And not only that, but the same person who lost this key also might have discovered Phil found it and that he was about to turn it over to the police—"

"And then they killed him in a hit-and-run," she said, finishing my sentence.

"Exactly." I leaned back, satisfied. Isabelle hopped next to me, and I pulled her onto my lap.

The other woman plopped the bag onto the table and frowned. "Jessica, are you okay?"

I almost said "yes" out of habit, but the frightening message I'd just received flickered through my mind. I gave her a slight nod instead. I'd report the threats I'd received through The Neighbor List after I'd laid out my theory.

She turned her face to the side and back again. "You seem a bit... out of sorts."

"I only want someone to listen to me, to look into what I'm saying."

"As I told you the other day, this scenario you've come up with is more than a little far-fetched. We had our best detectives at the scene directly after Barbara's body was discovered. Besides, I checked the file after I got your voicemail. The case is all but closed. And even if someone suddenly decided it was a homicide, Phil would have been the number one suspect. As you know, he's not around to face charges."

I squeezed my eyes closed, frustrated. "No. Phil didn't do anything."

"You can't possibly know that."

"He told me that he heard someone in the house. He wasn't lying. I swear, I could tell."

Officer Lang cocked her head, her lopsided grin suggesting Phil had sold me a bag of goods.

"How can Barbara's case be closed already?" I asked, ignoring her patronizing expression.

"It's not closed, officially. We're still waiting on the final toxicology report to see if Barbara had any drugs in her system. In that case, the medical examiner could change the manner of death to suicide. Either way, the official cause of death was drowning. Her lungs were filled with water."

"But there must be more to the story. What if they've missed something? It seems like the police only searched the perimeter of the house. The key was under some bushes. Why wouldn't you want to check that out? Barbara had so many enemies. It's not a crazy theory." My voice was ragged and frantic, and I stopped to gulp for air.

Officer Lang stared straight past me, tapping her fingertips on the table as if weighing the risk against the reward. I could almost see the scales balancing and tipping in her pupils.

"Please. Can't you test the key for clues? Fingerprints? That can't be too much trouble."

She grimaced. "I don't do that myself. The detectives who were on Barbara's case are busy with a double homicide over in Pontiac. They won't bother with this. But just between you and me, don't expect anyone in this building to go above and beyond for Barbara Draper. She treated us like garbage."

"Oh." I crossed my arms, remembering what Phil had told me about his mom's constant complaints to the police. "Isn't there someone else who can help? At the very least, we can return the key to its rightful owner."

The policewoman stared at the plastic baggy and released a drawn-in breath. "I'll tell you what. I have a colleague who owes me a favor. I'll ask him to run the prints. It might take a week or two, though." She offered a trite smile and I got the feeling she would have agreed to just about anything if it meant getting me out of her hair.

"Thank you. I'll feel so much better knowing whose key this is. Maybe the person who dropped the key has an innocent explanation. Then I promise to let this rest."

"We'll see." Officer Lang pinched the bag and stood to leave.

"Wait." I motioned for her to stop. "There's something else that's been going on. It might be related."

"What is it?"

"I've been getting strange messages through The Neighbor List app. They're from fake accounts and whoever sends them deletes them immediately after I read them. The messages are threatening." I dug through my purse to pull up the most recent message, but just as I feared, it had already disappeared.

Officer Lang tilted her head. "Threatening, how?"

"The first one said, *Enjoy your perfect family*. Then I got one from someone called RVenge that said, *You will pay*. I reported it to the administrator, but the accounts had already been deleted. Then, just a little while ago I got another one saying, *I hope you sleep well tonight*. The username was called, ISeeU666."

"And you don't know who sent them?"

I shook my head. "No idea."

"It certainly sounds like someone is trying to scare you. I can understand why you're on edge."

I nodded, feeling tears building but determined to hold them back.

"Are you aware of anyone with a grudge against you? Maybe an estranged family member or an old boyfriend? Perhaps things ended badly with a previous employer?"

"No. I can't think of anyone who would do this. That's what makes it so weird."

"I see." Officer Lang's face softened. "Faceless messages are a big problem with social media but are usually harmless." She tapped her fingertips together. "Have you noticed anyone strange lurking around your house? Anything concrete that I can check out?"

I dropped my eyes, remembering Luke Moreno in my backyard. But he was only a boy and he'd been there to give us a lawn quote. Sean Peale was always creeping nearby, but he lived behind us. I couldn't be certain either of them were behind the messages. "No. I can't think of anything."

"Do me a favor, if it happens again, take a screenshot immediately and text it to me. I'll see what I can do."

"Okay. That's a good idea," I said, feeling relief wash through me.

"Continue reporting the messages to the app's administrator in the meantime, just like you've been doing. I'll do a daily drive-by through your neighborhood this week, just to establish a police presence. Sometimes that acts as a deterrent. This sounds more like a teenage prank, though, so don't worry yourself too much."

I nodded. "Thank you."

"And Jessica."

"What?"

"Because I doubt this side investigation with the playground key is going to lead to anything material, I'm not going to ask you how you were able to retrieve this bag from inside the Drapers' house."

I could feel the heat creeping up my neck, remembering the day I'd stood across from the policewoman on the Drapers' driveway practically begging her to let me inside the house to look for the park key. I averted my eyes. "I found it in my mailbox. It turns out Phil left it for me there."

"Right." Officer Lang lowered her chin and flashed me a look to let me know she hadn't been born yesterday.

THE NEIGHBOR LIST
POSTED MAY 24

Username: StephPeale

Subject: Dr. Sean Peale for Glenn Hills City Council!

Let's bring good old family values back to Glenn Hills! Please join me and my husband Dr. Sean Peale for our upcoming fundraiser to boost his campaign for the open City Council seat. View all information by clicking this LINK. Thank you for your support!

FDoor: No politics allowed on The Neighbor List.

Aroberts75: Local politics are allowed.

GoneFishin: The current City Council is worthless. I attend every public meeting and nothing ever gets accomplished.

Click to view twenty-one more comments

TWENTY-SEVEN

At 11 a.m. the following day, Bree waited near the gate of the Ridgeview Pines playground, shaded by the wavering branches of a giant maple tree. Sunlight filtered through the canopy of young leaves, stretching strange shadows across her symmetrical features. Beyond the metal fence, the usual Tuesday morning crowd populated the park—a half-dozen toddlers and preschoolers occupying the sandbox, swings, and slide. The realtor relaxed in her natural state, long-limbed and studying her phone, oblivious to our approach. Isabelle raced toward her.

"Bwee!"

A pearly smile formed on my friend's mouth as she lowered her phone and opened her arms toward Isabelle. The breeze carried the faint citrus and vanilla notes of Bree's perfume past my nose.

"Thanks for meeting us." Bree didn't live in the neighborhood and didn't have a park key, so I retrieved mine. I unlocked the gate, wondering if the similar key I'd dropped at the police station was simultaneously undergoing some sort of elaborate infrared scan to identify the prints of a murderer. After receiving the *I hope you sleep well tonight* message, I'd double-checked the locks on all the doors and windows before going to bed last night, gripping the edge of my cotton sheets in my fingers. Mark looked surprised when I'd shown him the message earlier in the day. I'd informed him that I'd already reported it to the police, and he said I'd done the right thing. My husband thought whoever sent the message was an immature coward, some bored teenager who would never actually do anything to us. But he didn't know the true meaning of the message, which surely referred to how I'd sneaked into the Drapers' house in the early hours of Sunday morning. Even so, Mark made a point to stay up extra late watching TV in the living room with the lights on. We made it through the night undisturbed.

Bree gazed toward the sky. "It's so nice out. It'll be good to get some fresh air before heading into the office."

Isabelle squeezed through the opening and ran to her preferred spot in the sandbox as Bree and I found an empty bench.

"Congrats on getting the listing for the Drapers' house," I said. "I mean, despite the circumstances. You sure locked up that one fast."

"It will still be a couple of months before it's official. Lots of legalese to work through with the Drapers' estate, but I'm letting Kathy—that's Barbara's sister—and the attorney deal with that. It's so crazy about Phil. I'm sorry."

"Oh. Thanks." Something twisted in my heart, but I kept my face still. "I barely knew him, really."

Bree checked her phone and placed it back in her purse. "Kathy called me right away. She's the executor of the estate. I guess Barbara had mentioned my name to her a while back. I'm so thankful she did. Any house in good condition in this neighborhood will sell quickly once we get it listed."

"Sounds like Kathy is eager to cash out."

"No kidding. She's going to meet with the estate attorney in person when she comes back for Phil's funeral next week."

"Oh. I didn't realize anyone was planning a funeral."

"It's small. Just family, as Phil didn't have many friends. Kind of sad."

"Yeah." My butt scooched forward across the hard bench as all of the secrets I'd uncovered over the last few days shifted inside me, threatening to spill. Bree didn't know half the story. I yearned to tell her about my middle-of-the-night run-in with Sean Peale and to confide about Mom's murderous past, but I couldn't break my promises. Things had been even sadder for Phil than Bree realized. "Doesn't it seem wrong to bury the body before they even know the cause of death?"

"What's there to know? Phil was hit by a car. Or he jumped in front of it. Either way, surely the cause was that he died from the impact."

I shook my head, unable to keep one more secret. "I need to tell you something important." I leaned closer to Bree and lowered my voice, tracking the other adults in the park in my peripheral vision. "I think someone targeted Phil to prevent him from turning over the evidence he found."

Bree stared at me, disbelief stretching across her face. "Jessica. Please tell me you're kidding."

I set my jaw and stared across the playground, my gaze drifting past the children who squealed and bobbed in blurry amorphous shapes.

"Oh my God." Bree touched her mouth, realizing I wasn't leaving my neighbors' deaths alone. "This is out of control. The police are handling it. You should stay out of it."

"Why would Phil make plans to meet me at 4 p.m. only to jump in front of a car ninety minutes before we were supposed to meet? It doesn't make any sense. Someone must have targeted him."

"Phil wasn't exactly all there, in case you didn't notice." Bree furrowed her plucked eyebrows. "He was probably high when he made plans with you. Or maybe the driver of the car was going too fast and hit him by accident. It's not normal to assume someone murdered the guy."

"I'm not exactly normal, in case you haven't noticed."

Bree tipped back her head and chuckled.

I rocked forward and crossed my arms. There was so much more I wanted to say, but both Sean Peale and Mom had sworn me to secrecy. Anyway, Bree would be even more annoyed if she knew how much energy I'd dedicated to uncovering the truth behind the Drapers' deaths.

I debated whether to confide in Bree about the threatening messages I'd been receiving on The Neighbor List, but I didn't know how to do it without stepping too close to Mom's secret or revealing my actions last night. Before I could decide, the metal gate clamored, followed by a familiar, high-pitched voice. "Hi, Jessica!" My toes curled as Stephanie Peale waved her arm and her two boys darted ahead of her toward the sandbox.

"Oh, great," Bree whispered as the bright-eyed woman marched toward us, her unruly curls poofed out around her head.

I scooched over to make room on the bench.

"I'm so glad you're both here. We only have a little over two months until the election for the open City Council seat. I'm assuming Sean can count on your votes?"

The question hung in the air. I glanced away to hide what I knew about Stephanie's drug-dealing husband.

"Sure," Bree said lightly. "How's the campaign going?"

"Great. He's the most qualified out of all the candidates."

Bree straightened her posture. "I've always had an interest in local politics."

I studied Bree's face, not sure if she was joking. "You have?"

"Yeah. I was class president junior year of high school. Don't you remember?"

"I guess." It was a vague memory, but I remembered it now: Bree Bradley for class president. High school politics had been more or less a popularity contest, so it was no wonder Bree had won. "What kind of platform would you run on?"

Bree shrugged. "I don't know. School funding would be at the top." She waved her hand at the playground. "There should be more parks like this. For everyone, not just for people who can afford to live in the nicest neighborhoods. And I'd propose adding

dedicated bike lanes on every major street in Glenn Hills. We need
to do our part to encourage green transportation and reduce our
carbon footprint."

I nodded my approval. "And all the city's publicly-owned
buildings should be powered by solar panels."

Bree gave me a mock salute. "Noted."

"I like your ideas, Bree. I'd vote for you." I pumped my fist in
the air. "Education. Parks. Environment."

Bree smiled and waved me off. "I don't have enough time or
energy to run."

Stephanie turned away, but I caught her eye-roll. "Well, Sean's
got a real chance to be the first doctor on the city council. And it's
so important to instill strong family values in this community."

I cringed.

Stephanie continued, "We're planning a fundraiser two weeks
from Thursday at the Fourth Street Bistro. It's going to give his
campaign a real boost. Can I put you each down for a ticket or
two?"

"I'll have to check with Mark." The words left my mouth a
little too quickly, and Stephanie's smile flattened, but I didn't care.
A bold and potent force surged through me. A secret power
simmered in my veins. I knew what her husband had done.
Stephanie had no idea that Sean had been feeding Phil Draper's
addiction; Sean's drug-dealing scheme was even more extensive
than she was aware of. My fingers gripped the edge of the bench as
I resisted the urge to raise the silver bracelet encircling my wrist,
fist clenched in Wonder Woman fashion. By merely uttering a
sentence or two of the truth to other adults in this park, I could
destroy the run of Dr. Sean Peale, the crooked, aspiring politician.
But a promise was a promise, so I sealed my lips.

"I work a lot on weeknights, but I might be able to come last
minute," Bree said.

"Great. I'll pencil you both in." Stephanie slid her palms down
the length of her khaki capris. "Jessica, if Mark can't make it,
maybe you can invite your new friend, Rick. It seems like you two

were really hitting it off when you were here the other day." Stephanie's eyes gleamed, her voice dripping with a dangerous innuendo.

I glimpsed something dark shift in Bree's features; the face of someone who'd been betrayed. A stiff smile formed on her lips. "I didn't realize you and Rick have been hanging out." Bree stared at me, but she didn't look quite like herself.

"We haven't been hanging out. Rick walked to the park with Isabelle and me one afternoon. That's pretty much it."

"Pretty much?" Stephanie grinned and winked.

I could feel my frustration growing, the heat building in my face. "Oh my gosh, Stephanie. Stop it." I imagined myself leaping up on the bench, raising my braceleted arm toward Stephanie, and yelling, *I have the power to destroy your life.* Instead, I took a breath and focused on her smirk. "Rick is a friendly neighbor and nothing more. Anyway, he and Isabelle's babysitter are dating now."

"Sophie?" Stephanie asked.

"Yeah. I think she and Rick make a super-cute couple."

A crease formed on Bree's forehead. "Tell Sophie to be careful. Guys like Rick can't be trusted."

"Guys like what?" Stephanie asked, flashing a bewildered look. "Handsome, successful, and charming?"

Bree sighed. "All I'm saying is that Rick's a little too slick. Men who know they're good-looking and charming are the most dangerous. They're used to getting what they want, no matter who they hurt along the way."

I laced my fingers together, realizing Bree was describing her ex-husband, Alex, more than Rick. Alex had been charming and handsome and, as Bree had said, a little too slick. He'd been cheating on her for six months before she caught him in the act.

"Anyway, warn Sophie." Bree cleared her throat. "Tell her to be careful. She's young. He might be taking advantage."

"I'll mention it to her," I said, although I had no intention of doing so. Sophie was a strong young woman capable of making her own decisions. I suspected Bree was still bitter about Rick's interest in me during their date, and now he'd shifted his attention to Sophie. Maybe Rick was a player, or perhaps he was merely a single man looking for the right match. But I didn't blame him for dating around.

Bree carried herself with the confidence of a runway model, and she had the looks to back up her swagger—blonde hair that dripped in tendrils over her shoulders, toned limbs that stretched on forever, shapely curves in all the right places, and oceanic eyes. She wasn't the type of woman who men easily ignored. Her failed date with Rick seemed like a sore spot. Maybe it stung more than she wanted to admit.

I changed the subject to the new color of our kitchen walls, showing the others before-and-after photos on my phone. We discussed Phil's sudden death and how strange it was that tragedy seemed to seek out certain families for no reason in particular. When Stephanie brought up a recent post in her mommy blog about the best way to talk to children about death, Bree checked her phone and stood.

"Sorry to leave, but I've got to head into the office."

"Busy day?" Stephanie asked.

"Yes. I have an appointment for a potential new listing tonight. I need to put together my presentation."

I waved. "Good luck."

Bree blew kisses toward Isabelle and strolled away. My friend's sudden urge to leave was probably an effort to avoid a lengthy monologue by Stephanie regarding the fastest way to extinguish a toddler's temper tantrum or a never-ending analysis of the best remedies for diaper rash. Once Stephanie got hold of a conversation, she locked her jaw and flung it to pieces.

Once again, I found myself alone on a park bench with the mommy blogger as she blabbed about upcoming topics for her blog. The tip of a playground key poking above her pants' pocket offered a bit of reassurance. Here was something I knew for sure—there was only one key per family, so the key in the ziplock bag didn't belong to the Peales. But as I watched Isabelle dig in the sand, I could almost feel the secrets floating around us, blowing along with the breeze like pollen in the wind, prickling my skin and clogging my airway. I spied the other adults in the park, ticking them off my suspect list. And I wondered who in our neighborhood was missing their key.

TWENTY-EIGHT

My daughter and I returned from the park, tired, hungry, and over-heated. As much as I tried to act like everything was normal, the events of the last two days affected me. I could feel my suppressed emotions building inside me, the pressure behind my eyes intensi-fying. Once Isabelle was down for her nap, the dam finally burst. I cried over Phil's death, burying my wet face in the crook of my arm and stretching my shaky legs over the length of our living room couch. Ever since Bree had mentioned Phil's funeral, the vision of a dead man—a beaten-down thirty-eight-year-old who'd had no friends—lying in an empty room had etched itself into the contours of my mind. Phil's life had been all but forgotten the moment he died.

My neighbor's early demise might have been the only thing sadder than his lonely life. I thought of a young boy cowering in his room as his dad berated and beat his mom. I remembered the night at the playground when my friends had called Phil names like "son of the bitch" and "Draper the raper" until he hung his head and quietly walked away. I hated myself for not stopping the taunts, for not befriending the lonely boy in any of the previous years. I'd only known him recently and briefly, but it was enough to see that Phil had been a kind soul. How was it possible that not a single person outside of his aunt and cousins cared that he was gone? Well, I cared. That was obvious as loud, ugly sobs heaved from my chest. Roo perked his ears at me, concerned. I choked on a wave of emotion, worried I might wake Isabelle from her afternoon nap.

Eventually, the tears dried, and I gripped my phone, distracting myself by browsing new job postings. The meager search results only increased my melancholy. The house was too quiet around me, and I suddenly feared ending up dead and alone one day, just like Phil. Only one thing would free me from my mind's tangled web. I marched into the kitchen, drawing inspiration from the bright blue walls, inhaling the fresh-paint smell, and gathering my supplies—flour, sugar, eggs, vanilla. I plugged in the standing mixer and retrieved the measuring cups and spoons. A tattoo I'd seen online the other day had sparked my interest. The inked image was a dramatic close-up of a human eye hovering over a steaming coffee cup. The words "Sleep is for the Weak" swirled in gothic lettering above the wide-open eyelids and bulging eyeball. It would make the perfect design to complement my mocha-latte cake.

I got to work measuring, mixing, baking. Once the cake cooled, I would frost it with a speckled beige frosting and spend a good thirty minutes painting the red, white, and black tattoo design on top. Once I was satisfied with the look, I would then snap a photo. I could use the image on my website if I ever found a way to start a business. Or maybe I'd settle for an Instagram feed of cake images. At least it was something, a creative outlet to display my work.

Isabelle woke late from her nap, screaming bloody murder until I arrived in her room and found her clutching her pudgy cheeks; her skin was pink with distress. But when I got closer and felt the heat radiating from her face, I realized it was more than that. She was sunburned. She must have gotten too much sun at the playground, even though I'd slathered her sunscreen on before we left. The bottle sat on a shelf near the back door. I led Isabelle downstairs and turned the bottle of SPF 55 lotion over in my hand, confirming it hadn't expired. I bit my cheek, confused. It didn't seem likely, but maybe she'd wiped it off when I wasn't looking.

I gave Isabelle some children's ibuprofen and placed a cold washcloth on her forehead, followed by a moisturizer. She calmed down. The thought of taking her to the doctor's office tomorrow for the prescheduled appointment to remove her stitches made me uneasy. First, my daughter had fallen out of her recalled booster seat, then tumbled down the stairs, and now she was sunburned. I could only imagine what a horrible parent the doctor would think I was.

I eyed the caffeinated cake on the counter as I let Isabelle watch a couple of her favorite cartoons. Returning to the kitchen, I decorated my cake just the way I'd envisioned, and then plated an early dinner of veggie corn dogs and fruit for Isabelle, eating alongside her because Mark was working late. Bree had unofficially secured at least one exclusive listing with the Drapers' house and possibly another with whoever she was meeting tonight. My friend had been through so much in the past months and deserved a celebratory cake. Maybe I'd include a bottle of champagne next to it too. Bree was busy, and I didn't want to bother her, but I could surprise her by leaving the goodies on her doorstep. A quick text after I dropped everything would ensure she wouldn't miss it. I peeled off my socks, leaving them in a neat pile next to the back door as I slipped on my sandals and reassured Roo that I'd be back soon.

A few minutes later, I sped down the boulevard with Isabelle strapped into her car seat and the cake and champagne wedged into the floor on the passenger side. I turned into Bree's complex of townhomes, searching for a parking space in front of her end unit. A car occupied the spot where I usually parked. I recognized the navy sedan with the blue parking sticker in the lower-left corner of the back window and the familiar string of numbers and letters across the license plate. It was Mark's car. He wasn't at work. *What was he doing here?* My mind churned in slow motion, reluctant to gather the dangerous shards of information.

My husband wasn't working late. He was here with Bree at her condo. He'd lied again. She'd lied to me too. Today at the park, Bree said she had a listing appointment tonight. My knuckles turned white as I gripped the steering wheel, hot breath clouding my lungs, tears burning the corners of my eyes. I felt as if I might throw up.

"Puppy!" Isabelle squirmed in the back seat, leaning toward the window. Outside, a young man carried a fluffy brown puppy down the steps of a nearby townhome, setting him down on a patch of grass. "Puppy!" Isabelle jabbed her finger at the glass.

I swallowed back the surge of emotion and raised my voice a pitch. "Yes. That's a cute puppy, isn't it?" I craned my neck to get a view toward Bree's front windows. Although the sun hadn't yet set, lights were on inside. There was movement in Bree's living room, bodies passing close to each other. I was sure they were in there, but Bree's wooden blinds were only partially open, and I was too far away to see any details.

My car idled in place as Isabelle knocked on the window, attempting to get the puppy to look at her. "Hi, puppy! Hi, puppy!"

I tuned out the noise, wondering what Mark and Bree were doing. Unwanted answers barraged my mind. *Had Mark taken over carry-out for dinner, so they could snuggle on the couch and watch a romcom? Were they skipping the food altogether and tossing back a few drinks before heading up to the bedroom? Or maybe they were doubling over with laughter, amazed at how easy it was to fool me.* Every cell in my body wanted to leap from the car, pound on the door, and catch them in the act. When Bree answered with her plastic smile, I'd smash the cake into her smug face, yelling, "I know what you're doing, you selfish, lying pieces of shit," I'd berate the pair of them before driving home and drinking the bottle of champagne myself. Mark could sleep in his car.

I pulled in a long, slow breath and squeezed my eyelids closed. Maybe I was jumping to conclusions. Maybe Mark was helping Bree with her finances again. But why lie about it when I already knew she was in a tough spot? And I suspected Mark had wandered outside the boundaries of our marriage before. Perhaps the move to Glenn Hills hadn't changed our situation as much as I'd wanted to believe. My foot found the accelerator, and I sped home with Isabelle wailing about not getting to pet the puppy. I wondered if Mark had ever helped Bree with her finances at all.

TWENTY-NINE

I stumbled through the back door, lugging my daughter, who continued to scream for the puppy. My own face was hot with rage at Mark's betrayal, and I struggled to find my breath and keep it together. My ankle twisted as I entered the house. I cursed my flimsy sandals as I set Isabelle on the floor and unbuckled the straps on my shoes. The tears flooding my eyes caused my vision to blur. Even as Isabelle pounded the floor and Roo circled me, I felt alone. I reached for my socks, but only one of them was where I'd left it next to the rug. The second one lay in the entrance to the living room. My heart thrummed at the sight of the displaced object but quickly subsided when I spotted Roo wagging his tail. He picked up a tennis ball and dropped it next to me. Our playful dog must have moved it after I left. I picked up the second sock and put it on, then crouched next to Isabelle, telling her I'd find another puppy for her to pet tomorrow and that, in the meantime, she could play with Roo. The promise calmed her down.

Now Roo trotted toward the glass slider, scratching to go out to the backyard. I needed some air, so I opened the door and followed him, Isabelle trailing a step behind. The cement slab felt cold beneath my socked feet. Children's giggles sounded from beyond the fence, followed by Sean's voice. "Give the ball another kick, Braydon."

I closed my eyes, hoping Sean would ignore us. Roo sniffed along the fence line as Isabelle chased him, repeating to our oblivious dog that she loved him. I looked around the yard and back toward our house, wondering if I was going to lose it all. I couldn't afford this house without Mark, and I refused to stay with a cheating husband. I imagined a different family moving into the home that I'd called mine for as long as I could remember. Mark's betrayal seeped through me like poison, and I found it difficult to stay upright. I pulled back a chair and cringed as the metal legs scraped against cement. The noise would surely catch Sean's ear. Sure enough, just as I sat, a shadow wavered behind the fence, followed by a knocking sound. One of Sean's pale blue eyes peeked through a crack.

"Come here for a second," he said in a loud whisper.

With effort, I raised myself from the chair and walked toward him. The grass dampened my socks, but I was too far gone to care. I leaned toward the gap. "What?"

My neighbor's eye flickered toward Isabelle and Roo on the other side of the yard and then back to me. "You'd better be keeping quiet."

"I am."

"Because if you don't, I will express my concern to the authorities that you returned to the scene of Barbara's death." His eye stretched wider. "Maybe you were destroying evidence of a murder."

"I wasn't." I turned away, not able to deal with this right now.

"I know. But it could look that way." Sean paused, licking his lips. "Why were you really at the Drapers' house in the middle of the night, Jessica?"

"I told you already. My park key."

"I don't believe you. You're hiding something." His head shifted as he lowered his voice. "I'm warning you. There will be repercussions if you mention my... business to anyone. Something bad will happen to you."

Sean's threat should have frightened me, but I felt numb. The worst had already happened—my husband was cheating on me with my best friend. Sean was free to pile another brick on my already back-breaking load.

I hardened my voice. "If you're the one sending me those creepy messages, you need to stop it. Now."

"I have no idea what you're talking about."

"Daddy, kick the ball!" a boy yelled from behind Sean.

I jutted out my chin, unsure if Sean was being truthful. "I'm not telling anyone anything about you, Sean. Now please go away and leave me alone."

He removed his face from the fence. I rounded up Isabelle and Roo and closed myself inside.

Mark barged through the back door at 8:25 p.m., muttering apologies about having to stay late to finalize his spreadsheet. "George is making me earn my money. This portfolio is a pain in the ass."

I leaned my weight into the couch, willing the cushions to swallow me whole if only to prevent me from hearing any more of my husband's lies. A cooking show flickered across the TV. I stared at the host, who diced onions and carrots at lightning speed, the oversized blade slamming down again and again. I forced my eyes away from the TV and toward Mark. Some masochistic part of me wanted to see how far he would take his story, so I kindled the fire. "That sucks. Did you get to leave your office at all today?"

"Not really. I grabbed a sandwich for lunch and another one for dinner from that deli next door." He massaged his forehead with his fingertips. "Is Isabelle asleep?"

"I put her down at 8 p.m. like always."

Mark tilted his head, probably noticing the punch in my voice. "I guess you had a long day too."

"You could say that."

He shuffled toward me and flopped down on a nearby chair.

I stared at the TV as a few seconds of silence stretched between us. "Why are you lying to me?"

He tilted his head, mouth opening. "Huh?"

I mustered the courage to face him, locking my stare on his shifty eyes. "I saw you at Bree's place tonight. Your car was parked out front. You weren't at the office. So, why are you lying?"

Mark clutched his head in his hands and leaned forward. "Shit! I knew this would happen." His breath huffed several times before he stood up and took the spot next to me on the couch. My body stiffened as he squeezed my hand in his. "No. I'm not cheating on you if that's what you're implying. I did lie just now about being at the office all day though. I was helping Bree fill out some online bank forms. It took longer than I thought it would because she has an equity line too. She's about to lose her condo, and she made me promise again that I wouldn't say anything to you."

"Foreclosure?"

"Yeah."

"But why be so secretive? I already know she's in trouble."

"I don't know. Pride, I guess. It's one thing to seek investment advice. It's another thing to face losing your home to the bank."

I sat forward with my hands resting on my thighs, registering his explanation, weighing the intonation of his voice. His account was plausible, and his words sounded sincere, but I didn't want to play the fool. I refused to be one of those women people laughed at because they were gullible, so quick to ignore red flags that their husbands were unfaithful because it was easier not to know. "It doesn't make any sense."

"Bree's embarrassed. That's it." He reached for my hand, but I pulled it away.

"Are you attracted to her?"

"What? No. It's nothing like that." Mark leaned toward me, forcing me to look at his face. "I've already found my dream woman, and it's you."

I angled my body away from him. "We won't survive another Sharon situation."

"That's not what this is." His face contorted. "Anyway, nothing ever happened between Sharon and me. I told you that a million times." He squeezed my hand. "I need you to believe me."

I stared at his pupils, unwavering black circles. "Will Bree get to stay in her condo? Now that you've filled out the forms."

Mark released a breath. "I hope so. It should delay things several months, if nothing else. Please don't mention this to her though."

Tears leaked from my eyes, and I whisked them away with the side of my hand. "Okay."

"Jess. Why are you crying?" Mark wrapped his arms around me. His lips were warm against the top of my head, and I didn't pull away this time.

"I don't know." My voice squeaked out the words, even though they weren't true. Somewhere deep down, I knew the reason for my tears. A pit weighed in my gut, and it was impossible to ignore. I wanted more than anything to believe him, but I couldn't shake the feeling my husband was lying.

THIRTY

I pulled into afternoon traffic, exiting the driveway of the doctor's office and glancing at Isabelle's healing head in my rearview mirror. Her sunburned cheeks glistened with the layers of aloe vera lotion I'd applied. The last forty-five minutes hadn't exactly been pleasant, and I took a breath now that the appointment was over. The nurse had done a double take when she'd first laid eyes on Isabelle's beet-red face. A few minutes later, Dr. Greely entered the examination room, her stiff smile morphing into a frown as she sat at her computer, reading Isabelle's chart.

"Wow. It looks like you've had an exciting couple of weeks. Two trips to the emergency room?" The doctor peered over her glasses which sat low on her nose.

"Yeah. My mom was watching her both times. We're not leaving Mom in charge of Isabelle anymore." A nervous giggle escaped my mouth, but Dr. Greely didn't laugh.

"And who forgot to apply the sunscreen?" the doctor asked, her fingers clacking away at the keys.

"Actually, that was me. But I didn't forget. The bottle I bought must have been defective."

"Uh-huh." More frantic clicking.

I wondered how anyone could type so quickly and what she

was writing. Probably something about me being a negligent parent.

"You should buy a new supply of sunscreen every season to prevent this." The doctor motioned toward Isabelle. "Sometimes, even when the expiration date hasn't passed, the active ingredient goes bad over the winter."

I gave a solemn nod. "I should have realized that. I'll pick up some new bottles on the way home."

At last, the intimidating woman rose from her computer and focused on Isabelle's stitches. Dr. Greely announced that the cut had healed nicely, and she sent us on our way. It had been a relief to get out of there.

Now I took a longer route through downtown so I could stop at the pharmacy for new sunscreen. As I turned the corner onto Main Street, the person who I least wanted to see caught my eye. Sean Peale stood on the sidewalk in between Frederick's and the children's clothing store next door, waving a handful of shiny fliers in the air and accosting anyone who tried to pass him. A woman crossed the street to avoid the aspiring City Council member, probably creeped out by his serial killer's grin. I ducked lower. Why couldn't I get away from him? No doubt, Sean was trying to sell as many tickets as possible to his fundraiser. His self-promotion was shameless, but I supposed politicians had to toot their own horns. It took every muscle in my body not to lower my window and yell, "Dr. Sean Peale is a drug dealer!" But I believed Sean's threats were good, so I clenched my teeth.

Sean's balding head swung toward me as I rolled to a stop behind a slow car, his eyes connecting with mine for a fraction of a second. I glimpsed a flash of terror on his face before it vanished just as quickly and transformed into an icy stare. He set his jaw and squared his shoulders as if to remind me that he knew my secrets too.

The car in front of me pulled into a parking space, and I careened around the corner, thrown off balance by the confrontational stare-down. Something moved in my peripheral vision.

Before I realized what was happening, a man stepped off the curb, landing directly in front of me. I swerved to miss him and slammed on the brakes.

"Watch it!" The wayward pedestrian threw up his arms, glaring at me through the windshield as I slunk behind the wheel.

My heartbeat pounded against the wall of my chest. "Sorry," I muttered, although it hadn't been my fault. The man was jaywalking, too lazy to cross at the well-marked crosswalk further up the block. The near miss sent jitters through me, but I continued straight, anxious to put space between the agitated man and me.

I focused on the road, but only Phil's tortured eyes peered through my mind as I drove toward home. I'd nearly hit that pedestrian. The same way someone had run over Phil. I couldn't help wondering how Phil's last moment had been. Had he seen the vehicle before it hit him? Had he suffered? And why would the person who ran over Phil flee the scene, especially if it had been an accident? Most people would stop their cars and attempt to call for help. Wouldn't they?

I turned the scenarios over in my head as my SUV rumbled along the boulevard. The timing of Phil's death had been more than suspicious. What were the odds that he'd die only an hour and a half before he was supposed to turn the key over to me? I was sure Phil's death wasn't a suicide. If he'd been planning to kill himself, he would have at least told me where to find the key before he jumped in front of a moving car. Then there was his mother's unexpected death less than two weeks earlier. Phil believed someone had been inside his house the night Barbara died. I'd heard Barbara's scream too. Something dangerous was going on. Here, in the place where I thought we'd moved to be safe. I had a vague feeling of knowing the answer without fully understanding the question. I couldn't find order in my churning thoughts.

I guided my mind back to the day of Phil's death. I'd been upset that morning because I'd spotted Mark and Bree entering the diner together the night before. They'd both lied to me, and I feared for the future of my marriage. Sophie had arrived to watch

Isabelle just as I received Phil's text about the key. I confirmed with Phil that I'd meet him at 4 p.m., then I headed over to Mom's condo, seeking comfort about Mark's suspected infidelity. Bree reassured me Mark was merely helping her straighten out her finances—something I still wasn't sure I believed. But I was relieved enough at the time to tell both Mom and Bree about Phil's discovery of the neighborhood playground key and about my plans to pick it up from him at 4 p.m. Bree immediately hung up, claiming she had to take another call. Mom insisted that I stop looking into Barbara's death before dropping her bombshell confession that she'd killed Ed Draper twenty-eight years ago. *What time had that been? 11 a.m.?* I returned home, ate lunch with Isabelle, and put her down for her nap. By the time I showed up at Phil's house at the agreed time, he was dead, run over by a car.

So who knew about the discovery of the key? Sophie, Bree, and Mom, for sure because I'd told them. But any of them could have mentioned it to someone else. I thought about Sophie first but couldn't imagine the aspiring kindergarten teacher repeating what I'd learned to anyone. Sophie wasn't a gossip. In fact, a couple of the other moms had mentioned how my daughter's babysitter always kept to herself when she took Isabelle to the park. Sophie didn't live in the neighborhood. She wouldn't have had a playground key other than the one she borrowed from me once in a while. And, as far as I knew, Sophie had never even met Barbara or Phil Draper, which meant she lacked any motive to want them dead.

I supposed Phil could have told someone else about our planned meeting, but Phil didn't have many friends. Sean Peale's dodgy eyes darted across my mind. The beads of sweat on the podiatrist's brow as he passed out fliers betrayed his desperation. He was a man living a lie, a man who needed to achieve at any cost. What if my backyard neighbor was hiding more than a side drug-dealing operation? What if Barbara discovered that Sean was her son's supplier? Maybe she'd threatened to turn Sean over to the police, which would have caused him to lose his medical license and destroy his reputation in the community. Perhaps Sean had reacted by killing Barbara before offing Phil, leaving no loose ends. Now that I'd returned the secret stash of pills to Sean's possession, he could get away with it. Maybe Officer Lang was correct that the playground key had nothing to do with anything, that a curious neighbor—not the killer—had accidentally dropped it. Perhaps the timing of Phil's death was a wild coincidence.

I stopped at a red light, my thoughts circling back over my list of suspects. A troubling idea nagged at me. *What if Barbara had a sudden change of heart and threatened to turn Mom over to the authorities for pushing Ed down the stairs all those years ago?* I bit my cheek, shaking my head at the ridiculous idea. *Mom had acted in Barbara's defense. She wasn't a murderer!* Besides, Mom had been at our house watching Isabelle when Barbara's scream had chased me through the night and back onto my own front steps. I was confident in crossing Mom off my list. She possessed a genuine soft spot for Phil and, although she'd killed his father, she viewed Phil as a blameless victim. And the playground key couldn't have been Mom's anyway because Mark and I had inherited her key when we purchased the house.

The light turned green, and my foot pressed the accelerator with more force than I intended. I caught a glimpse of Isabelle in the mirror, thankful she was still asleep. A *For Sale* sign in a passing front yard sparked a vision of Bree's Hollywood smile. She'd become one of my closest friends since I'd moved back to Glenn Hills two years ago. But now I wondered how well I really knew her. My so-called friend felt comfortable enough lying to me and sneaking around with my husband behind my back. Whether her lies had been about something innocent or not, I wasn't sure.

Bree had been at the Drapers' house the night Barbara died. She'd left before I'd completed my loop around the neighborhood. What if something ugly had transpired between the women during the meeting? Maybe Bree had merely parked a couple of streets over and returned on foot. My stomach turned as another memory took hold. Mark hadn't been home that night. He'd claimed he was working late, but now I wondered if he'd met up with Bree instead.

But while my husband and my best friend had proven themselves to be liars, I didn't want to believe they were capable of something as sinister as murder. What motive could they possibly have to eliminate Barbara Draper and her son? Bree's business had been struggling, compounded by her recent divorce. Still, a double murder seemed an unlikely way to secure a listing. And why would Mark help her do something like that? I couldn't imagine it. On the other hand, they'd both been so quick to discourage me from questioning the police findings, telling me to drop it at every opportunity. Why? The chalk message I'd discovered on the driveway unscrolled in my mind, followed by the anonymous messages on The Neighbor List:

Mind your own fucking business!

Enjoy your perfect family.

You will pay.

I hope you sleep well tonight.

I'd suspected Luke Moreno for the chalk message, had even discovered him lurking in my backyard. But the other messages didn't seem an appropriate reaction to me inadvertently telling his mom he'd sneaked out on a Saturday night.

I sucked in a deep breath, aware that my thoughts were spiraling with wild theories and unlikely scenarios. I was about to remind myself that Bree didn't even have a playground key when Rick's smooth voice replayed in my ears. *Bree must have forgotten to give me a key.* Bree's failed love interest hadn't even known about the neighborhood playground until I told him about it. Was it possible Bree had pocketed Rick's key? Maybe Bree planned to sell it to a desperate mom in a neighborhood bordering ours to make some extra money. Had she dropped the key in Barbara's yard that night when she returned to murder the woman? If so, it would have provided a motive to run down Phil. Bree knew that Phil had found the evidence and that I was meeting him at 4 p.m. A shudder traveled through me as I turned down Mapleview Lane, questioning everything I thought I knew.

I didn't want to believe the evil theory I'd concocted, so I forced myself to come up with another possibility, my thoughts creeping along with my SUV past the houses of Mapleview Lane. Rick Smith had only just moved into the rundown house across from Barbara Draper a couple of weeks before she'd died. While the timing was suspicious, I couldn't think of a motive the new neighbor might have to kill a woman he'd never met. Rick's surprise and delight when I'd informed him of the existence of a neighborhood playground seemed genuine. The flirtatious house flipper had won me over with his flattery, but he'd raised Bree's suspicions with his slick and charming demeanor. Now I wondered if I'd been too quick to give him a pass.

I slowed in front of the silent facade of the Drapers' house, my gaze snaking through the backyard and beyond the fence to the Morenos' looming second story. Three of their upstairs windows overlooked Barbara's otherwise private backyard. Avery Moreno had been happy at the news of Barbara's death. Gleeful, even. Had Avery exceeded the amount of abuse she could endure from her neighbor and taken matters into her own hands? Maybe someone in the Moreno household happened to spot Phil through the window as he discovered the key they'd left behind. Maybe the threatening messages weren't about Luke sneaking out on a Saturday night. Perhaps they were warnings not to probe any further into Barbara's death. *I hope you sleep well tonight.* I shuddered at a new and terrifying thought: *What if Avery Moreno or one of her sons had spotted me entering Barbara's house the other night?*

My temples throbbed as I continued down the street and

pulled into our driveway. All of my theories had holes. None were solid enough to take to the police, and some were downright laughable. And so I held a breath of air in my lungs as I parked in the garage, unable to shake my hunch: There was a murderer in the Ridgeview Pines subdivision, and I had no idea who it was.

I entered the house through the side door, frazzled. Roo sniffed Isabelle's cheek and jumped on me as we made our way toward the kitchen. Out of habit, I tousled Roo's soft ears and kissed him on top of his head, thankful for my loyal four-legged friend. He jumped down, nails clicking over the linoleum as he trotted toward his water dish. I stared after him, my brain reluctant to register what my nose had just smelled. A hint of vanilla and citrus clung to my dog's coat, overpowering his usual musty scent. It was Bree's perfume. She always hugged Roo when she saw him. I froze as a horrible realization crashed through me. Bree had been inside our house while I was out.

THIRTY-ONE

The doorbell chimed at nine the next morning, sending Roo into a barking frenzy. The sight of my dog caused thoughts of Bree to sift through me. I'd called her yesterday, telling her Roo smelled of her perfume, and asking her straight out if she'd been in my house. Bree had laughed and said of course not. She'd spotted Roo in the front yard earlier that morning as she'd driven to the Drapers' house to take a few photos of the exterior. She'd stopped and gotten out to give Roo a hug, led him back into our fenced backyard, and then continued on her way. She apologized for not knocking to let me know, but she'd been in a rush.

It was possible that either Mark or I had left the back gate open yesterday, so Bree's story was plausible. Still, I noticed how she'd hesitated for a split second after her bout of laughter. I wasn't sure if I believed her.

The person at the door rung the bell again, and Roo's barking intensified. Today was Thursday, but I'd canceled Sophie's regular visit this morning. The strange happenings and threatening atmosphere had overwhelmed me, and it felt reckless to let Isabelle out of my sight even for a couple of hours. But now I wondered if Sophie had forgotten about the schedule change and shown up anyway. I closed my laptop, ending my effort at self-distraction—a search for a fiery volcano tattoo to inspire my design for my next molten-lava chocolate cake. I shooed my dog away with my foot and cracked the door, finding a middle-aged woman with a head of frizzy gray hair and a clipboard clenched beneath her arm.

"Hi. Jessica Millstone? Isabelle's mom?"

I opened the door a little wider. "Yes."

"I'm Rachel Zettlieg, a social worker with Child Protective Services for the Tri-County area."

My eyelids lowered. I didn't understand why this woman was at my door.

"I'm stopping by today because someone has expressed concerns about your daughter's care. When we receive a complaint, by law, we're required to do an in-person wellness check."

A wellness check on Isabelle? I could almost feel the blood draining from my body, as if time dripped in slow motion. My mouth stammered, and I used the solid wood of the doorframe to stay upright. I could admit to failing at other aspects of my life—my career and marriage, to start with—but I was a good mother. I straightened my shoulders and found my voice. "I'm sorry. You must be mistaken. My daughter *is* Isabelle. But she's perfectly fine."

"There's no mistake. Isabelle is the one who I'd like to see." The woman pursed her lips and craned her neck, looking over my shoulder. "It won't take more than ten minutes. Assuming everything is fine, I'll be on my way."

I tugged at the hem of my shirt, debating whether to slam the door in the woman's face but realizing that would make the situation worse. My face grew hot as I remembered all the notes Isabelle's doctor had been typing at yesterday's appointment. "Who complained? Was it Isabelle's doctor? I already explained everything to her."

The social worker gave me a sideways look. "It was an anonymous call. I'm sorry. I'm not allowed to leave without performing the checklist."

I stepped away from the door and allowed the social worker to enter. Isabelle sat on her beanbag in the living room, wearing her enormous pink headphones and entranced by an alphabet game on her iPad.

"Isabelle. This nice woman is here to ask you a few questions."

My daughter peeled off the headphones and trained her round, brown eyes on Rachel Zettlieg. Isabelle's pink and blistered skin was impossible to ignore, but the social worker didn't comment on it. The two proceeded to chat about my daughter's favorite activities and what she usually ate for lunch and dinner. I clenched my jaw when Isabelle proclaimed that she liked cake and cookies the most.

"We eat a lot of fruits and vegetables too. Don't we, Isabelle?" I edged between them, unable to stop myself from butting into the conversation.

Isabelle nodded.

The social worker pointed to her arm. "It looks like you got a little sunburn there."

"Yeah."

"Do you wear sunscreen when you go outside on sunny days?"

"Yeah."

My fingers curled into fists at the continued questions aimed at a child who'd barely turned three. This investigation was ridiculous.

The social worker touched her forehead. "And you had a cut on your head recently? How did you get that?"

"My chair fell."

"I see. And you also fell down the stairs?"

Isabelle nodded.

"How did that happen?"

Isabelle shrugged.

I cleared my throat, Mom's guilty face floating through my mind. "We have a safety gate. Someone had accidentally left it unlatched."

"Gwamma," Isabelle said, and I wished I could put a plug in her innocent little mouth.

The woman took more notes. "I see."

At last, the questions for Isabelle ended, and the social worker asked to see the gate, the booster seat, Isabelle's bed, her car seat, and the contents of our refrigerator. I led the woman to each location as she nodded and wrote notes beneath each of her checkpoints.

"Okay. That's it for today. Everything looks good here, so there's no need to worry. As I said, we're obligated to check these things out."

"I understand." I ushered Rachel out to the front steps and didn't let myself breathe until the door closed behind her.

Several hours later, I positioned Isabelle's sun hat further forward on her head, feeling the bulk of the new sunscreen bottle in my bag. I'd already rubbed a thick layer of protection over my daughter's vulnerable skin, but I brought more to reapply later. My insides still shook from the social worker's surprise visit. As soon as the woman had left, I'd called Mark and burst into tears. After I explained what had happened, he'd assured me it must have been a misunderstanding by the overzealous doctor at Isabelle's appointment yesterday. Who else would have known about all those incidents? Besides, the social worker had seen for herself that Isabelle lived in a happy, loving, and safe home. I knew Mark was right, but I couldn't help feeling someone had violated my trust.

Now I stepped onto the sidewalk with Isabelle in tow and headed toward the park. A grumbling motor cut through the air as Luke Moreno pushed a lawnmower around the side of Mr. Delaney's house. The boy wore black headphones and kept his head down as he followed a straight line across my neighbor's front yard. He'd never given me that quote for his mowing services, but we didn't need it anymore now that Mark promised he'd keep up with our lawn.

As Isabelle and I continued our stroll, a car rumbled behind us. I turned, surprised to find Sophie's rusted hatchback approaching. I wondered if she had a date with Rick.

Sophie's face brightened as she eased to a stop next to us, lowering her window. "Hi, Jessica. Hi, Isabelle! I missed you today." Her eyes hovered on Isabelle's pink face, then landed on me. "Is she sunburned?"

"Yeah. The lotion I used yesterday was expired. There's always something, right?"

"Right." Sophie bit her lip but forced a smile.

I got the feeling the babysitter was mentally cataloging my failure somewhere along with the recalled booster seat and the out-of-range monitor incidents. I was so thankful I'd canceled on her this morning. I definitely wouldn't tell her about the social worker's visit. I'd never tell anyone, for that matter.

"Are you visiting Rick?" I asked, noticing Sophie's shimmering lip gloss and the jeweled clip in her hair.

She nodded as pink blotches appeared on her pale cheeks. "He's been filling up the pool. He said I could be the first person to swim in it."

"Oh, that sounds fun. You two make a cute couple, by the way."

"Thanks." A bashful smile spread across Sophie's face. I could tell she wanted to say more but decided against it. She refocused on Isabelle. "I'll see you on Saturday night, Isabelle."

Isabelle hopped up and down. Mark and I had dinner plans at Frederick's on Saturday despite my husband's recent tangle of lies. I wanted things to be good between us, to believe that nothing scandalous was going on between him and Bree. I pulled my thoughts back to the sidewalk, where we said goodbye to Sophie and watched her pull into Rick's driveway.

My fingers gripped Isabelle's clammy hand as we continued along the sidewalk. Bree's red Mercedes drew my eye from its position at the top of the Drapers' driveway. A white car with out-of-state tags and a rental car sticker sat behind Bree's sedan. I realized the second car probably belonged to Barbara's sister, Kathy. Bree had mentioned the other day that Kathy was coming into town for Phil's burial and would hand over the keys and paperwork necessary for selling the house. She must have arrived a few days early. I imagined the two women inside, going through Barbara and Phil's personal belongings, and I was thankful I'd sneaked into the house in the middle of the night and removed the bag of pills.

I exhaled, relieved I didn't have to face Bree just yet. Isabelle and I walked the two-and-a-half blocks to the playground entrance, where I unlocked the gate and entered. A bored-looking nanny stood in a patch of shade near the sandbox, trapped in a conversation with Stephanie. Isabelle darted ahead to join Ben and Braydon in their shoveling. Stephanie's distracted gaze flickered my way. She merely offered a nod instead of bombarding me with her usual boisterous greeting.

I waved and headed to a nearby bench, secretly relieved the mommy blogger hadn't insisted I join their conversation. I could only imagine what mind-numbing topic spewed from Stephanie's mouth as she ignored her listeners' social cues—the glazed eyes, the fake yawns, the glances at watches. Suddenly, I wished the old version of Bree were sitting next to me, telling a funny story about a difficult buyer or giving me the heads-up on the latest Netflix shows. But things weren't the same now that she'd lied to me—more than once. I worried my friend had changed. Maybe I'd been so desperate for female companionship that I'd never really known who she was.

Stephanie's head swung toward me, a polka-dot sunhat sitting atop her nest of hair. The nanny's stare followed. They saw me see them and immediately turned back toward each other, but not before I'd glimpsed the devious look in their eyes and the sneer on Stephanie's lips. As Stephanie leaned closer to the younger woman and continued talking, I got the feeling she was talking about me.

What was my gossipy neighbor saying? Acid churned in my stomach as I imagined possible answers. I wondered if Sean had cracked. Maybe he'd confessed to his wife about his drug dealings with Phil. He could have revealed that he'd found me inside the Drapers' house the other night retrieving a ziplock bag from a secret hiding place. Or maybe Stephanie had spotted Isabelle's sunburn. Or, even worse, she might have seen the woman from Child Protective Services at our house this morning. I'd had the door to the patio open. Perhaps the seemingly perfect mom had been in her backyard and overheard the social worker. There were several possible reasons for Stephanie's juvenile behavior, and none of them were good.

Before my thoughts plunged any further, the nanny followed a wobbly two-year-old toward the swings. Stephanie snapped her fingers at the boys as a breeze carried her words over to me. "It's time to go."

I rolled my shoulders, eager for Stephanie to leave. But when I looked back, she was marching toward me, her pinched face void of warmth. "Hi, Jessica. Have you had a chance to order tickets to the fundraiser yet? Sean is counting on his neighbors to support him."

"I forgot to mention it to Mark. I'll let you know."

She turned toward the sandbox. "C'mon, boys. We're leaving."

"Sean definitely has our votes, though," I said, lying.

Stephanie's mouth settled into a cool grin. "Great. I'll tell him."

"You're taking off early today."

"I've got tons of catch-up work to do on my blog." She paused and nodded toward Isabelle. The layers of aloe and sunscreen I'd slathered on my daughter's face glistened beneath the floppy brim of her hat, probably drawing more attention to the fact she'd gotten burned. "Speaking of my blog, you should read my post from last month about toddler sunscreen."

My jaw tightened. "Yeah. The lotion I used the other day was expired."

I waited for a lengthy explanation about sunscreen product ratings. Stephanie only hoisted her bag higher on her shoulder and ushered the twins out through the gate without saying goodbye.

I stared after her, seeking comfort in the sunlight warming my face or the melody of chirping birds, but I felt unsteady instead, as if someone had sawed off one of the legs of the park bench beneath me. Isabelle kneeled alone in the sandbox, focused on digging a hole beneath the shadow cast by her sunhat. My eyes drifted from my daughter and across the nearly empty playground, landing on the gate. A woman I'd seen here last week approached the park with a baby strapped to her chest. I rotated my body to get a clear view as she dug into her pocket and removed a key, using it to let herself into the enclosed area. She wasn't the murderer.

I continued this exercise for another forty-five minutes, watching each person who entered the park, waiting for someone without a key. But my amateur detective work proved futile. Everyone had one.

At 12:30 p.m., Isabelle had tired of the sandbox, and my twisting stomach demanded food. We retraced our steps along the sidewalk toward home. A black SUV hummed toward us and stopped. The window lowered, and Avery Moreno smiled from behind her oversized sunglasses. "Hi, Jessica."

"Hi, Avery."

She tilted her head at Isabelle. "I love your sunhat, sweetie."

I stepped to the side, a little confused by Avery's sudden effort to make small talk. She had never stopped to chat with me before.

She continued, "Sorry to interrupt your walk. I just wanted to let you know that Paul and I are having a party a week from Saturday in our backyard, starting at seven. We'd love it if you can come. A lot of the neighbors will be there." She smiled toward Isabelle. "Kids are welcome."

"Oh, thank you. That sounds fun. We should be able to make it."

"Wonderful."

"Can we bring anything?"

She waved me off. "No. Just show up. It'll be super casual." She glanced in her rearview mirror, then back at me. "Did you have fun at the park?"

"Yeah. The usual." I shrugged. "Isabelle loves the sandbox."

"I miss those days." She cocked her head, smiling. "Enjoy it while you can." A car approached from behind, and Avery frowned, fluttering her fingers in the air. "See you later."

"Sounds good." I watched Avery drive toward her house, mildly confused at her sudden attempt to be neighborly. As her vehicle turned the corner, it struck me again how happy Avery was that Barbara and Phil were dead.

THIRTY-TWO

I'd been flattered by the unexpected invitation to the Morenos' backyard party. Still, an uneasy feeling expanded in my gut as I returned from the park and entered our shadowy house. I removed Isabelle's hat in the foyer, noticing the front rug sitting askew, a piece of mail laying upside down beneath the console table, and a dust bunny floating across the floor. I hadn't seen this mess earlier, and I wondered if the social worker had made a note of the disarray. Her surprise visit still reverberated through me.

Roo danced around my ankles, wagging his tail, as I placed the envelope back on the table and straightened the rug. It had been a few days with no new threatening messages. I'd spotted Officer Lang drive down our street a couple of times, keeping tabs on the neighborhood as she'd promised. Perhaps her presence really had scared away whoever had been harassing me. I wouldn't let my paranoia get to me. Our hyper dog was probably the one who'd messed up the house. I shooed him away. "I'm going to make us some lunch, Isabelle. You can go play until it's ready."

Isabelle nodded and skipped toward her corner of toys in the living room. As I passed the stairway to the basement, a narrow gap between the safety gate and the doorframe halted my feet. My fingers grasped the plastic fencing, and the gate swung back with ease. It wasn't latched, which didn't make any sense. I scanned the room, following a clear path down the stairs. I'd only just demonstrated the securely locked gate to the social worker, and I hadn't opened it since. A warning crawled up my spine and over my scalp.

"Mom?" I yelled toward the cellar. Maybe she'd stopped by to retrieve one of her boxes. I waited for a response, but only my own voice echoed back from the stairwell leading to the basement door. I secured the gate's latch and wandered back into the living room, pulse racing. My feet edged toward the study, where the door sat slightly ajar. I peeked inside the small room, finding no one there. But my gaze hovered on the nearby shelf, the one where I'd found our family photo face down and cracked. I'd replaced the frame a few days ago, propping the photo back into its usual position. Now it was knocked over again, laying face down. My mouth went dry and I felt like I might vomit. Was someone messing with me? Or had a gust of wind toppled it a second time?

Without righting the photo, I paced into the living room, eyes sweeping for anything else out of place. Isabelle stood at her play kitchen with her back to me. My eyes flickered toward the glass slider leading out to the patio, catching on the handle. I'd forgotten to lock the patio door when we'd left for the playground. Our backyard was fenced, and I sometimes overlooked that door unless it was nighttime or we were leaving the house for a long time. Roo stayed close to me, panting. I stroked his head, wishing he could speak and tell me if someone had been in our house. He'd always been friendly with strangers, which made for a horrible watchdog. A faint creak sounded from behind the kitchen wall. Was someone here now? A flash of hot terror surged through me at the thought.

"Isabelle, come over to Mommy. We're going to go out the front door." I struggled to keep my voice even as panic rose inside me.

Isabelle turned around, holding up an object. "Look." The blade of a butcher's knife glinted in the light, its razor-sharp tip wavering inches from her pink cheeks. Her pudgy fingers clutched the handle as she raised the weapon higher.

Oh my God! Fear surged through me, white and hot, but I didn't want to scare her. "Set that down. It's very sharp." Isabelle froze, sensing the panic in my voice. Her wide eyes brimmed with tears as she lowered the knife to the floor. I lunged toward her and scooped her up in my arms.

The knife pointing at my feet was the same expensive French brand as our cutlery. It had come from our kitchen. I'd been using that knife to chop melon before the social worker arrived. But I'd set the dangerous object in the sink out of Isabelle's reach. I was sure of it.

I pulled away from my daughter so I could see her face. "Where did you find that knife? Did you take it out of the sink earlier?"

"No." Isabelle's lower lip protruded as she pointed toward her play kitchen. "It was on top of my pizza."

I followed her gaze to the wooden pizza resting on the counter of her Fisher Price kitchen. I stumbled backward, a realization blowing through me like a cold wind. Someone else had placed the knife there. Someone was trying to harm my daughter.

My arms tightened around Isabelle. I bolted through the front door with Roo chasing after us. When I reached the edge of our front yard, I pulled my phone from my pocket and dialed 911.

It only took five minutes for a patrol car to arrive, and I was relieved when Officer Lang emerged from the driver's seat. A partner accompanied her today, a man in his early twenties, sporting a crew cut and a stunned expression that made him appear as if it was his first day on the job. They listened as I explained what had happened—the messed-up rug and fallen mail, followed by the unlocked gate that I knew had been locked when we left for the park and our family photo laying face down for the second time. And most importantly, I told them about the butcher's knife in Isabelle's play kitchen.

"Was anything stolen that you could see?"

I hugged my arms around myself. "I don't know. We were only in the living room when I realized something wasn't right. I left the sliding door to the patio unlocked. Whoever it was might have gotten in that way."

Officer Lang jotted a few notes on her pad and set it aside. "We'll go inside and do a thorough search. You two wait out here."

I perched under a maple tree bordering Mr. Delaney's freshly cut grass with Isabelle next to me, and Roo on a long leash. I called Mark but only reached his voicemail, telling him to call me back. Every once in a while, a passing car slowed to gawk at the police car in our driveway. My mind churned, trying to think of who would possibly want to harm a three-year-old girl. I couldn't think of anyone. I considered a different angle. *Who had known we were at the park and not home?* I'd mentioned our afternoon plans to the social worker. We'd passed Luke working in the yard next door and Sophie on her way to Rick's house. Then I'd spotted Bree's car in the Drapers' driveway. I stood and peered down the street. Both of their vehicles were gone now. I supposed anyone in the neighboring houses could have seen me walk past. My thoughts circled back to Stephanie Peale. She'd been acting especially cold toward me and had left the park in a hurry after we arrived. Then Avery had stopped her car to chat as we were on our way home, something she'd never done before. Had she been delaying our return, giving someone else time to leave? But why would any of them break into our house to unlatch a gate and move a knife? I wondered if the terrifying happenings were somehow related to the deaths of Barbara and Phil Draper. But the more I dissected the facts, the less it all seemed to fit together.

The front door flung open, and Officer Lang and her partner marched toward me.

"All clear," Officer Lang said as she neared. "Looks like nothing else was disturbed, but you should go through your jewelry and other valuables to be sure. We'll wait for you."

I nodded and entered the house. It felt less scary now that I knew no one was hiding in a closet. I peered into the kitchen, where all the drawers and cupboards were closed. My feet padded up the stairs. Checking Isabelle's room first, then ours. Nothing appeared out of place; no clothes had been yanked from drawers and tossed on the floor. I raised the lid of my jewelry box with shaking fingers, finding my diamond earrings and ruby necklace shining back at me. The jewelry was worth thousands of dollars, and I wondered why the intruder hadn't stolen them.

I returned to the first floor, where Officer Lang waited in the lobby. I could hear her partner laughing with Isabelle outside.

"All of my jewelry is there, even the diamonds. That's weird. Isn't it?"

The woman pinched her lips together and glanced at the floor. "Yes. It's unlikely someone would break into your house and not take something so valuable."

"I think someone is trying to harm my daughter. Or maybe my whole family."

Officer Lang sighed. "Who would want to do that?"

"I don't know. But remember that anonymous message I told you about? The one that said *Enjoy your perfect family*. And now there's a knife sitting on my daughter's play kitchen. Whoever put it there can't stand the sight of our family photo. It can't all be a coincidence."

"Have you received any other messages since then?"

"I got one that said *You will pay*. And then another that said *I hope you sleep well tonight*. I told you about them the morning I met you at the station. Remember?"

The police officer rubbed her forehead. "Listen. The messages are certainly alarming, and I understand that you faced a scary situation with the knife in your daughter's hand and the open gate, but my partner and I don't think this feels like a break-in. You probably left your safety gate unlatched without realizing it. Or maybe the latch is defective and your dog knocked it loose somehow. And picture frames fall over sometimes. I'm guessing you're still on edge because of those text messages and your neighbors' recent deaths."

"No. The gate works fine. It was locked this morning. I checked it to make sure it was secure."

"There was a step stool near the counter in the kitchen," Officer Lang continued without acknowledging my response. "Your daughter could have used it to reach the knife earlier in the day when you were doing something else."

"I guess it's possible. But Isabelle wouldn't do that. She knows better."

"Isabelle finding it and moving it seems like the most logical explanation. Three-year-olds don't always have the best impulse control." The policewoman winked in what seemed like an attempt at solidarity. "I'm sure you know that."

I clutched my head and squeezed my eyes closed. I didn't think I'd imagined anything, but now I doubted myself. For the past few weeks, scandalous ideas had congealed in my mind, clouding it up until I couldn't think much of anything else. I'd been watching my friends and neighbors through a darkened lens, viewing them as potential criminals. Now two law-enforcement professionals were standing on my property telling me I'd freaked myself out, concocting a story that wasn't true. I wasn't sure if I trusted my senses anymore.

I straightened myself up and clenched my hands together. "What about fingerprints? On the knife? Can you check?"

"Yes. We dusted the knife and lifted a few prints already. But most intruders wear gloves, so I'm not sure if it will get us anywhere. The prints could very well belong to you or Isabelle."

"What about the key I gave you? Did you get the results back yet?"

"No. I'm still waiting. I'll call you as soon as I hear anything, but don't get your hopes up. As far as law enforcement is concerned, no crime was committed against Barbara Draper. Or Phil."

I lowered my head, resisting the urge to argue and wondering if I was a total head case. "Okay, thank you for looking into it."

"We're happy to help."

I followed her outside, where the other police officer threw a stick across the lawn. He and Isabelle clapped their hands as Roo retrieved it and brought it back to them.

Officer Lang chuckled and waved her partner toward the cruiser. "We've got another call."

"Bye, Isabelle. Stay safe." The other officer tipped his head toward me. "Ma'am."

"Thank you," I said again as I gathered Isabelle and Roo close to me and watched them pull away.

Isabelle and I went inside, where I locked all the doors for good measure. I buckled Isabelle into her booster seat and gave her a cup of chilled apple juice. As I placed a few slices of bread on the stove to start some grilled cheese sandwiches, my phone buzzed with a notification. The Neighbor List icon showed a new message waiting for me, and, ignoring my pounding heart, I clicked on it.

The sender was JDelaney. I did a double take at the username: Jim Delaney, my next-door neighbor. I nearly toppled over as I processed the words on the screen:

Back off or you'll be next!

THIRTY-THREE

The phone shook in my hand as I stared at the threatening message. I couldn't imagine mild-mannered Mr. Delaney, who I'd known since I was a child, sending something like this. He had long since retired from his sportscasting career and must have been pushing eighty. Other than glimpsing him through his window watching TV at night, I sometimes ran into him working in his yard, where he always greeted me with a smile and a friendly comment about the weather. But Mom's words spun through my head. She'd always worried that Mr. Delaney had seen her leaving the Drapers' house the day she pushed Ed Draper down the stairs.

Isabelle pounded on the table. "I'm hungry."

I took a screenshot but held off on sending it to Officer Lang. I felt someone was monitoring my every move, and I didn't want to put my family in even more danger. Hiding the shocking message in my pocket, I slapped together a cold cheese sandwich for her and scooped some melon cubes onto her plate. My head felt light, so I forced myself to eat a few bites of a second sandwich, even though my appetite had vanished. As soon as Isabelle finished her meal, I led her out to the backyard, handed her a plastic bucket, and told her to collect as many rocks as she could find. She got to work as I peered over our slatted fence. Mr. Delaney hummed to himself, watering the plants around his patio.

"Hi, Mr. Delaney." I waved, projecting my voice into the neighboring yard.

He looked up, turning off the nozzle and walking closer to me. "Hi, Jessica. The weather's getting warmer."

"It sure is."

"How's your mom doing?"

"She's fine."

"Well, tell her to stop by and say hello next time she comes over." He raised his hand. "Nice to see you." The man began to turn away.

"Wait. Mr. Delaney."

He paused, turning back.

"I was just wondering, have you posted any messages on The Neighbor List app lately?"

He raised a bushy eyebrow at me. "What's that?"

"The Neighbor List. It's an app you can load on your smartphone and post information for your neighbors to see, like job openings or road closures. You can also send messages to people. Do you have an account?"

"No. I don't do social media." His jowls sagged as he shook his head of white hair. "My granddaughter signed me up for Facebook a few years back, and it was a headache."

"Yeah. Facebook is a nightmare."

"I prefer calling people on the phone, I guess."

"That makes sense." I reached into my back pocket for my phone, debating whether to tell the kind man that someone had assumed his identity on The Neighbor List. But when I touched the icon on my screen, my inbox contained zero messages. The message from JDelaney that had appeared minutes earlier was already gone.

. . .

Mark sat at the kitchen table, sipping a can of seltzer water and tapping his foot against the floor. After my third time calling him, he'd finally picked up. The day's unsettling events tumbled from my mouth in a frantic, tangled mess. I begged him to leave work early and come home, and to my surprise, he did.

Now, Mark's gaze ricocheted from the living room to the step stool I'd shoved into the far corner of the kitchen. "Listen, the police might be right about that gate. Maybe the latch comes loose sometimes. And I've seen Isabelle climbing up on that step stool a lot recently. It's not out of the question that she moved the knife."

"What about the family photo?"

"Roo probably bumped into the shelf. Or maybe a gust of wind got it, like you said."

"So you don't think it was a break-in?"

"I don't know. You were right to call the police. All I'm saying is that a break-in where the intruders don't take anything seems weird." He crossed his arms in front of him as if protecting himself from my reaction. "I'll pick up a new safety gate tomorrow. We'll chuck that one."

I paced across the linoleum, feeling a little like I was drowning within our kitchen's blue walls. "What about that message from JDelaney? Who would do that?"

"That I can't explain." Mark released a long breath and massaged the bridge of his nose. "Maybe some teenagers playing a prank? They all know how to program high-tech stuff like creating fake accounts and messages that disappear after thirty seconds. No one our age or older would have a clue."

My mouth went dry as I remembered Luke Moreno lurking uninvited in our backyard, just days after I'd discovered the threatening chalk message on the driveway. If someone had entered our house this morning, it had likely been through the back sliding door. Maybe Luke never gave me a lawn-mowing quote because he'd only been in our backyard to scope out a break-in.

"What if Luke Moreno is messing with me? I blabbed to his

mom about seeing him that night when she had no idea he was out, and then we never hired him to do our lawn mowing."

Mark eyed me. "Leaving threatening messages for your neighbors seems like an extreme reaction to either of those things. Doesn't it?"

"Yeah. On the other hand, I didn't always make the best decisions when I was a teenager." My thoughts tumbled backward over dumb things I'd done in high school. Perhaps karma was worming its way back for me. Still, while I could see why Luke might have written a couple of those angry messages, breaking into someone's house and moving a knife to a toddler's play kitchen took things to another level. It was difficult to imagine what a soft-spoken fifteen-year-old boy would gain by threatening the safety of a toddler.

Mark chuckled, but he must have recognized the fear radiating through me. He stood up and looped his arm around me. "Just to be safe, I'm going to take the day off work tomorrow and stay here with you and Isabelle. Then it will be the weekend. I bet by Monday all this will have blown over."

My knees almost buckled with relief, and I realized just how terrified I'd been at being left alone in the house again. My need to have another person with me outweighed my doubts about my husband's secret visit to Bree's home. I decided to give him the benefit of the doubt.

The next day, I never ventured further than ten feet from Mark or Isabelle. I felt safe with my husband home and our doors locked, but my nerves from all the unusual events of the last few days hadn't subsided. I caught myself hiding behind the curtain and peering out toward Mapleview Lane, searching for a wayward teenage computer geek who'd been up to no good. Only the usual joggers, dog walkers, and parents with strollers passed by our house.

I skipped my regular trip to the neighborhood playground and, instead, we buckled Isabelle into Mark's car and drove to the nearest big box store to purchase a different brand of safety gate to guard the basement stairs. Then we stopped at Isabelle's favorite restaurant on the way home and treated ourselves to ice-cream, laughing as her rainbow-colored dessert covered half her face and dripped down her shirt. Once we returned to our silent house, the afternoon passed uneventfully, with Mark taking some work calls while Isabelle napped. Meanwhile, I organized and cleaned room by room. I wasn't leaving anything to chance. This time our home would be spotless if that social worker made another unnecessary visit.

That night, I lay awake in bed, convincing myself that everyone else was probably right, and my nerves had fueled my overactive imagination. Isabelle must have moved the knife before we left for the park. The social worker's visit had most likely been caused by Isabelle's doctor's appointment the day before, and I could see that the two things were unrelated. The mysterious message on The Neighbor List from someone posing as Mr. Delaney was probably another harmless prank by some loser on the app with too much time on their hands, maybe someone from high school held a grudge and had discovered I'd moved back into town. I pulled the sheets up to my neck, deciding to temporarily back off my laywoman's investigation of my neighbors' deaths. No matter who had sent the threatening message, it simply wasn't worth putting my family at risk.

By 6:30 on Saturday evening, I was showered and draped in a sleeveless black blouse and a flowing gray skirt, a spritz of seldom-used perfume lingering on my neck. Mark and I had already booked Sophie for the evening and were eager to enjoy a dinner out at Frederick's. The thought of an evening out with my husband felt like I'd finally come up for a breath of air. A brighter future was waiting for me; I just had to make an effort to get to it. After clipping my ruby necklace around my neck, I changed Isabelle into her pajamas and led her downstairs. Mark looked up from his seat on the couch and whistled at me, and I couldn't stop the smile from stretching over my lips.

Five minutes later, Sophie arrived, wearing a floral sundress paired with a denim jacket and heeled sandals. Eyeshadow glimmered from her usually bare eyelids.

I stepped aside to let her enter. "Wow. You look too nice to be hanging out with a three-year-old."

"Oh. Thanks." Sophie smoothed down her dress and waved at Isabelle, who bounded toward her. "I might go see Rick after you and Mark get back from dinner. No rush, though."

"That's great. I'm glad things are going well with you guys. We shouldn't be gone more than two hours."

I ran through Isabelle's instructions for the night, reminding Sophie to keep the doors locked without adding any additional details. A text buzzed through my phone just as I kissed Isabelle goodbye:

Hi Jessica. I'm in the area. Can I stop by to see Isabelle for a few minutes? Sorry for the short notice!

A pained sigh rushed from my mouth.

"What's wrong?" Sophie stretched her head toward my phone just as Mark wandered into the foyer.

"My mom has the worst timing. She's in the area and wants to stop over and see Isabelle."

Mark grunted. "Seriously? Right now?"

"I'll tell her we're heading out. We can push it to tomorrow."

Sophie shrugged. "Your mom can hang out here for a while if she wants. I don't mind. She's so nice."

"Are you sure?"

"Yeah."

I glanced toward Mark, who shrugged. Mom hadn't been to the house in over a week. With everything that had been going on lately, I hadn't even thought to invite her to check out the new wall color in the kitchen. Guilt needled through me as I imagined Mom driving around our bustling neighborhood, missing her grand-daughter and waiting for a response.

"I'll make sure she keeps it brief," I said to Sophie. "I know my mom can be pushy sometimes, but don't let her pay you to leave. We need you here."

"Sure thing."

I responded to Mom, letting her know that Mark and I were leaving for our 7 p.m. dinner reservation but that Sophie was here and open to having her hang out for a few minutes.

Mom responded:

That works. Thanks. I'll be there in five minutes. You don't have to wait for me.

I gave her a thumbs-up and added,

I hope you like the new color in the kitchen!

Mark and I headed toward the garage, eager to escape to our relaxing dinner. But a sudden surge of unease rose within me as I approached the door; it was the fear of separating myself from Isabelle, of having my daughter out of my sight, if only for a short time. I brushed away the feeling, telling myself the warning grip-ping my insides was understandable paranoia after the recent string of near misses. Still, I couldn't stop myself from turning back and yelling over my shoulder, "And, Sophie. Don't forget to lock the door when my mom leaves."

THIRTY-FOUR

We sat at a white-clothed table in a private corner of Frederick's, a melting candle flickering between us. As I lifted the wineglass to my mouth, I had the sensation of having completed a marathon and collapsing beyond the finish line as someone handed me a cold bottle of water.

"What a week, huh?" Mark shook his head, and I felt as if he'd read my thoughts.

"It's been so crazy and stressful."

"Is everything okay? With you?" He reached across the table and squeezed my hand.

"Yes. It will be."

"You just seem so..." He looked around the restaurant as if struggling to think of the perfect word. "Distracted. Or distant. Like you're not telling me something."

I laughed at the irony. "Really? You're the one running around with Bree behind my back."

Mark pulled his hand back. "That was absolutely nothing." He paused, his face softening. "I should have told you, though. I've been thinking about it, and you were right about that."

I nodded, wanting to believe him. "You didn't meet with Bree at our house, did you? That morning I took Isabelle to her doctor's appointment?"

Mark's lips pulled back.

"To help her with her finances, I mean."

"No. Why?"

"Nothing. It's just that I smelled her perfume on Roo. I asked her about it later and she said she spotted Roo in the front yard that morning and stopped her car to lead him into the backyard. But it seems like a strange thing to do without telling one of us."

Mark twisted his lips to the side, considering. "Yeah. That's a little weird, but I don't think she'd lie to you. It sounds like she was trying to help. Maybe she was in a hurry."

"That's what she said. I feel like I'm going crazy lately."

He sipped his drink.

The secrets I'd been hiding from my husband spiraled through my mind: Mom pushing Ed Draper down the stairs nearly thirty years ago, and my break-in at the Drapers' house in the middle of the night, followed by my run-in with Sean Peale.

Mom had held her secret close for so many years, never even mentioning it to Dad. I wondered how she'd been able to keep it to herself. As much as I wanted to tell Mark what she'd done, I wouldn't break her trust.

On the other hand, I didn't owe the Peales anything. I inhaled a long breath and leaned closer to him. "There is something I've wanted to tell you, but you have to promise not to get mad."

His chin turned slightly to the side. "Okay."

I checked over my shoulder, making sure no one at nearby tables was listening, then I lowered my voice. "About a week ago—a day or two after Phil died—I let myself into the Drapers' house in the middle of the night to recover a playground key Phil had found in his yard."

"You did what?"

"I used a house key I found under their flowerpot to get in."

Mark angled his head to the side, then looked back at me, incredulous. "Why would you do that?"

"Someone dropped the playground key in the Drapers' yard the night Barbara died. Phil heard footsteps in the house that night after Bree left. Remember when we stopped to help Phil in the front yard, and he said it wasn't an accident? The key was evidence of an intruder, but the police didn't believe him because of his... altered state. I promised Phil I'd turn his findings over to the police, but someone ran him over right before we'd planned to meet. I had to break in and get the key because one of our neighbors might have killed Barbara Draper and then taken out Phil to prevent him from sharing the evidence."

Mark stared at me, his lip twitching as if he wasn't sure whether I was joking.

"Don't worry. I delivered the playground key to Officer Lang. They're supposed to be testing it, but it's not a priority."

"Jessica, why would you do that?" Mark asked again, then took a swig of his drink and shook his head. "This HAS to stop! You sound like a mad woman. I thought we'd dropped all the conspiracy theory nonsense."

"Yes. But that actually wasn't what I wanted to tell you. There's something else, even worse."

He lowered his chin. "Really?"

"When I was leaving the Drapers' house—after I'd found where Phil hid the key—I ran into Sean Peale. He was standing in the doorway with his creepy, weird smile."

Fear washed through my husband's eyes. He leaned toward me. "Seriously? Did he hurt you?"

"No. Sean told me to hand over the pills. That's why he thought I was at the Drapers' house. Sean Peale, the podiatrist, Mr 'Family Values' himself, was the person supplying Phil Draper with painkillers, illegally."

Mark rocked backward in his chair, eyes stretching wide. "Holy shit. That slimeball."

"I showed him where Phil hid his stash in exchange for keeping each other's secrets. I told Sean I was merely there to retrieve our playground key, but I don't think he believed me."

"Oh my God, Jess. Why didn't you tell me? How did I not hear you leave in the middle of the night?"

"I thought you'd be mad. And you were sound asleep." I smiled.

"Just when you think you know someone." My husband's eyes held a dazed stare.

"Doesn't it make you sick how Sean and Stephanie walk around all high and mighty? The perfect parents, family values first for City Council, blah, blah, blah. I want to scream the truth to the whole town, but I can't tell anyone because he saw me there too."

"Jess, this is dangerous. Sean is probably the one who sent you that message on Thursday. Maybe he saw the police car in our driveway and thought you were going to turn him in."

I'd already wondered if Sean was behind the messages, but I hadn't considered the possibility that he'd seen the police at our house and decided to escalate his threats. I remembered how he had threatened me through the fence, telling me something bad would happen if I talked. "Yeah. You might be right. Or it could have been Stephanie. Her image is everything, and she knows her way around a computer."

Mark's eyes darted around the bustling restaurant. "It might even explain why one of them would sneak in and move the knife. Maybe it was some kind of sick threat."

As Mark spoke, I felt the weight of a thousand bricks slide off my shoulders. It was a relief to share my worries, to have someone I trusted on my side, for my husband not to think I was crazy.

We took our time ordering and eating, losing ourselves in conversation in a way that hadn't happened in a while. We discussed every angle of the mysterious happenings in our neighborhood. Mark still believed that Barbara died in an accident, but he was willing to hear me out. He listened to my various tales of our neighbors' strange behavior, then grimaced, pointing out holes in each of my theories. But he didn't shut me down like he'd done so many times previously. I assured him we'd know more when Officer Lang got back to me with the print results.

No sooner had I mentioned the policewoman when my phone vibrated from within my purse. I pulled it out, fearing a text from Sophie. But when I looked at the screen, I could see it was a phone call, not a text. I'd saved Officer Lang's number in my phone, and now she was calling me at 8:30 on a Saturday night.

"Hello?"

"Hi, Jessica. This is Officer Lang. I'm afraid I have some troubling news."

It felt like my heart plummeted through my body and onto the floor. I forced myself to ask the question. "What is it?"

"One of my colleagues has just arrested a woman named Marilyn Tyler for a DUI. Is that your mom?"

I stared across the table at Mark, barely able to speak the word. "Yes."

"I recommend you come down to the station and get her."

And just like that, our dinner was over.

THIRTY-FIVE

Mark drove us to the police station, his stunned expression mirroring my own. I couldn't believe this was happening. The police had arrested Mom for drunk driving. Her behavior surprised me in all the wrong ways lately; she was turning out to be someone completely different than the happy, responsible home-maker I'd always made her out to be.

Mark furrowed his eyebrows as he leaned over the steering wheel. "What's going on with your mom?"

"I have no idea."

"Was she drinking at our house while she played with Isabelle?"

"I can't imagine it. She's never done that before."

"Not that we knew of."

We drove through a sea of thick silence, and I could tell we were both thinking the same thing—the two accidents with Isabelle had happened while Mom had been in charge. *Had she been drinking then too?* I'd never known her to have a problem with alcohol, but maybe she'd been using it as a crutch to get through her loneliness.

When we arrived at the parking lot, I insisted I could handle things, that Mom would be ashamed and not want extra people around. I suggested Mark go home so that Sophie could leave and keep her plans with Rick. I had no idea how long the process of getting Mom out of here would take, but Officer Lang had mentioned another officer had driven Mom's car to the station, so hopefully I could use it to deliver her back to her condo and drive myself afterward. Mark reluctantly agreed, watching from the driver's seat as I entered the police station doors.

I rushed toward the counter, fearing Mom would be hand-cuffed and locked in a cell with prostitutes and drug dealers. I told the receptionist my name, and she called Officer Lang, who gave me a sad smile and escorted me to a tiny room with no windows. Mom hunched over a metal table, resting her head in her hands, but sat up as we entered.

I almost didn't recognize the person sitting in front of me. Mom's skin sagged with a grayish hue. Her lids weighed heavily above bleary and bloodshot eyes, and remnants of black mascara swirled with dried tears across her cheeks. Her face crumpled when she saw me.

I ran over and hugged her. "It's going to be okay."

Mom wiped her eyes. "I don't know what happened."

Officer Lang waited in the doorway. "I'll give you two a minute while I put the paperwork together. Marilyn, you'll get a tempo-rary license until your court date is set sometime in the next four-teen days, but we can't let you drive home tonight."

"I'll drive her," I said.

Officer Lang nodded and left the room.

"Mom, were you drinking at our house? Or after you left?"

She nodded. "I was upset after I saw what you did to the kitchen. Those blue walls look so... different. I guess it felt like you'd painted over a piece of my life. That sounds silly, I know. I don't deal well with change."

"I'm sorry. I should have warned you about how different it looks."

"Sophie saw that I was having a hard time with the new look. I asked if she'd mind if I made a drink to take the edge off. She said that was fine and that I could stay as long as I wanted. She could tell that Isabelle enjoyed having me around. I poured the drink myself. It was a very weak gin and tonic. I barely added any gin at all, and I stuck around for another hour after that without drinking anything. I just don't understand how this happened."

"Mom, your blood alcohol level was much higher than one weak drink."

"I know. I can't explain it."

I pinched my lips between my teeth, wondering if she was losing it. She might have misremembered things, but it didn't seem like she was purposefully lying. Or maybe there was another explanation.

"Maybe your blood pressure medication interacted with the drink somehow?"

"That's never been a problem before."

"And Sophie didn't slip an extra splash of gin in there?" I asked, grasping at straws.

Mom threw her head back. "Of course not. Why would she do that?"

"I have no idea." My eyes lowered. I didn't know much of anything anymore.

Officer Lang slipped back into the room, rustling a handful of papers. She went over each one with Mom, who signed where necessary. Our next step was to hire a lawyer and wait for a court date.

I helped Mom out to her car, my heart squeezing with each wobbly step she took. I drove to her condo, parking in the garage and helped her inside. As she changed her clothes and washed her face, I scrounged through her refrigerator and made up a plate of cheese and crackers, along with a tall glass of water.

I rested on Mom's couch, watching her approach; the thick lines etched into her face made her appear sad and defeated. "I can hang out for a while if you feel like it."

"Sure. I'm exhausted, but I don't think I can go to sleep right away after such a shock." She plucked a cracker from the plate and bit into it, followed by gulps of water.

"I'm sorry you don't like the new wall color. I promise the kitchen will look stunning when it's finished."

She waved her hand in the air. "I'll get over it. It's just difficult to get old, to see everything and everyone around you change so much. People die. Houses get knocked down and rebuilt, and it's almost like they were never there at all."

Mom's eyes were glazed, and I wondered how much the alcohol was still affecting her.

She continued talking without looking at me. "Your house— that neighborhood—holds so many good memories for me. A few bad ones, too, I guess. It's almost like I left my entire life within the walls of 627 Mapleview Lane when I moved. I didn't realize it at the time."

"Do you want to come over tomorrow? Only if you feel up to it. We can fix a nice brunch."

"That would be lovely." Mom's eyelashes flickered. "Sophie told me she's dating the man who bought Greta Washburn's house. I was happy to hear he isn't knocking the place down. It's good to keep some character in the neighborhood's architecture."

"Yeah. I heard Rick just finished redoing the pool."

"Oh, I remember when the Washburns had that put in. Gosh, I even remember who owned that house before them. That's a whole different story, though." Mom's voice dropped in temperature as she spoke that last sentence.

I leaned closer, intrigued. "What's the story?"

"Well, it takes me back a long time—you were still pretty young —and I'm a little fuzzy on the details, but there was a woman with three kids who lived in the Washburn house. She was a horrible alcoholic, but I guess I'm not in a position to judge anyone anymore." Mom made a face at me, and we giggled, despite ourselves. "Anyway, she was terribly neglectful of those kids. The oldest one was a scrawny boy, maybe a year or two older than you. Then there was another boy in the middle and a baby girl. I guess the woman's husband had left her, and she couldn't cope. I remember how the two boys would try to take care of the baby, three blonde heads of hair fumbling about in the yard. They weren't equipped, of course. They were only babies themselves." Mom pursed her lips and took another sip of water. "Barbara Draper was so upset at what she saw going on over there. She reported the family to Child Protective Services. That was just a few days before the stairway incident with Ed."

My mouth had gone dry. "I don't remember the kids."

"You wouldn't have. We didn't interact much. You were only about six when they moved away. It only took a week or so after Barbara filed the complaint for the state to intervene and remove the kids. They sent the mother to a rehab facility. That's what I heard, anyway. I'm not sure what happened to any of them after that. Now what was her name again? Mary something... Kensington, that was it."

"Kensington?" I straightened up at the mention of the name.

"Yes. Why?"

"That's the name of Rick's company. Kensington Renovations."

"Huh. Is that his last name?"

"No. It's Rick Smith."

"Still, that's quite a coincidence."

This new set of facts clicked and turned in my head. Too many coincidences... "Do you remember the kids' names, Mom?"

"Let's see. Bobby was the middle boy. He was the one who was always wandering into our yard. I don't remember the baby's name. The older boy was Ralphie. No, it was Richie, I think."

"Richie? Like Richard?" *Or Rick.* Beads of cold sweat formed on my forehead. The walls of my chest seemed to crumble like a dilapidated house. "Oh my God." I pictured my new, charming neighbor, Rick Smith. I'd been mesmerized by his southern drawl, easy humor, and inviting eyes. Had he been up to something evil all along? Bree had warned me to watch out for him. She'd sensed during their dinner date that Rick's slick exterior was hiding something. I'd ignored her warning, writing off her fears to her recent divorce.

Rick's words echoed in my head: *It must be nice to have such deep roots.* Now, I attributed a different meaning to them. I wondered if the man had returned to reclaim his childhood home. Maybe he blamed Barbara Draper for taking his mother away. Perhaps Rick's heavy footsteps were the ones Phil had heard upstairs the night of his mother's death.

My mind tumbled back over recent events. Bree said that Rick had asked numerous questions about me during their dinner, about my childhood, and about Isabelle. *Why the interest in me?* He'd accompanied us to the park that day, acting as if he had no idea a neighborhood playground even existed. His previous statements circled again in my mind:

Is this what happy families do?

I wish I had someplace like this to play when I was a kid.

It seemed he'd been hinting at the truth, toying with me. He said he'd never received a playground key at his closing, and I'd believed him.

With shaky hands, I clutched my phone, found Bree's name, and typed a question:

Did Rick get a Ridgeview Pines playground key when he closed on his house?

I sent the text and waited.

I thought of Isabelle's string of recent mishaps, followed by the visit from CPS. Was Rick targeting my daughter? Was he trying to get her taken away from me? Or separate Isabelle from her grandma? But why? My gaze veered back toward Mom, who propped her hands on her knees and leaned forward.

"Mom? Did you have anything to do with the Kensington kids getting taken away from their mother?"

"No. Barbara filed the complaint." Mom picked up a cracker, then set it back down, tilting her head. "Except that... now that you mention it... Barbara showed up on my doorstep one afternoon and asked me to sign a form. Something about needing a witness to corroborate her claims about the Kensingtons. I was worried about those kids, too, so I was happy to do it. With everything that happened with Ed in the following days, I guess I'd forgotten all about that."

I could almost feel my guts spilling from my body, replaced by a surge of cold, liquid panic. Rick must have discovered Mom had signed Barbara's complaint to CPS. Surely, he would have been able to access files related to himself, even if they weren't part of the public record. I wasn't sure how Rick had accomplished it, but he must have been framing Mom, making her appear negligent so she'd lose contact with Isabelle. And now he'd turned his sights on me.

"Mom, did you ever let Rick into the house when you were watching Isabelle?"

Mom narrowed her eyes, confused. "No."

I wondered if Rick had broken into our house, messed with the gate, moved the knife, replaced plain lotion for the sunscreen, added drugs to our bottles of alcohol. It would have been easy enough for him to spy on us from behind his windows or through the slats of his dilapidated fence. He would have known whenever Isabelle and I left for the park. I thought of the sudden love connection between Rick and Sophie, and realized that was an act, too; merely another way for Rick to infiltrate our household. Bree had even urged me to warn Sophie about Rick, and I hadn't listened.

My phone buzzed as Bree's reply lit up the screen:

Yes. Slick Rick got a key just like everyone else. I told him it was worth more than gold.

I reread Bree's words, not wanting to believe them because then I'd have to admit how stupid I was. So gullible. So naïve not to have thought to ask Bree about this before. He'd known about the neighborhood playground all along. Rick must have dropped his key that night outside of the Drapers' house.

"Jessica, what's wrong?" Confusion clouded Mom's eyes, her question cutting through my terror.

I stood up. "Rick Smith isn't who he says he is. He's Richie Kensington, and I think he killed Barbara Draper. And Phil."

"Oh my goodness."

"I need to leave right now. You'll be safe here if you lock all your doors and windows behind me, and don't leave until I come back in the morning."

"Why?"

"Because our family is Rick's next target."

THIRTY-SIX

The ball of my foot pressed against the accelerator as I careened Mom's Oldsmobile through a yellow light and around a corner. I tried to focus on the road in front of me, but my fears sped faster than the car. The headlights illuminated a line of orange construction cones, and I swerved to miss them. I'd called Mark from Mom's condo, but he hadn't picked up. Now I worried Rick had shown up at our door, pretending to be a caring neighbor or a loving boyfriend, all the while planning his next scheme to frame us as negligent parents. The memory of the butcher's knife he'd left on Isabelle's play kitchen terrified me. It seemed there was no limit to how far Rick would go to get revenge, even threatening my child's life. I reminded myself to breathe and remain calm. I worried for Sophie's safety too. Our babysitter could be lying on Rick's couch watching a movie, unwittingly enveloped in the arms of a smooth-talking killer.

At last, I turned onto Mapleview Lane and pulled into our driveway, only releasing a breath when I spotted a few lights on inside our home. I made myself believe Mark was inside watching TV and that Isabelle was sleeping, tucked safely into her toddler bed upstairs. I stretched my neck toward Rick's house, also seeing a couple of lights glowing from within those windows. My eyelids flickered as I fumbled through my purse for my house key, hoping my imagination had run away with me, that Mark and I would laugh about my outrageous mistake tomorrow. I wanted to be wrong.

My fingers pinched the metal key ring as I exited Mom's car and hurried up the front steps, letting myself into the foyer. Roo trotted over to greet me, but his tail wasn't wagging. He circled my legs, whining and ears pinned back. The TV sounded from the other room, playing the jingle of an insurance commercial. "Mark?" I closed the door behind me and turned the lock, waiting for an answer. I patted Roo's head, wishing he could speak. The silence caused a chill to radiate from my core and out through my limbs, my own animal instincts alerting me that something was very wrong.

I couldn't breathe as I entered the living room. My husband's head tilted sideways, resting on the couch cushion. "Mark?" I stepped in front of him and could see now that his eyes were closed. A few melting ice cubes glistened from within a highball glass on the table in front of him. He was asleep. I squeezed his shoulder and shook him. "Wake up. I'm home." His chest rose and fell, but he didn't budge. I tried to rouse him two more times, but my efforts failed. Mark had always been a sound sleeper, but I'd never seen him completely non-responsive like this. My eyes landed on the nearly empty glass, then bounced toward our wet bar, where a bottle of gin and a bottle of vodka rested on a mirrored shelf. Rick must have slipped something into our alcohol when he broke in the other day. That would explain the amplified effects of Mom's drink too.

My spine straightened, my neck arching toward the stairs, toward Isabelle's room. *Please, God! Please!* I took the stairs two at a time as I bounded toward my daughter's bedroom, reaching the second level. Her door was flung wide open, and I knew something terrible had happened. I rushed into her room, where her toddler bed sat empty—only a tangle of twisted sheets and blankets remained. A primal scream unfurled from my throat and pierced through the air. Tears leaked from my eyes. "Isabelle! Isabelle!" My feet tumbled over each other as I barged into the two remaining bedrooms, finding them empty.

Fueled by terror, I raced downstairs and through the front door, closing it behind me so Roo couldn't follow. "Isabelle!" I ran toward Rick's house, crossing the shadowy street as my vision blurred at the edges. I focused on the faint lights glowing within the ranch house. My ankles twisted above my sandaled feet when I landed on the opposite sidewalk, but I didn't let the pain slow me down. "Isabelle!" I screamed again as I approached the front door. Had Rick tricked Sophie into bringing Isabelle over here? Or maybe he'd threatened our babysitter. With clenched fists, I pounded. No one answered, but other noises reached my ears. Laughter from beyond the fence. The splashing of water. Sophie's high-pitched voice. I darted toward the gate and fumbled with the latch as I yelled for my daughter.

"Mommy." Isabelle stood next to Sophie on the other side of the pool.

"Isabelle." Relief flooded through me at the sweet sound of her voice.

"Look who's here." Rick opened the gate and allowed me to enter, but only so far. "Stop right there." He glanced toward the phone clutched in my hand. "Throw your phone into the water, and maybe no one gets hurt." He stood like a wall, blocking my path. His charming smile had transformed into something cunning and grotesque. "I guess your husband's usual after-dinner drink hit him a little hard tonight."

Sophie wavered next to Isabelle, grabbing her hand. Underwater lights illuminated the water, making the crystal-blue surface smooth and inviting. My daughter wore her pink-footed pajamas and clutched a small panda bear in her hand. Isabelle stared at me with wide and solemn eyes as if she knew she shouldn't be here, as if I'd caught her with her hand in the cookie jar.

I edged toward them, frightened for my daughter and her babysitter. "Sophie, are you okay? Why is Isabelle here?"

Rick pointed at my hand. "Throw your phone into the pool, and I'll tell you."

My hand shook, hesitating for a second before I tossed my smartphone—my lifeline—into the liquid, watching it sink to the bottom. Danger charged the chlorine-scented air. "This isn't okay. Sophie, please bring Isabelle over to me now." I ignored the tears streaming down my cheeks and motioned toward Rick. "This man isn't who you think he is."

Sophie's eyes stretched wide as she cocked her head. "Who is he?"

"Rick used to live in this house when he was a kid. He has returned to hurt my family. Don't listen to him."

Sophie's lip twitched, her stance shifting. "Wow, Jessica. You're smart. But not as clever as you think you are. You only got part of that right." Sophie flashed a cold grin at Rick as she tightened her grip on Isabelle's arm.

I stared across the pool, stunned. Sophie's voice had changed into something sharp and hateful. This young woman who I'd entrusted with my daughter was mocking me. Whatever was happening here, Sophie was in on it.

THIRTY-SEVEN

The gap in Sophie's front teeth lost its endearing quality. Isabelle gazed up at her trusted babysitter, who suddenly appeared ugly and menacing under the harsh patio lights, a piece of Halloween candy with a razor blade hidden inside.

I wanted more than anything to run to the other side of the pool and yank Isabelle away from Sophie, but the bulk of Rick's body kept me in place. All at once, I felt as if I might throw up. "Why are you doing this? Please don't hurt my daughter. She's just a little girl."

Rick squared his shoulders, the muscles in his tanned arms flexing as he faced me. "That's funny because we were only little kids when Barbara Draper and your mom destroyed our family."

Sophie fastened her eyes on me. "Our brother, Bobby, is dead because of Barbara Draper and your mom. Our mom died in prison before we ever had a chance to reconnect. I don't even remember her."

I gasped, realizing Sophie was Mary Kensington's third child, Rick's sister, the baby Mom had mentioned. Sophie and Rick had never been dating at all. The two fit together so perfectly because they were brother and sister. The strange and deadly happenings in the neighborhood rearranged themselves in my mind, more pieces of the puzzle falling into place and forming a harrowing picture.

I held my palms up, hoping to calm her. "I'm so sorry that happened to you, but I had nothing to do with it. I was only a little girl. And Isabelle is completely innocent too."

Blue veins strained along Sophie's pale arms. "Your mom has to pay. Hurting Isabelle is the best way to punish her."

My jaw went slack. "No. Please. Don't."

Rick leaned closer to me, a storm brewing in his eyes. "Do you know what it's like to be seven years old, ripped from the only home you've ever known, separated from your brother and sister, and thrown into the foster care system?"

I stepped back, closing my eyes and shaking my head. My phone lay at the bottom of the pool, useless.

"It's hell. And my foster family wasn't too bad—they only emotionally abused me." He nodded toward Sophie. "My brother and sister weren't so lucky."

"I'm sorry," I said again. "I can't imagine how traumatic that must have been."

Rick's mouth pulled down in the corners. "Bobby got dealt the worst hand. I left Georgia and hunted him down when he turned eighteen. He told me how his new parents beat him every day and made him believe he was worthless. He'd been all alone, and I couldn't protect him. No wonder he turned to drugs."

"My brothers found me several months after that." Sophie's voice projected across the glassy water. "Mom was already dead by then. When I turned eighteen, the three of us pooled our money and shared an apartment for a couple of years." She paused, blinking.

"That must have been nice for all of you to be back together," I said, hoping to talk my way out of the situation, to convince Sophie to walk Isabelle over to me.

"It was good for a while." Sophie's voice was eerily calm, like the eye of a hurricane. "But one night, Bobby overdosed. We couldn't save him."

Rick cleared his throat. "He didn't deserve that. None of us did."

"No. Of course you didn't. But what you're doing here, it's not going to change anything."

"Stop talking!" Sophie scowled at me. "I know you got the messages I sent on The Neighbor List. And the one I left on your driveway."

I looked away, breathless. It had been Sophie the whole time. My face burned as I blinked back tears. "But why?"

Rick squared his shoulders. "Sophie and I started looking into why the authorities took us from our mom in the first place. I remembered being a kid, living in a nice house with a big backyard and a park down the street. Sophie was too young to remember, but we'd been happy here."

I rolled back on my heels, crossing my arms in front of me and remembering the story Mom had told me about the Kensington kids. I didn't want to hear whatever was coming next.

Rick's jaw pulsed. "It's amazing what I uncovered by searching public records. A woman named Barbara Draper had filed a complaint with CPS, accusing our mom of neglect and abuse. Another woman named Marilyn Tyler corroborated Barbara's account." He shook his head. "Only five days later, CPS carted us away, divided us, and placed us in new homes that were so much worse."

I pinched the inside of my cheek between my molars, my body taut with fear.

Sophie's voice carried across the pool. "A couple of years ago, I started doing my own research. I learned all about Barbara and her miserable life. She had a son who was only a few years older than us and who'd graduated from college before his drug addiction took hold."

I pressed my feet into the cement, taking in each word. I thought of Phil's sad and lonely life, his lifelong battle with addiction.

"We saw firsthand how those drugs destroyed our brother. It

might have evened things up a bit if Barbara's son suffered the same fate." Sophie dipped her toe in the water. Isabelle squirmed, wriggling her arm, but the wayward babysitter only tightened her grip. "Except the universe never works that way. Phil never overdosed. He received the best treatment at the most expensive private facilities. He moved back into his quaint childhood home with his mother. That was a luxury Bobby never had."

Rick looked from his sister to me. "We've bided our time, waiting for tragedy to strike Phil. But, let's face it, karma works too slowly. When we discovered our old house was for sale, it was like the stars had aligned. We came up with a new plan to take back what was ours."

I gasped, realizing their resentment had been building for years. Now it boiled over into something dangerous and deadly.

Rick continued talking. "It took a few months to save the down payment, but my construction business had been doing well." He raised his chin toward Sophie. "We figured out the financing and closed under my new surname—Smith. We'd hoped to wait longer before deciding what to do with Barbara Draper, but she showed up at my door on moving day complaining about the noise from the moving truck. I couldn't take it. The sight of her face made me want to kill her."

I lowered my head, feeling no satisfaction that my hunch had been correct.

"Sophie and I met for a minute at the playground that night to finalize the plan. We didn't want to risk you spotting Sophie or her car at my place, so she parked a few streets over. That's why I had that stupid key with me in the first place."

Sophie looked worn and haggard in the patio light, but her eyes gleamed with hatred. "We waited until Bree left and Phil was high out of his mind. We'd been watching him long enough to know it was a nightly occurrence." She inched in my direction. "You could have ruined the whole thing when you almost saw me in the bushes."

Her revelation felt like a punch to the stomach. It had been Sophie hiding behind the branches, acting as Rick's lookout.

Rick spoke again. "Barbara's murder was clean, finished. No questions asked. But then you started poking your nose into it."

"What about Phil?" I asked, afraid to hear the answer.

"Sophie told me about your meeting with Phil to collect the key that had fallen out of my pocket. I couldn't let that happen. I'd been watching him and I knew he had an appointment with his psychiatrist every Thursday at 2:30 p.m. It was easy enough to track him down, side-swipe him with my truck as he cut through an alley."

I sucked in a deep breath, Rick's words confirming that he'd killed Phil too. I focused on Isabelle, struggling to keep my face calm so she wouldn't be scared. I would die before I let them hurt her.

"We researched your mom, even months before we bought the house. She still lived in Glenn Hills, and she'd sold her house to you and your husband. Sophie followed you on The Neighbor List. She saw your post looking for a part-time babysitter. It was that easy."

My mind spun backward through time. Sophie had been the second person to respond to my post, but she'd followed up the next day, offering referrals, telling me about her plans to become a kindergarten teacher. I'd eaten up her lies and set up a meeting. I'd called one of them, too. A man who'd raved about her. Now I realized that person could easily have been Rick, acting. I'd been so careless, hiring Sophie on the spot.

Isabelle whined, trying to pull her hand away and come over to me, but Sophie only grabbed her other arm. "It didn't take long to figure out that Isabelle is the most important person in your mom's life. Isabelle... and you."

The ground felt as if it tilted beneath my feet. "Whatever you're thinking of doing, please don't."

Sophie lifted her chin. "Here's what's going to happen. We're going to throw Isabelle into the pool."

"No. She can't swim!" I ran forward, but Rick stepped in front of me, slamming my body to the ground. I could hear Isabelle crying.

Rick hovered over me, eyes blinking and lips parting as he peered toward his sister. "We don't need to hurt the kid, Sophie."

"Shut up, Rick." Sophie shot him a death stare. She was the one in charge. "We're going to rescue the spoiled brat after a few minutes. What's the worst thing that's happened to her?" Sophie yanked Isabelle's arm, causing Isabelle to squeal. "She got a few stitches, a little sunburn, and thrown into a pool. This is nothing compared to the years of trauma we suffered."

Rick placed his foot on my back, keeping me down. I looked up at him, glimpsing the doubt flickering across his face. He seemed to be suffering a crisis of conscience, but his sister was calling the shots.

Sophie directed her stare at me now. "We'll even call an ambulance. I'll say we heard a noise and I found this little girl floating in our swimming pool at eleven o'clock at night. The police will look into it and see that CPS had already been out to visit you after Isabelle's other two spills, one that even required stitches. They'll see that your husband drank too much, not to mention Isabelle's grandma with the DUI. They'll start asking around. Neighbors will comment on the recent accidents, the sunburn, the cries of a three-year-old from behind your walls. I'll tell them about how you left your terrified toddler home alone as she screamed for her absent mother." Sophie widened her eyes. "Oh, no. It isn't going to look good."

I steeled my voice. "I'm going to tell them who you are and what you did."

Sophie chuckled and shook her head. "Oh, sweetie. You're the only one who knows what's going on here. We're not going to let you live."

"Mommy!" Isabelle squealed, arms flailing.

I tried to get up, but Rick's foot pressed harder on my back. Fear panged through me, gripping my throat.

Sophie glared at me, a sick smile cracking her lips. "The only person Marilyn Tyler loves as much as Isabelle is you. Don't worry. People will assume you drowned trying to save your daughter."

A scream formed in the pit of my stomach, a desperate noise clamoring up my windpipe and unfurling from my mouth.

"Do it." Sophie nodded toward Rick, giving the order. I wished for him disobey, to snap back into himself and tell his sister that enough was enough. But Rick's large hands tightened around my torso and pulled me into the water, silencing my cries. The liquid surrounded me, cold and slippery. I writhed my arms and kicked my legs but couldn't break free from the man's death grip. He was in the water next to me, the weight of his body refusing to let me rise to the surface. A reel of what must have been Barbara Draper's last moments flashed in my mind: Rick holding the woman down beneath the tepid bathwater.

Another object splashed at the far end of the pool. Through the swirl of chlorine, a pink blur began to sink. I screamed again, realizing it was Isabelle, but no one could hear me. Liquid filled my lungs as I gulped for air. My daughter sank lower, and I couldn't break free. I couldn't save her because my oxygen had run out. I was going to die.

THIRTY-EIGHT

All at once, the hands released me. Watery colors churned in the distance as someone else dove into the pool. I thrashed toward the surface, surprised at the easy movement of my body. A violent string of coughs spewed from my mouth as I reached the air, hooking my elbows over the pool's cement edge and expelling the liquid from my lungs. My chest heaved. I looked back, finding Rick floating on the surface of the pool, a large gash glistening beneath his hair. Blood mixed with the water, turning it pink. His sister splashed toward him, hurrying to reach him.

I didn't understand what had happened, but there wasn't time to figure it out. I sucked in a long breath and prepared to dive back under to rescue my baby girl. But before I could, someone else splashed up through the water's surface, gasping for breath and holding Isabelle in her arms. Bree kicked her way to the edge, where I rushed to meet her. I pulled myself out of the water and reached for my daughter's limp body, dragging her to dry land. Bree climbed onto the cement, her soaked clothes sticking to her skin and her hair dripping with water. She began chest compressions, followed by puffing breaths of air into Isabelle's mouth. I kneeled nearby, guarding my friend and my daughter against the two monsters in the pool.

Isabelle coughed and then began to cry. Bree looked at me, tears shining in her eyes. "Your mom called me. She was worried."

I sobbed as I hugged Isabelle, so thankful she was still here, that we were together.

In my peripheral vision, Bree stood and moved with purpose. She picked up something from the grass. The object in her hand was a hammer, a splash of red glistening from its metal edge. She bent down again and collected her phone with her free hand.

Now it was Sophie's sobs that pierced the air. "You killed my brother." Sophie splashed as she pulled Rick's motionless body through the water toward the far edge of the pool.

Bree didn't respond. She held her shoulders tall as she faced the woman in the pool and punched three numbers into her phone. "This is Bree Bradley. We need an ambulance and the police to 638 Mapleview Lane right away."

THIRTY-NINE

We gathered around our living room table as Isabelle stacked cardboard blocks and knocked them over to our cheers. Mark draped his arm around my shoulder. Mom cradled a cup of tea in her hands. Bree leaned forward, wearing a terrycloth tracksuit and white sneakers. The impromptu gathering filled me with gratitude. Last night's near-death experience made every second feel precious.

"There's never been a better excuse to take the day off of work." Bree lowered her long lashes at me. I touched the heavy bags under my eyes and wondered how she looked so perfect after what she'd done last night to save us. The EMTs had arrived quickly and loaded Rick—who was not dead, but unconscious and severely injured—into the ambulance. He remained in the hospital in critical condition. The police had cuffed Sophie and loaded her into a police cruiser as she screamed and sobbed. Bree accompanied me, Mark, and Isabelle to the hospital, where we were all examined and then questioned by police, who finally believed me. Thankfully, the ordeal had left us with only minor injuries.

Mark leaned into me. "I'm sorry I couldn't help you last night. I didn't see it coming."

I rubbed his leg. "They drugged you, Mark. There's nothing you could have done."

Mom pinned her lips together, deep lines forming around her mouth. "I'm just so thankful you're all okay. How could they do that to a little girl?"

"We owe our lives to Bree."

"Not entirely." Bree nodded toward Mom. "Marilyn is the one who called me and urged me to check on you. I'd just gotten your weird text asking about Rick's park key, so I knew you were up to something. No one answered when I showed up here, and I worried you might have gone over to Rick's place. When I heard Isabelle crying, I ran toward the noise and into the backyard. That's when I saw Rick on top of you in the water. Some tools were lying around. I grabbed the first one I saw—a hammer— jumped into the pool and hit him on the head. It was pure instinct."

Mom gasped. I'd already heard the story a few times, but I looked at Bree in awe.

"Then Sophie threw Isabelle into the water. I couldn't believe what was happening. I didn't even think about what I was doing; I just reacted."

"Thank goodness you went over there. I had such a bad feeling when Jessica left my condo." Mom pursed her lips, looking from Bree to Mark. "I knew she wouldn't bother with the police again after they disregarded her previous concerns. Once Jessica gets an idea in her head, she never lets it go."

I smiled at Mom's habit of talking about me as if I wasn't in the room.

Mark rubbed his forehead and chuckled. "No kidding."

A furtive look passed between Bree and Mark.

"She's stubborn," Bree said.

Everyone giggled except for me.

Mark leaned forward, staring at Bree. "What do you think? Should we let Jessica in on our little secret?"

Bree raised her chin. "I think she deserves to know."

Tension strained my chest as I immediately thought the worst. But I closed my eyes, reminding myself to breathe. If my husband and Bree were confessing to having an affair, surely they wouldn't do it now, here, in our living room with Mom and Isabelle present. Surely they wouldn't be laughing about it. I was confused.

"Marilyn, you can ride in my car." Bree waved toward me, Mark, and Isabelle. "You guys drive separately."

Mark popped up from the couch and grabbed my hand. I stared at my husband as a smile played at his lips. "C'mon, Izzie. We're taking your mom on a road trip."

Mark didn't give anything away as he drove, heading toward downtown Glenn Hills. Isabelle clapped her hands behind us, buckled into her car seat, and belting out the alphabet song. I savored each note as I sang along with her. I would never again take these moments for granted. Five minutes later, we turned from Main Street onto Fourth Street, followed by another left onto a side street. Several angled parking spots lined a row of quaint storefronts, built like tiny, old-fashioned houses and painted in complementary bright colors. I'd never been down this side street before and realized the center was brand-new construction.

"What's this?" I asked as Bree and Mom pulled into the spot next to us.

"You'll see," Mark said, still not giving anything away.

We exited our cars and unbuckled Isabelle, who hopped over cracks on the sidewalk. Mark pulled a small white envelope from his pocket and handed it to me, excitement sparkling in his eyes. I opened it, reading the words:

To the most talented artist and baker we know, welcome to the future home of Inked Cakes. We hope this is the first step to all of your dreams coming true! Love always, Mark and Isabelle

A shiny silver key clung to the inside corner of the envelope, and I spilled it into my open palm. I looked at Mark, astonished.

"It's this one." Bree motioned in front of us to the blue storefront with the white door. "Isn't it perfect?"

"My own shop?" I inched closer, a sign taped to the inside of the glass becoming visible. It was an enlarged version of the sketch from my notepad, printed in vibrant colors—red, black, and white.

Inked Cakes.

An image of my cake tattoo design popped behind the writing. My tagline ran across the bottom in smaller print:

T*aste the* R*ebellion.*

I studied the vision before me, emotion rising in my throat. I hugged Mark. Isabelle jumped up and down next to me, and I crouched to hug her too. "Thank you. I can't believe you did this for me."

Mom patted Isabelle's shoulders and gasped. "It's lovely."

Mark pulled away, squeezing my hand. "Bree discovered this new development. The builder hasn't been able to fill all the spots, so we got a good deal on a two-year lease."

Bree nodded. "We thought it was perfect for you. You can build out the inside with a commercial kitchen."

"Can we afford that?" I asked, eyeing my husband.

"I took out some equity from our house. I had to jump through a few hoops, but it's all set." Mark's fingertips caressed my hand. "Those times you saw me with Bree... We were meeting to find you the perfect spot for your bakery and complete the paperwork. I'm sorry I lied to you. I wanted it to be a surprise."

I studied my husband's earnest face, knowing he was telling the truth. What an idiot I'd been to think anything different.

Bree fluttered her eyelashes. "My finances are bad, but not *that* bad. Besides, I'm your friend. I would never do..." she waved her hand in the air, "whatever you thought we were doing."

WE LIVE NEXT DOOR

"I should have known." I could feel red splotches forming on my cheeks. "I don't know what I was thinking."

Bree nodded toward the sign. "I had to let myself into your house the other day to take a photo of your sketch so we could get it to the marketing person at my office in time. Mark was supposed to get the photo but he forgot. Of course, I couldn't resist hugging Roo while I was there."

I tipped back my head. "I knew you were lying about finding Roo in the front yard. I'm not completely insane."

"Only partially." Bree grinned and nudged me forward. "You've got the key. Don't you want to see inside?"

I let us into my future cake shop, flanked by the people who'd made it happen. Natural light poured over my face as I stepped into the empty space. Isabelle skipped across the cement floor. It was easy to envision where everything would go—the counter, display cases, the back kitchen with its ovens, cooling racks, and sinks, the spray-painted urban art on the walls. After I'd inspected every inch and described my idea for the sign out front and some new cake designs, we filed back outside into the warm breeze. Twenty-four hours ago, I couldn't have imagined this scene.

"I'm guessing you might need some help with Isabelle. I'm available whenever you need me. I won't even charge you." Mom winked.

I glanced toward Mark, who gave a sheepish nod, then looked back to Mom. "That would be great. Isabelle would love that."

The neighboring stores huddled around us like new friends—a salon specializing in kids' cuts, a shoe store, a specialty paper store, a chiropractor, and a gift boutique.

"There's one more surprise," Bree said, flashing her polished teeth. "Check out your next-door neighbor."

The mint-green storefront next to mine sat vacant with blackened windows and no sign over the door. I edged closer, spotting a white piece of paper taped inside the corner of the front window. Isabelle followed a ladybug down the sidewalk in the opposite direction as Mom trailed her. Mark stepped next to me.

I read the sign out loud, "Future Campaign Headquarters of Bree Bradley for City Council." I reread it, wondering if my eyes were playing tricks on me. "Are you serious? You're running for City Council?" I looked at Bree, whose smile had grown wider.

"It's a long shot, but the developer is a friend of mine. He offered me free space for the next two months—until I get elected. I'm officially entering the race tomorrow."

"This is so great." I pumped my fist in the air. "Education. Parks. Environment!"

Bree chuckled. "Something like that. I guess you inspired me to go for my dreams."

I turned toward Mark. "Did you know about this?"

Mark shoved his hands in his pockets. "Only for a few days. It was hard to keep it from you." He lowered his voice. "Especially after what you told me about Sean."

The mention of Sean's name caused a memory of the strange man's unsettling gaze to pierce through me.

Confusion swam in Bree's eyes. "What about Sean?"

"Nothing." I spoke the word a little too quickly, and Bree shot me a suspicious look.

"Yeah. Nothing," Mark said, backing me up. He coughed, then straightened his shoulders. "Only that Jessica and I feel confident that you'll beat out Sean Peale for the City Council seat."

I looked down to hide my smirk. "Easily," I added.

Mark's strained features settled as he flashed me a sideways smile. Bree didn't know what we knew about her competition, and she never would. I locked eyes with my husband, understanding we shared a powerful secret. We could destroy Sean's political run with a single sentence. It would only take one threat of exposure to the unsavory man who resided beyond our backyard fence. In my attempt to uncover the truth behind Barbara and Phil's deaths, I'd accidentally glimpsed behind the curtain of the Peales' perfect lives, and the view had been ugly.

I looped my arm inside Mark's, leaning into his weight, feeling his body's heat next to mine, cementing our bond. It turned out my boring and safe suburban life hadn't been boring or safe at all. Now I would do whatever it took to protect it. Mark, Isabelle, and I were survivors, but we almost hadn't made it. Rick and Sophie had nearly gotten away with three murders—Barbara's, Phil's, and mine. I shuddered, terrified by how easily Rick's charming accent and Sophie's gap-toothed grin had won me over, how quickly I'd been willing to suspect those closest to me of horrible things. While I didn't have to worry about Rick and Sophie anymore, Sean Peale's shadow still loomed at the edge of my mind, the memory of his eyes still peered at me from between the slats of our backyard fence. But not for long. I planned to banish that lingering presence, to send it scurrying far away.

I surveyed my new surroundings, feeling a little like a wild animal emerging from its cage, prowling the suburban savannah of Glenn Hills, and letting out a triumphant roar. I no longer felt trapped, worried, and paranoid. Our decision to move back to my childhood home had been the right choice. I was sure of that now. This scene before me was proof that the life I was building for myself and my family was the life I was meant to live. As long as I stood in my truth, no one could bring me down.

Mark wove his fingers through mine as courage coursed through me. And I felt another tinge rippling alongside my bolstered confidence. This new realization flowed slightly to the left, just outside the bounds of the law; it was delicious and evil. I thought of Sophie and Rick Kensington, and their traumatic past and tragic present. The brother and sister had misused their power, almost getting away with their deadly scheme. I would use the same knowledge to protect my family because I now understood what Sophie and Rick had already figured out.

There are few things more dangerous than knowing your neighbors' secrets.

THE NEIGHBOR LIST
POSTED JULY 30

Username: JMillstone

Subject: Inked Cakes Pre-Grand Opening Celebration!

Please stop by the Pre-Grand Opening of my new bakery, Inked Cakes, today between 1-5pm. Locally owned and operated, Inked Cakes features unique and delicious custom-made cakes with tattoo-inspired designs. Perfect for any occasion! Taking pre-orders now! Website HERE.

Wolverine8: Cool concept!

AMoreno: Congrats! We will be there!

BHall: Do you do wedding cakes?

Click to view sixty-three more comments

THE NEIGHBOR LIST

POSTED JULY 31

Username: BreeSells4U

Subject: New Listing in Ridgeview Pines Neighborhood – 784 Pine Tree Lane!

Quaint 4-bedroom, 3-bathroom single family home on quiet, tree-lined street features updated kitchen, and spacious fenced-in backyard. Walk to private neighborhood playground. Highly motivated seller moving out-of-state. All reasonable offers considered!

AMoreno: The Peales are moving out of state?? What about the City Council race? The election is only four days away!

WaterLilly: I guess I need a new podiatrist. Any recommendations?

NerdGirl: Sean Peale dropped out of the race last week. Anyone else think it's strange that he listed his house with the person running against him?

Click to view eight more comments

A LETTER FROM LAURA

Dear reader,

I want to say a huge thank you for choosing to read *We Live Next Door*. If you enjoyed it and want to keep up to date with all my latest releases, just sign up at the following link. Your email address will never be shared and you can unsubscribe at any time.

www.bookouture.com/laura-wolfe

We Live Next Door was partially inspired by a well-known app where local people can ask questions, share information, or express concerns about regional or neighborhood issues. I am one of the millions of people active on this app and am often entertained and informed by my neighbors' posts. Other times, though, I can't believe the petty things people have the time and energy to complain about. In my city, there is one user in particular, who I do not know personally (thankfully!), but who regularly posts unpopular, obnoxious, and sometimes abusive comments. These comments always ignite a firestorm of angry responses to follow. (After talking to others in various regions of the country and world, it has become clear that every town has at least one of these people!) This particular unnamed person has been twice banned from my local app. Somehow, though, he continues to find his way back into the forum. After reading one of this man's offensive posts and the combative thread that followed, a couple of fleeting thoughts passed through my psychological thriller writer's mind. First, what past events must have happened to this person to make him think it's okay to act in such a horrible manner? Secondly, how many dozens of names would make the suspect list if this person ever died under suspicious circumstances? Shortly after having these thoughts, I created Barbara Draper's character, and what fun it was to write her, especially her cantankerous posts on my fictional version of the app, The Neighbor List. In uncovering Barbara's painful past, I hoped to answer my own questions about why some people behave the way they do and the potential repercussions of their actions.

I hope you loved *We Live Next Door*, and if you did, I would be very grateful if you could write a review. Reviews make such a difference in helping new readers discover one of my books for the first time.

I love hearing from my readers – you can get in touch on my Facebook page, Goodreads, Instagram, or my website. To receive my monthly book recommendations in the mystery/suspense/thriller genre, please follow me on Bookbub.

Thanks,

Laura Wolfe

www.LauraWolfeBooks.com

 facebook.com/LauraWolfeBooks

 instagram.com/lwolfe.writes

 bookbub.com/authors/laura-wolfe

ACKNOWLEDGMENTS

While writing a novel is mainly a solitary endeavor, there have been many people who supported and assisted me in various ways along the journey of writing and publishing this book. First, I'd like to thank the entire team at Bookouture, especially my editor, Isobel Akenhead. She helped to smooth out my novel's rough edges and continually reminded me to raise the stakes. Her insights into my story's structure, pacing, and characters made the final version so much better. Additional gratitude goes to copyeditor, Lucy Cowie, and proofreader, Shirley Khan, for their keen eyes, and to Bookouture's top-notch publicity team led by Noelle Holten and Kim Nash. Thank you to those who continuously support my writing and provide inspiration and encouragement, especially Lisa Richey and Karina Board. Thank you to the many book bloggers who have helped spread the word about my books. I'm so thankful for the authors in the Bookouture Authors' Lounge Facebook group, who are always there to prop me up, offer laughs, and answer questions. It's a joy to be a part of such a supportive group of talented writers from around the world. Thank you to my parents, mother-in-law, and other extended family for supporting my books in one way or another. I appreciate everyone who has taken the time to tell me that they enjoyed reading my stories, has asked me "How's your writing going?" or has left a positive review. Thank you to my "writing partner," Milo, who inspires all the canine characters in my books. He sat by my side (and only occasionally barked) as I wrote every word. Most of all, I'd like to thank my kids, Brian and Kate, for always cheering for me and for finding creative ways to occupy themselves, so that I could have time to write, and for my husband, JP, for supporting my writing. I wouldn't have made it to the end without his encouragement.

CPSIA information can be obtained
at www.ICGtesting.com
Printed in the USA
BVHW071111021121
620548BV00005B/132